MW00586318

LONG
TIME
GONE

LONG TIME GONE

A NOVEL

HANNAH MARTIAN

CROOKED
LANE

NEW YORK

Published in the United States by Crooked Lane Books, an imprint of The Quick Brown Fox & Company LLC.

Crooked Lane Books and its logo are trademarks of The Quick Brown Fox & Company LLC.

Library of Congress Catalog-in-Publication data available upon request.

ISBN (hardcover): 978-1-63910-969-2
ISBN (ebook): 978-1-63910-970-8

Cover design by Nebojsa Zoric

Printed in the United States.

www.crookedlanebooks.com

Crooked Lane Books
34 West 27th St., 10th Floor
New York, NY 10001

First Edition: October 2024

10 9 8 7 6 5 4 3 2 1

For Anna.
We did it, brother.

Part 1

The Missing Woman

PROLOGUE

Wild Child

*S*HE WAS FLYING; *she was sure of it.*

The Wyoming night was brittle cold as it rushed in through the open window of the passenger side door. Her cheeks hurt from the chill as she tilted her face toward it, but in that moment she couldn't have moved if she had wanted to.

For the first time in her life, she was running—and it was her choice.

It was glorious and freeing, even if she knew it would all end soon. It had to. She could already see the sirens in the rearview mirror, hear them blasting through the otherwise silent night.

Or maybe it wouldn't end.

After all, if they found her, how would they explain the existence of the girl next to her?

The one who shined brighter than the stars hanging in the Wonderland sky.

The one she would, and had, gone to war for.

The one who was driving them directly into the heart of the rest of their lives.

CHAPTER

1

. . . Ready for It? (Now)

M Y PHONE IS ringing.

It takes a minute for the sound to drag me out of the deep, dreamless sleep I'd been under. Then I'm groaning, groping to my left, hand finally closing around it on my nightstand.

I prop myself up on an elbow, squinting against the brightness of the screen. Fucking five AM, and I'm getting a call from a number I don't recognize in—

Wyoming.

Wonderland, Wyoming.

And suddenly I'm wide awake.

I go still, the ringing somehow growing louder, the screen getting brighter.

The woman lying next to me grumbles something incoherent, the bed dipping beneath us as she rolls over, throwing her arm around my bare waist. "What time is it?" she groans, trying in vain to pull me back to her. She's Jessie or Jaime; another face, another name I won't remember come the sunrise.

But I remember Wonderland, Wyoming, as much as I wish I didn't.

And the only person who would be calling me from there—yeah, I'd like to be able to forget her too.

I sit up, my hand shaking as I bring the phone to my ear and answer with a short "You've got a lot of fucking nerve calling me, Cora."

Silence. For so long that I think that surely my long-estranged aunt has simply misdialed and is now realizing what a terrible, horrible mistake she's made. A mix of anger and anxiety is making my pulse pound so hard I can feel it against the inside of my temple.

"Not Cora," a deep female voice responds.

"Then who the hell is this, calling me at five in the god-damn morning?"

"Didn't realize it was too early to call."

Fucking Wyomingites and their ranching hours. "What do you *want*?" I demand.

The woman next to me releases her grip on my stomach, pulling away in alarm, as the one on the other end of the line offers me no reply. I already know what Jesse/Jaime is think-ing, wondering exactly who she went home with tonight: *"What's wrong with her? How could she talk to someone like that?"*

But that's the good thing about one-night stands: they know nothing about me and my past and one tiny town in the most miserable excuse for a state in this entire country.

"Cora wants you here," she replies, quiet and terse.

"She shouldn't have sent me packing eight years ago, then."

"Well, your aunt's missing now. Maybe that'll change your mind."

Either the woman on the other end hangs up or the phone slips from my hand, landing somewhere below me in the tan-gle of skin and sheets—which one, I don't know.

CHAPTER

2

Kerosene (Now)

THE SOUTHWEST WYOMING Regional Airport is so small it shouldn't be allowed to legally operate. The airport in Spokane is small. A handful of flights to Seattle, one or two to Canada, throw in a special trip to Boise or Missoula every once in a while. But this is one compact, concrete slab of a building with a landing strip in the back. There's no food, no gift shop; only a small baggage claim and a couple rows of seats.

I throw my backpack over my shoulder and drag my carry-on out, closer to the door. A few people run past me, jumping into the waiting arms of loved ones, tears and shouts and laughs making this place even smaller.

I've always wondered what it's like to have that—someone waiting for you. Someone excited to see you, welcome you home. Or even just someone to pick you up from the airport.

The last time I was in this airport, there was someone to drop me off—accompanied by a vow that it'd be the last time I'd ever see the inside of this shitty place.

"Well, your aunt's missing now. Maybe that'll change your mind."

Missing. Gone. Vanished. One of only two family members I have, and now I don't know where either of them is.

The woman who'd called me from Wonderland followed up her call with an email from Cora's account not twenty minutes later. A plane ticket, already booked in my name, for August 3rd, was attached, complete with the message: *Cora said you worked for an investigator, the kind she used to be. I'll be at the airport if you reckon to use this ticket.*

I won't, I'd told myself. I deleted the email without a reply. Eight years ago, my aunt turned her back on me when I needed her, when she *knew* I needed her—karma would suggest it only appropriate that I return the favor now. She's been missing from my life for almost a decade. Let the good people of Wonderland, Wyoming, get a taste of that feeling.

And yet.

Here I am.

In fucking Wyoming.

There's only one person still waiting by the time everyone else has cleared out. A woman, roughly the same age as me, clad in a red flannel button-up, dark-wash denim jeans, and a light brown cowboy (cowgirl?) hat. The jeans she wears are worn and torn in a way that I've only ever seen mimicked in department stores, which I doubt they've even got within fifty miles of here. Her hands are tucked into her pockets, shoulders back, eyes forward. Her brown hair is cut bluntly, like she did it herself with a pair of kitchen scissors, and hits right at her chin, which looks sharp enough to cut me if I were to get too close.

She's familiar, maybe—but I can't quite place her. If she wasn't so clearly a Wyoming product, I might've guessed she was a hookup I'd forgotten about. Everything about her is easy and relaxed, comfortable and in control; exactly the kind of woman I'd approach at the bar, a drink or two humming through my veins, tossing my hair over my shoulder as I smiled and fed her a line.

The woman is motionless, waiting for me to come to her. And she's staring at me. Though the way she's doing it makes

staring seem like an insufficient description. It's like she's trying to burn her way down to my bones. Maybe it's just her
eyes that are making me feel that way. The color of them is
shocking, even from ten feet away—haunting, almost. The
shade makes her pupils nearly blend in with her irises: a blue
that's nearly as dark as the Wyoming night sky, far different
from the lighter, icier shade that mine are. No, that's the feeling her eyes remind me of—standing outside of Cora's ranch
house at midnight, so much emptiness above me it made it
impossible to even ponder what lay beyond it, feet bare and
the wind nipping at my shoulders, holding me in place and
forcing me to exist solely in that precise moment.

If I missed anything about this state, it was that feeling.
Now it's staring right at me.

I make the first move, crossing into what I've known for
years is unwelcome territory. As I come to stand in front of
her, I clear my throat, blink a couple of times to disperse my
plane daze. "I take it you're the one who called me at five in
the morning to let me know my aunt's missing?"

The woman in front of me reacts as if I hadn't spoken at
all. Enough time passes that I raise my eyebrows. *Well?*

"I take it you're the niece?" she finally replies. Her voice
is even deeper than it sounded on the phone, rougher, like
she hasn't used it in a while, and it's putting her out to do
so now.

"Quinn Cuthridge," I say.

A once-over, quick and clinical, then she meets my eyes
again. "Let's go."

"I need my other bags—"

"You got more than this?"

I snicker. "I doubt that you've got everything that I need
out here in the middle of—"

"Didn't ask for the whole kit and caboodle," she says, rubbing at her forehead.

"What in the hell does that even—"

"It means get your bags and let's go," she says irritably. "I've got work to do."

I take a step closer, hating that I have to look up to meet this woman's eyes. For a moment, they throw me off, so familiar, the memory just out of reach. "You asked *me* here," I say.

The stranger echoes me, moving so we're right in each other's faces, the brim of her hat tipped toward the sky, as she retorts, "And if you didn't wanna come, you shoulda stayed right where your feet were planted."

Oh, she's certainly not a once-upon-a-time hookup I forgot about. This woman would've taken whatever pickup line I'd fed her and stuffed it right back down my throat. This woman I wouldn't have given up on, wouldn't have forgotten.

This is a woman I want to go toe to toe with just for the thrill of seeing what happens.

"I ain't got time for this," she says, backing away. "Either get your stuff and let's go, or you can catch the first flight headed north."

"Are you going to help? Or just stand there and keep making demands?"

She doesn't move. For so long that I think we're going to be locked in this staredown until this tricked-out barn of an airport closes, but then this angry, gnashing woman reaches down, grabs the bag at my feet, and gestures for the one on my back.

She jerks it out of my grasp as I hand it over. "I'll be in the truck."

That's all she says before she's gone, and I'm standing in this airport, alone again, wondering what in the hell has happened over the course of the past eight years to get me right back to where I started.

I turned six in the spring, sixteen years ago. Every summer after that I spent in this wasteland of a state—up until Cora banished me, no reason given, the summer before I turned fourteen.

The memories are faded around the edges, time dulling the sharper points—that old saying about remembering how someone made you feel, but not their words. Still, I don't recollect it taking this long to drive back from the airport. I watch what feels like the same strip of land flash by over and over again, the most incredibly dull landscape of green and gold and brown. Occasionally there's a sign for a town, but half of them advertise "No Services."

How does someone even end up living out here? How haven't they all gone completely insane yet?

It's been silent the entire drive, not even the radio playing. All I've done is watch the sun slowly make its descent toward the Wyoming horizon, and ponder exactly how old this truck is. It's well taken care of—no holes in the brown upholstery beneath me, hardly any scratches or stains—but dust covers nearly the entire span of the floorboard. I wouldn't have the slightest idea how to drive it; the stick shift and dials on the dash make me nauseous just looking at them. I keep hitting the window hand crank on the door with my elbow, and my knees keep knocking against the glove box.

"You're going to have to speak to me if you want me to find Cora," I remark at one point.

It's disorienting out here, especially in the silence. The speed limit is eighty, but it still looks like everything I see is standing still.

"Once you actually say something worth responding to, I'll talk."

I shift on the bench seat. "Who are you, for starters?"

"Hunter Lemming," she says finally—*something*. Some shred of evidence that this is all real, happening, and not some sick daydream my mind has concocted.

"How old are you? What do you do out here?"

"I'm twenty-one. And I work for Cora."

"Doing what?"

"Whatever she asks me to. Includin' drivin' three hours to get her overly-chatty niece from the airport."

I bite back a response to her insult, instead asking, "She's missing, so how's she still issuing demands?"

Hunter's hands tighten on the steering wheel. They're tan and strong, wrapping around the steering wheel like they have a right to be there, and it makes me wonder what else they'd look good wrapped around. "It's what she would want. It's been long enough."

"What do you mean—"

The truck suddenly comes to a stop, cutting me off. I face forward, looking right at the ranch house that's been in the Cole family since Wonderland, Wyoming, has been in existence. It's been renovated several times over the past few decades, but some of the original features remain. The exterior is all wood, a hazelnut color, with high ceilings and big windows. The porch wraps around the entire house, and there's a sign that reads "Cole" above the front door, in gold letters. I used to dream of owning a house like this, once. I used to dream about a lot of things that I don't anymore.

Hunter's out of the truck in a flash, and I follow her, walking to the back of the truck. She throws the tailgate down, then lifts my incredibly full suitcases effortlessly out of the bed. She's moving again before I even have time to register it. Everything is exact and precise with Hunter; no energy or time wasted, as if her mind is always already three steps ahead of her body. She reminds me of a wild animal tracking its prey: her eyes, the tone of her voice, the way she moves.

The ranch house is one story, a mostly open floor plan that sends the entryway to the kitchen, then to the living room without breaking stride. Rugs are thrown over the hardwood in front of both couches, with a large glass coffee table sandwiched between them. The appliances are all gleaming silver in the kitchen, the countertops obsidian black. It's a similar setup to the one in the guesthouse, which is back down near the edge of the property. Everything's as I remember, as if this place has been frozen in time, waiting for my return.

And then, of course, there's Cora.

The last time I was here, the last time I'd gotten a glimpse of my aunt, she was gorgeous in an easy, straightforward way: bare feet and blue jeans and a big tousle of brown hair. Eighteen years the junior of Elain Cuthridge—my mother, by legal definition—making her thirty-nine now. Half sisters, the two sharing a mother, but not a father. Family tradition, seemingly, to fornicate with the wrong men. Maybe that's why the universe made me a lesbian—*"enough of this bullshit; no more men."*

It's always been just me, Elain, and Cora. The former I haven't seen or heard from in six years, the latter in eight. Another family tradition, I suppose: abandonment. Mothers running, fathers never having existed in the first place.

"It's all yours," Hunter says suddenly, tossing a set of keys onto the kitchen table. "Bedroom's down the hall, bathroom's right next to it, laundry's at the very end. I'd say you could take your old bedroom, but Cora had everything cleared outta there. I'm in the guesthouse if you need anything, though I hope you won't."

"You *live* here?"

"What I said, ain't it?"

Hunter's boots echo behind me as she starts to leave, but I stop her. "Where would she go?"

"What?"

I turn. She's leaning against the wall, arms crossed over her chest. Cora used to stand in that exact same spot in that exact same way, and seeing it replicated so precisely by a woman I don't know from Adam isn't a feeling I ever want to get used to.

It hadn't hit me at the airport, or on the ride here, that I'm *back*, in this place that's felt more like home—and hell—than anywhere else in the world. This place I never thought I'd see again. But oh, is it hitting me now.

"You seem to know her better than anyone," I reply, trying in vain to keep my tone even. "So. She goes missing. Where would she go?"

"Nowhere else to go around here."

"She had a life before all this ranch shit. She could've up and decided—"

"She was an investigator, like you're fashionin' yourself to be," she says, cutting me off again. "She gave that up when her dad died. She missed this place, and this is what she was raised to do. This is her life now—and I know her well enough to know she didn't run off. No, she's . . ." Hunter swallows, shakes her head. "She's in trouble. I know it."

"Is that what the cops think?"

"Some of 'em."

"What—one out of three?"

"Somethin' like that."

Goddamn her with all these half answers. "And how long has she been missing?"

"Two weeks."

"She's been missing for *two weeks*? Why's it taken you so long to pick up the goddamn phone?"

She shrugs, like the timeline doesn't even faze her. "Guess I finally got desperate enough to ask for your help."

"I need to get started now, then."

"Nothing of importance's open around here till Monday."

"Is there internet here?" I only have one bar of cell service, making it nearly impossible to do any research on my phone.

Hunter jerks her chin down the hall. "Only thing left in your old room's the computer. It's ancient, though. I tried doin' some searchin' before I called you, and couldn't get much to load."

"What about the house, then? Have you looked around at all or—"

"Of course I have. If I'd found anything, I wouldn't have had to call you to *investigate*."

The way she says the word makes me grit my teeth. The insinuation wrapped around them, like I'm just some silly girl playing Nancy Drew; like I haven't been shadowing the top private investigator in Spokane since I was fifteen, camera in one hand, learner's permit in the other.

"Do you want me to find her or not?" I demand.

Something flashes in her eyes, some violence-tinged form of anger. *Good,* I think. *Let me get under your skin like you're getting under mine.* "What's to say she didn't just run off?" I continue. "I'm surprised she lasted as long as she did out here in this black hole of a state. Maybe she rubbed a couple of brain cells together, looked at all the *literal* cow shit surrounding her, and left."

A muscle jumps in Hunter's jaw with how hard she's trying to swallow down her retort. It's the reason I said it in the first place: to get a reaction out of her.

"You could leave too, you know," I offer. "No one's heard from her in over two weeks? Odds aren't good for finding her alive. And I'd imagine it's pretty hard to collect a check from a dead woman."

It's too far, and I know it before the words are even out of my mouth. Hunter goes deathly still for one long, pregnant moment, as if in shock that I've said it.

I'm right, though. If something bad has happened to my aunt, we're probably not finding her alive. Time means everything when someone's missing, and maybe Cora would already be home, safe and sound, if these idiots had called me earlier, or if Cora hadn't banished me from here in the first place. *If, if, if.*

"Well, now I know," Hunter finally says, her voice low, calm.

"Know what?"

I meet her gaze from across the room. Those goddamn eyes cut into me, and my breath catches in the back of my throat, realizing that I've miscalculated. I might've landed the first blow, but Hunter is about to deliver the next one.

"Now I know why she told you never to come back," she says. "Good to know Cora's always been a good judge of character."

* * *

I can't sleep.

I've set myself up on the couch tonight, which is comfortable but still a couch. Sleeping in Cora's bed, in her room . . . the idea makes my skin crawl. Even though I deserved them, I can't get Hunter's words out of my head either. Needless to say, I can't sleep, my brain running a million miles an hour.

Was she taken or did she leave?

Where would she go if she did leave?

What has she gotten into these past eight years?

How much have I missed her?

Is she dead? Because, statistically, if she was taken—

I shove my feet into the old pair of flip-flops I brought along, and head for the front door.

Two things that would be impossible in Spokane: seeing the moon, so bright and unobstructed by all the light pollution from the city, and walking alone at night. The ranch is so far from anyone and anything else that I feel pretty safe walking under a dark sky by myself. But I'd be lying if I said the hairs on my neck don't prickle the slightest bit as I make my way down the driveway. I'm too seasoned, have seen too much, to believe there are any truly safe spaces left in this world.

It's cold tonight, but not unbearably so because I'm wearing long sleeves. My flip-flops smack against the cement, which soon turns to gravel beneath me. I swerve right and left, avoiding the largest potholes.

When I reach the end of the path, I inhale long and deep before letting my breath back out. I used to spend every summer here, on this land, staring up at this part of the sky. Cora and I, doing nothing and everything for the whole summer. We'd drive to Cheyenne for ice cream, the radio cranked up high in Cora's old truck. We'd make a trip to Mount Rushmore every year; Casper and Denver and Cody, lakes and rivers and mountains passing and blurring until all I could remember was *I can't wait for the summer.*

Cora was born a bastard, her father already married but childless when she was conceived by my grandmother, who left her here in Wonderland and took off shortly after she was born. Cora didn't find out about Elain, or me, until I was six.

Her father raised her on this land, just the two of them after his wife divorced him. Cora learned to run the ranch but moved to Denver when she was eighteen and became a private investigator. She worked disappearances mostly—a stabbing that the police had no idea on, one time. Cora solved them all, but then her father died, and she came back to run the ranch. I asked her once why she didn't just sell it and stay in Denver, but she shook her head and said, "It's the last thing I've got left of him. This place, the couple of things inside of it. Maybe it'll all tell me the things he never did."

Cora loved her dad, but he became more reclusive after his wife left. He never married again, and he didn't have any kids after Cora, leaving everything to her when he died. I don't know if Cora kept the memories and stories of him from me to honor the way he lived, but whenever I'd ask about him when I was younger, she'd clam up. She moved to Denver because it was easier to become a PI there, but she never wanted to be too far away from him, from this place, in case one day Wyoming came calling again.

I tip my head back, close my eyes. I wonder if Cora's somewhere along the map we carved out, laughing and remorseless, not even thinking about the people she's left behind. It certainly wouldn't be the first time, or even the second or third, that it's happened to me.

In my eyes, it's fifty–fifty whether she left by choice or by force. Cora had dug back into this place. Her place. Her home. By what Hunter said in the house, it doesn't seem like any of that's changed.

But I know how fast things can change. How people you've known and loved and looked up to for so long can become strangers overnight; how they can look you in the eye and not even flinch as they cut through the last feeble stitch holding your heart together.

Once upon a time, I thought I had my aunt all figured out. I thought I knew all her secrets, all her tricks. Then she threw all my shit in the back of her truck, drove me to the airport, and told me never to come back.

Getting hurt like that . . . I swore I'd never let it happen again. I couldn't let it, and thus everything became a never-ending game of *hurt them before they hurt you.*

My mind keeps churning, relentless, as it always is. The wind sings through the openness, the moon and the night my only companions.

Or so I think.

"What are you doin' out here?"

I jump what is surely an impressive height into the air at the voice behind me. When I turn, Hunter stands a few feet away, jaw set in a hard line, hair a mess.

"Jesus," I breathe. "You scared the shit out of me."

"Imagine how I felt when I heard someone outside my window at three AM." She crosses her arms over her chest, which draws my attention to that part of her body. I hadn't noticed what she was wearing before, but I certainly do now: long red flannel pajama pants, a tight black tank top, no bra. She's got her arms right under her breasts, pushing them up toward the neckline of her top. Her arms are toned and tan,

same as her hands, which makes me wonder what other parts
of her are—

She clears her throat, and I realize how long I've been staring at her chest. "What are you doin' out here?" she repeats.

Definitely not letting an old ghost keep me awake. Or gawk-
ing at your tits. "Just going for a walk."

"At three AM."

"Yes."

She scoffs, runs a hand through the back of her hair. It's
sleep messy, standing up in the back. "Go to bed, Princess,"
she says. "I'm sure you need your beauty rest."

"What's that supposed to mean?"

She shakes her head, and I can tell she's fighting back a
laugh. "Nothin'."

"Why do you keep calling me that?" I demand, stalking
toward her.

Shrugging, she replies, "Just a hunch I had. You city girls
tend to all act the same."

"Act like *what*?"

"Spoiled," she replies. "Stuck-up. Wouldn't know a hard
day's work if it slapped you upside the head."

"It's shitty of you to make assumptions like that."

"Is it, now?"

"Yeah," I retort, stepping closer. Close enough that my flip-
flops brush up against her bare toes. Close enough that I can
make out every single one of the freckles painting her nose and
cheekbones. Close enough to feel her breath on my face, my
neck. I may be angry and irritated with this girl, halfway to hating her, but it doesn't hinder my attraction to her in the least.

Her eyes drop, and I watch her gaze linger on my right
wrist. This close, my birthmark is easy to clock. Plenty of
people have thought it was a scar before I patiently explained
that I was born with the jagged, deep tan mark on the inside
of my wrist.

I wait for her to ask about it, but when she doesn't, I continue on. "Then I guess you're just some rude, ignorant country-girl hick."

"What's to say you're wrong?" she asks, her voice dropping low, eyes meeting mine again.

"Am I?"

Her nostrils flare, but she says nothing.

"What about you?" I continue. "What are you doing here? Where's your family?"

Hunter flinches like I've slapped her across the face. I'm hurting her without even realizing it now, and it doesn't give me the same sense of security that it usually does. Something about her reaction, about all of this, makes me want to apologize, explain that I didn't mean it, any of it. Tell her that Cora's alive and we'll find her, and it'll all be fine.

It scares me, how much I want to do all those things. Because the last time I gave someone the opportunity to strike first, it nearly killed me. Since then, I've told myself that it's better to be hard than to be weak. Better to be the villain who lives than the hero who dies at the end of the story.

I wonder if she'd understand that—the reasons why there is a method to everything I do. That I can't afford to be the girl I was when I was just Cora's niece anymore; that the days of drives for ice cream and playing at the shitty little park in town—

Wait. *Wait.*

"I do know you," I breathe.

It all falls into place so suddenly. Her hair was far longer, almost down to her waist, so it hid the sharpness of her jaw. Long and shiny, made lighter by the rays of the sun. There were a couple of other kids in town that I knew, who ran and screamed and laughed the heat of a mid-Wyoming summer away. But *she*—the girl with the brown hair and those blue eyes—she was different. Quieter. She watched more than she joined in.

"The summers I was here, you were too," I say. She's gone pale and deathly still. I don't even know if she's breathing or not. "You'd come over to the ranch sometimes. But you'd come with your—"

"*Stop*," she gasps out harshly. "You're here to find Cora. That's it. So go back to bed and forget you ever remembered me."

"*Forget you ever remembered me.*" As if it would be that simple.

3

Fool's Gold (Then—March 1981)

I T WAS RAINING. Holly Prine hated the rain.

It wasn't *supposed* to be raining—the forecast that morning had announced clear skies for as far east as Cheyenne. Holly had heard it over the radio in the motel lobby, her mother packing up the last of their things into their secondhand 1965 Ford Mustang. It was a fine car—Holly's mother, Lenora, had purchased it from a particularly unsavory man when they were on their way out of San Francisco. All you had to do was ignore the dark red spot in the back seat, pretending it was a tomato sauce stain instead of what Holly suspected it was.

But maybe that was just her imagination running wild. They'd been living like this—motel to motel, gas station to gas station, an occasional abandoned or foreclosed house for a night or two—for the past five years. Lenora's mother had died, in unsurmountable debt, and by the time the bank was done, all Lenora had was a car that barely ran and her twelve-year-old daughter.

Holly was seventeen now, and she read mystery novels to pass the time. She'd read a stolen library copy of *In Cold Blood* so many times she had it nearly memorized. But her true love was Nancy Drew novels. On the long trips to a new home, or the even longer nights when Lenora was working her shift at a diner or wherever else she'd managed to find work, Holly pretended she was right there beside Nancy: finding clues, solving mysteries, and catching bad guys.

She wasn't, though; she wasn't even close. She was in her mom's car, riding shotgun as the rain started pouring down the stretch of Interstate 80 they were on. Holly wondered how much longer they had to go to their next destination—it had been about thirty minutes since she'd seen a sign for a town, an hour since they'd crossed over the Utah border into Wyoming, a big sign with a cowboy and his horse welcoming them—but she knew better than to ask.

Lenora took her hand off the wheel—the other had a lit cigarette in it and was tipped against the glass of the window, open a crack to let the smoke escape—and changed radio stations. The broadcaster droned on about gas prices and the stock market.

Lenora had never told Holly her age, only that her birthday was the third of September, which was a handful of months away. Holly guessed she was somewhere between thirty-five and forty—young to have a seventeen-year-old daughter. Lenora's hair was the palest shade of blonde Holly had ever seen, thin and frizzy, the ends desperately in need of a trim. Holly's own hair was deep brown, cut right at her chin. *"Your father's hair,"* Lenora had told her so many times she'd lost count, though Lenora had just as many times told her she had no idea who Holly's father was.

Their eyes, though—the Prine women had the same eyes. Every Prine woman had them for as long as the family tree could be traced back: a brilliant green with flecks of hazel, so distinctive that Holly almost resented them. It was the only thing that linked them, it seemed. Where Lenora was rail thin, Holly's chest and hips and thighs curved in ways she often wished they didn't. Where Lenora was the life of the party, Holly was in the corner, standing by the chip bowl, without a word to say.

They were nothing alike, so much so that Holly wondered sometimes if they were really related. One look in the mirror, one glimpse of her eyes staring back at her—that erased any doubt. Any hope.

"Look at this," her mother remarked suddenly, gesturing out the window. "Beautiful. No government regulations out here, Holls. Just as God intended."

Holly said nothing. Her mother spoke of God sometimes, though Holly sincerely doubted Lenora actually believed in Him. *Did God intend for us to live in motels, fleeing town after we've been kicked out, never having a real home?* she wanted to ask sometimes. But she knew it'd be no use. Lenora would get a glazed-over look in her eyes, like she had no idea what Holly was talking about. Like they had everything they could ever need and wanted for nothing.

There were so many things that Holly wanted for. Friendships that lasted longer than a handful of months; books that she didn't have to steal from the shelves of libraries; clothes that didn't come from thrift stores, with tiny holes in the neckline or the armpits before she'd even gotten a chance to wear them for the first time.

Lenora had promised that Wyoming was going to be their big break. Wyoming was booming with oil money, uncharted territory that reeked of promise and opportunity. A few months back, a friend of a friend of a friend had told Lenora that she and Holly could stay at a house in a tiny town called Wonderland, should they ever need to.

And yes. They needed to.

The rain tapered off as Lenora took the exit for Wonderland. Holly still couldn't believe the town was actually named that. She thought that maybe, somehow, it was a sign. That things were going *right* for once.

There were a few small buildings that didn't appear to be in great shape, a wooden sign that welcomed them to the town, and the railroad. Lenora took a left, navigating down dirt roads, swerving to avoid potholes. The engine revved as she pressed particularly hard on the gas to get over the railroad tracks. She turned onto Swift Lane slowly, tentatively, as if she were dreading it.

"There it is," Lenora announced, pointing to a tiny, dilapidated house on the end of the block. The grass had grown high and untamed in some places, was completely dead in others. A huge tree stood in the front yard. Trash was strewn all over the narrow deck that led to the front door.

Suddenly, the motel in Utah looked like a palace. The urge to cry overwhelmed Holly, and she swiped at a few rogue tears that leaked from the corners of her eyes. *This isn't right*, she thought.

Lenora pulled the car into the driveway. She reached over, wrapping an arm around her daughter as she said, "Welcome home, Holls."

CHAPTER

4

Outlaw State of Mind (Now)

I WAKE TO THE smell of bacon.

At first I think I'm hallucinating. I can't recall the last time I made a real breakfast—everything is usually takeout and delivery. But then I come to my senses, feel the unfamiliar couch beneath me, and remember where I am.

Cora's house. I'm in Cora's house. And someone else is here with me, making bacon. I whip around, the open floor plan giving me a straight view into the kitchen. I blink a few more times. *Maybe I am hallucinating.*

"What are you doing?"

Hunter looks over casually from her spot in front of the stove. She stands, looking completely at home in a blue-checkered flannel and jeans, a grease-stained towel slung over her shoulder. "Oh, good. I thought you were gonna sleep all day."

I throw off the blanket I grabbed from the closet last night, and run my hands over my face. "What time is it?"

"Eight."

"And you thought I was going to sleep all day because I wasn't up by *eight in the morning*?"

"I've been up since five thirty," she replies. That's only . . . two and a half hours after she caught me wandering around outside. "Cora was always up by then too. I guess they run on different hours up in the city."

"Yeah, normal ones," I snap, coming to stand in front of the fridge.

Hunter sneers, her gaze turning back to the pan in front of her. Eggs, I notice, as she uses a fork to fluff them. "Nothin' normal about wastin' nearly three hours of sunlight."

"Well, we're not out in the fields hoeing and plowing, or whatever it is that you do."

"Mighty nice for y'all," she replies, not missing a beat.

"Forget you ever remembered me." Her words come back to me in a rush as I cross my arms over my chest, leaning against the fridge. Last night, she cut me off right before I was about to ask more about her family—her parents were friends with Cora, and I think she had a brother. I could be wrong, though. Truthfully, I've tried to forget as much about that time as possible.

Hunter came back to me. She was important enough to remember.

The idea that she's here and her family isn't . . . "You didn't answer my question," I say, distracting myself.

"Which was?"

"What are you doing?"

"Y'all don't have eggs up in the city?"

"Why are you making eggs at eight in the morning in my kitchen?"

"Cora's kitchen," she corrects, a slight edge to her tone that I don't miss. "And it's Sunday. It's tradition."

"Tradition?"

"Sunday mornin' breakfast before headin' out for more work."

"You work on Sunday?" I snort, then adopt a poor rendition of Hunter's accent and say, "What, y'all don't have weekends down in the country?"

She says nothing for a moment, all her attention on the sizzling pan in front of her. She reaches for a plate, then dumps the eggs out onto it.

I clear my throat. "Look—"

"I'm the only one keepin' this place afloat right now, so yes. I work on Sundays." She thrusts the plate in my direction, looking up. Her gaze is hard and unwavering, not revealing anything, so unlike the way she looked at me last night under the stars, like she was a few words away from unraveling completely. "Bacon and potatoes and toast are already on the table. You can eat, or you can starve. I'm headin' into the city later today, so if you need anything, I suggest you let me know."

I take the plate from her. Without another word, Hunter turns, walking straight past all the food she prepared and tugging her boots on.

"I'll need a ride to the police station tomorrow."

"Fine."

"What about you?" I ask, holding the plate of eggs, watching as she methodically laces up her boots, then double-knots them.

She grabs her hat from the rack, tucks it onto her head one-handed. "I already ate. And I told you, Sunday breakfast is a tradition for me and Cora. You're Cora's niece, whether you like it or not, and down in the country—that means somethin'."

Her words stick like hot asphalt in my stomach, eviscerating any semblance of an appetite. "Must be nice," I say sarcastically as she pulls open the door. "Being the one that she wanted. The one she allowed here."

Standing in the doorway, Hunter drops her head, letting out a long, heavy sigh. "You ain't got the slightest idea what it's like bein' the only one left standin'."

*   *   *

I'm just out of the shower and pulling on a pair of fresh leggings when I hear Hunter's truck rumble to life.

A very large part of me wants nothing more than to lie back down on the couch and pray that the blanket smothers me. That would be admitting defeat, though—letting Hunter know that all her shots are piercing my armor in the worst kinds of ways.

So that's how I end up pulling up the right leg of my leggings and hopping to the door in the same motion.

"What the hell?" I exclaim, catching her as she's getting into the truck.

She glances over the driver's side door. "What?"

"You asked if I wanted to go into the city with you, and now you're gonna leave without me?"

Her eyebrows pull down. "I asked if you *needed* anything, not for you to road trip with me."

"So you were gonna leave me here?" I demand.

"Planned on it."

The contempt that she has for me would be staggering if I weren't so used to it. "Are you gonna let me come with you or not?"

Her gaze drops south, taking in my appearance. "You gonna go out like that?"

I glance down at my leggings, black tank top, bare feet. "I was going to put some shoes on first."

"Be quick, then," she says dismissively. "Some of us got things to do."

I double back to the house, putting on a pair of socks before slipping on my tennis shoes. Grabbing my purse and my phone, I storm back to the truck, then climb into the passenger's side and slam the door. "You hate everyone this much, or am I special?"

I know I've done everything in my power to make her hate me, so it's a stupid question to ask. But then something close to a smile crosses her lips. It's the first time that I've even come close to seeing her make such a gesture. "How'd you get that mark on your wrist?" she asks instead of answering.

"Birthmark," I tell her. "Been waiting for you to ask about it since I caught you staring last night."

"I know someone who's got one that looks like that, is all," she replies. "Don't flatter yourself, Princess."

"Stop calling me that."

She laughs derisively, hooking a left. "I'll make a note."

"What did I do to deserve—"

"Oh, you wanna talk about *deserve*? Did Cora deserve a niece who didn't even know she was missin'?"

Shock forces the air from my lungs. "Did I deserve an aunt who hasn't talked to me in eight years?"

"Did I deserve to have to arrange for you to get down here, just so you could complain and whine and waste my time?"

"Then drive me to the airport right now," I bark. I'm showing her all my cards, every last one of them, and I desperately need to pull them back before she notices. "I'll grab my shit and you can send me right back to where I came from, and you'll never have to see me again."

"No."

"No?"

"No," she repeats. "Cora needs you."

"If she *needed* me, where the hell has she been for eight years?" I yell.

Jesus. *Jesus.* I've been here not even twenty-four hours, and I'm already unraveling, already letting Cora and this place and the woman next to me get back inside my bones. All the work I have done to protect myself, to ensure that I continue to see another day—so close to crumbling to dust.

There's a subtle curiosity that thrums through me, nearly drowned out by the searing hate and irritation that rattles alongside it. I'm itching to know how Hunter can pinpoint all my triggers, all my buttons, with such preciseness and so little effort; how she knows exactly where to push, exactly how hard, and exactly when.

Maybe because she's got the same ones. Family, Cora, abandonment. It'd make sense. The two of us, tied to this place differently, but no less irrevocably.

Hunter goes quiet as she throws the truck into gear, checks her rearview, and starts reversing. I wonder if any of the same thoughts are dancing through her mind, if the similarities between us have caught her attention. She must hate it, if so—sharing so much with some silly *city girl*.

Cora's house is set far back off the main road, at the end of a long, winding dirt one that Hunter goes down at twenty miles an hour. There are no other houses out here—just dirt, and animals I have no interest in engaging with at any point. Cora and I used to ride four-wheelers up and down this road all day, to the point that I knew where to swerve, to avoid the biggest potholes, with my eyes closed.

Leave, I think. *Go back to where you belong, and don't look back.*

"Phones work both ways, you know," Hunter says suddenly, though her voice is quiet. "You could've tried to fix things first."

"I did. Right after she made me leave, I tried calling—"

"What about in the past year? Or the past three years? Past five? Cora could've called you, yes, but you could've called her too."

I want to be mad at Hunter—she makes it so easy, after all—but a part of me knows that she's right. I could've called. Hell, I could've gotten on a flight and showed up at her doorstep. But I'm here now—and since I can't change the past, this has got to be enough.

Of all the cases I've helped Carson—the investigator who took me under their wing—solve, this is the one I've wanted to solve the most. To find out why, after so many summers, twilight struck for the final time eight years ago. The only way I'm going to do that is by finding Cora; and if she's still adamant I vacate this hellhole of a state, I'm stronger now. Harder. Ready to demand answers, even if they'll hurt more than help.

I need to know. I'm *entitled* to know why the one and only person in this godforsaken world I thought loved me proved so thoroughly and definitively that she did not. This is a mystery, and I solve those for a living. Regardless of whether the person I'm trying to find wants to be found.

*   *   *

Hunter fails to mention that "into the city" means a two-and-a-half-hour drive north to Casper. A quick Google search tells me it's the second-biggest city in the state, with a population of just over fifty-five thousand. It's the seat of Natrona County—two high schools, a summer collegiate baseball team, and a Target. The biggest fish in the littlest pond.

Most of the trip is spent out of cell service range, so all I'm left with to do is stare out the window. I wonder vaguely what it's like to grow up here. Not in a town like Casper, which I realize as we drive through town semi-resembles actual civilization, but in a town like Wonderland, where everyone knows you, your reflection, and your shadow. Where you can't draw a breath without the wind changing. Where you could disappear into the gold and the open sky and never be found again.

But isn't that what people flee to this part of the country to find? Big Sky Country. Wide open spaces. Freedom and air and peace.

Maybe Cora realized, same as she did at eighteen, that this life of dirt and dust wasn't enough for her. Maybe she got tired of five AM wakeups, of her tires hitting the same bumps in the same roads. Maybe she ran back to Denver or maybe somewhere else this time: the East Coast or Mexico or Australia.

Maybe she just ran, deciding finally and absolutely that anywhere else was better than here.

The first thing Carson taught me is that there are no facts, just truths that can change should the circumstances be right. I'd like to believe it's a fact that Cora wouldn't up and leave without telling anyone; that she wouldn't run for one of the four borders of this state, hopping in her truck with nothing but the clothes on her back. But believing that would make me a fool, something I can't afford to be ever again.

It's funny, almost. In a place where there's nowhere to go, there are so many places to hide.

Hunter gets off the highway, jarring me from my thoughts. We pass a couple of gas stations and a pair of hotels that have surely seen better days, before she hooks a sharp right. She pulls into a small parking lot, the road that leads to it full of holes and bumps that rival the ones back at the ranch.

Hunter exhales as she turns the truck off. There's a chain-link fence, a small building, and a sign that reads "Players and Coaches Only." Then she reaches over, her hand brushing across my knees, as she opens the glove box and pulls out a handgun.

It's not my first time seeing a gun. Carson used to leave the office with them sometimes when we were doing something particularly dangerous, something that we probably shouldn't have been doing in the first place. But it's certainly the first time I watch as someone tucks one into their waistband, up against the small of their back, closes their eyes, and grips the steering wheel in front of them like it's a lifeline.

The worry tensing her neck, the way her knuckles are quickly going white, the shades of this woman that keep emerging . . .

"What the fuck is going on?" I ask in a small voice.

A gust of wind passes by us, rattling the truck. It does nothing to calm my quickly fraying nerves. "Work," she says after a moment.

"What kind of *work* requires you to bring a gun to a baseball field?"

Hunter runs her hands along the circumference of the steering wheel. She takes a deep breath, lets it go. Does it again, then a third time. I'm sure, she's convincing herself.

We all have monsters inside of us; I learned that at a young age. They take different shapes, different forms, but each of us has one, rattling around, waiting to be unleashed. The difference between a *good* person and a *bad* one, most of the time, is control—how much time it takes before they lose their grip on their monster.

For the first time, I wonder what it would take for hers to come roaring to the surface, exploding from her throat like a tornado.

When she finally opens her eyes and looks over at me, I see her control. It's there, still firmly in her grasp, even if the gun at her back has caused her to loosen her grip a touch.

"My kind," she says.

Hunter offers me nothing more than a gruff "Stay here" before she's out of the truck and moving.

She walks toward the front of the building. There's a door there, and when she approaches it, she knocks twice. Her hand goes to her back, then she drops it, shaking it out at the wrist. An instinct, to go for her gun before there's a clear and present danger.

Reckless. Puts herself in potentially unsafe situations. Quick on the trigger.

The door opens. A man steps out, and Hunter moves back, just a step. He is clean-shaven, a ball cap with a horse on it pulled low over his eyes. Gray T-shirt, pair of old jeans, cowboy boots.

He looks her up and down in a way that has me reaching for my door. It's not even noon yet, the sun beating down without a single cloud to block it. And both of us still wary about what this man might do.

It's easy to dismiss the caution, the gut reaction, as typical man-hating lesbian behavior, silly and stereotypical. But the minute you drop your guard? The minute you leave your gun in the glove box, your keys in your purse, your drink uncovered? It's the same ending, over and over again, an infinity loop, a never-ending cycle of violence and pain and suffering.

I'll take the names, I'll take the dismissals if it means I'm safe. Hunter seems to accept that trade-off too.

Outside the safety of the truck, the man reaches behind him to the small of his back. All the air seizes in my lungs. Hunter's fingers twitch but stay at her sides.

Not a word is exchanged as he hands her a medium-sized envelope. He holds onto it for a beat too long, and she has to tug on it, but he lets go. Then he turns around, throws the door open, and storms back inside the building.

She stands there for a moment, motionless, as if she's in shock. Just as I'm about to go after her, she turns on her heel and starts back toward me.

The door closes with a slam. She puts the gun back, touches my knee again. When she exhales, there's nothing sure about it.

Then she puts the truck into reverse, backs out of the space, shifts into drive, and we're gone.

* * *

Hunter's driving again; at least I think so.

There's a buzzing in my ears, a fuzziness around my vision that's throwing off all my senses.

I should already be looking for Cora, already assembling leads and clues and tracking her down. Instead I'm doing . . . whatever this is.

Nothing is fitting like it should. There's no rhyme or reason to any of this, no path forward. What I originally thought would be cut and dry is unwinding into something far more complicated.

I hate it. I hate not being in control. I hate not being able to anticipate the next two, three, four moves. I hate that Cora is missing, that she hasn't spoken to me in eight years, that she never—

"You alright over there?"

I startle, flinching as if Hunter had reached out and slapped me. I realize that her hand is on my thigh, dangerously high, though I doubt she even notices. "What?"

"I asked if you were hungry."

"Hungry," I repeat.

"Yeah. Am I speakin' French?"

It all comes rushing back, everything clicking into place: the sweat on my hands, the squeak of the leather beneath me, the envelope she has resting between us, the gun tucked away just beyond my reach.

I've held a gun before, one of Carson's, but it wasn't loaded. I've certainly never fired one before. Suddenly I want to. I want to feel the weight in my palm, feel the impact of the ricochet, my heart beating in time with the bullet as it leaves the chamber.

I exhale, flexing my fingers, then curling them back in, feeling the bones press together and release. "What's in there?" I ask, jerking my chin at the envelope.

She scratches at the skin above her eyebrow. "None of your business."

I pause, letting the words sit for a moment to ensure that I've heard her right. "You call me from a thousand miles away," I begin, "to summon me to come find my missing aunt, and you don't think to mention that your line of *work* entails guns and mysterious packages? You didn't stop to think for even one second that that man you met up with, the one you were so afraid of that you approached him *armed*, might have something to do with this?"

"No," she says slowly, like she's explaining something to a child. "This is part of ranch business. I've been doing it for years, and there's never been a problem. There's no connection, so there's no need to get all excited—"

"Then what's in this envelope? Drugs? Money? Something else entirely?"

She says nothing for so long that I'm surely about to come out of my skin. She keeps driving, winding us through downtown, passing shops and people going about their day.

"I swear to *God*—"

"It's money," she says, finally relenting. "In the envelope. Last month Cora sold him some old ranch equipment we weren't usin' anymore, and that's the cash for it."

"Then why the gun?"

She shrugs. "Don't make a habit of trustin' folks easy."

"That's all it was?" I ask, still not quite believing all that was over some tractors. "You promise?"

The truck comes to a stop. I don't look to see if we're at a red light or parked somewhere or hanging off the edge of a cliff—my attention is entirely on Hunter. This woman who keeps dodging my questions with incomplete answers she thinks will satisfy me; who keeps trying to slip through my fingers like sand. Who has so many different faces and sides that I cannot even remember the last one she showed me, let alone decipher the one that's staring back at me now.

Her hand is still on my thigh, searing through the thin fabric of my leggings. Her eyes flicker over my face like she's searching for something in my features. *No*, I think. *Someone.*

"I promise," she says, dragging me out of my head, her fingers digging lightly into my thigh. "That's all it is. Now, are you hungry?"

I don't reply, and we don't move—not an inch, either of us. I'm too shell-shocked thinking about how this morning could start with bacon and eggs and lead to an armed exchange of cash, all before noon. Or maybe I'm waiting to see what Hunter does, if she'll offer up some new piece of information or touch me somewhere more interesting.

"You're asking me to trust you," I continue. "You realize that, right?"

"I do."

"Well, I don't trust easy either."

"Hard not to notice that, Princess. Another thing we've got in common."

So she has noticed. All the similarities, all the ways we fit together.

I regard her carefully. "I could eat."

The hand from my thigh is gone as soon as the words are out. "Then let's go."

*   *   *

The waitress sets down two menus and asks what we'd like to drink.

"Whiskey, please," I reply, flashing my ID. A real one, my actual age and name printed on the material after countless years of using top-of-the-line fakes, courtesy of Carson. "A double on the rocks."

The waitress gives me a blank look before nodding, probably wanting to know why I'm ordering straight liquor at noon on a Sunday, but she's not making nearly enough to raise any objection to it.

Hunter orders a water, which I could've seen coming from a mile away. "You alright?" she asks as the waitress disappears.

I lean back in my chair. "Let's talk about you."

"That's not what I—"

"How'd you end up as a ranch hand for Cora?"

A muscle in her jaw jumps. "She took me in when ain't nobody else would."

"And now you arm yourself while picking up payments for busted tractors."

"Nothin' else in the world I'd rather be doin'."

"Really?" The waitress returns with our drinks, and I take a long sip, leveling my gaze on the woman across from me, waiting for her answer.

"It ain't so bad, livin' out here," she replies. "'Specially the way you make it seem."

"I'm assuming you've lived here your whole life?"

"I have."

The question about her family, the one she skirted last night, I want to ask her again. I want to find out exactly how Hunter ended up out here with Cora. But I know if I ask again, I'll startle her. Lose any sort of miniscule ground that I've gained in the handful of hours I've been here. I need her if I'm gonna solve this, and I'm only starting to make headway.

"What do you want to do once you're done here?" I ask.

"You miss what I said the first time around?"

"You want to work for Cora for the rest of your life?"

"I do," she says solemnly. "I won't explain it, 'cause you prob'ly wouldn't understand it all anyway."

"It's a lot of assuming you do."

As if on cue, her eyes flicker to my drink. "How old are you?"

"Twenty-two."

"You're Cora's niece on your mom's side, then?"

I go still, glass frozen halfway to my mouth. "Remember how you reacted last night, when I asked about your family? Same goes for me."

She gives me an oddly open look, like she understands exactly what I'm saying. I wonder how bad things must be with her family, then, if I make sense to her.

The waitress comes back, and Hunter looks down at her menu. She orders for both of us, two of the same thing.

"You ain't a vegan, are you?" she asks.

"Feels like that was a question you should've asked prior to ordering for me."

She exhales through her nose, slow and annoyed. "What is it you do up in the city, exactly?"

"I've been shadowing the top private investigator in the region for the past six years," I explain. "We handle mostly missing persons cases, so you called the right woman."

A beat. "How many folks you find that are still alive?"

"Most of them," I say carefully. "The earlier we start looking, the better the odds."

"Two weeks ain't good odds, then?"

Hunter knows the answer. She wants me to refute it to make her feel better, and maybe if I were a kinder person, I'd do it. Honestly, I think the truth—no matter how terrible and ugly—is the kindest thing of all.

"Yeah," she says when I don't reply. "That's what I'd worked out."

Our burgers come. Hunter digs right in, rolling up her sleeves, juice dripping down the sides of her mouth. I sip my drink slow, eat a couple of fries, and watch.

Hunter is someone who does what she wants, regardless of what anyone else thinks of her. Maybe that's what this kind of isolation does to you, when your best friends are the deer and raccoons that prowl around your property at night. Maybe it gives you fewer reservations, less caution when it comes to other people.

Cora knew what people are capable of. She was the first one who taught me to be wary of them. Denver had chipped away at the naivety that growing up on a Wyoming ranch and staying here your entire life breeds—exactly what's taken root in Hunter.

She juts her chin at my plate. "You ain't gonna eat?"

"Jesus, I'm working on it."

She grunts something noncommittal, then goes back to devouring her burger. I finish my fries, polish off my whiskey, feeling the heat start to buzz through my limbs.

It's surely the liquor that makes me ask, "You got a boyfriend?"

A strange, choked sound emerges from deep in her throat, and I raise my eyebrows. "No," she replies around a bite of burger.

"Why not?"

Wiping at her mouth, Hunter shakes her head. "Just don't."

A horrible, terrible thought throttles into my mind, a sinking feeling taking hold in my gut. I've been wondering why she won't expand on how she got here, what her relationship is with Cora. *What if—*

"Were you two together?"

She pauses, burger halfway to her mouth. "What?"

"Were you and Cora fucking?"

Her entire body locks up, her back going ramrod straight. And for one long, trembling moment, I think I'm right, that I've figured out this part of the puzzle, especially when she makes no move to correct me.

The waitress collects our plates, offering me a box that I decline. She gives me another strange look before disappearing, then comes back with the check.

I reach for it at the same time Hunter does, our fingers brushing. Before I can blink, she's wrapping those very fingers around my wrist, applying enough pressure that it's noticeable, but not quite painful.

"Do not ever ask me something like that again," she says, her voice low, the line of her jaw hard. Her eyes are wide, her nostrils flared.

"Alright, calm down," I tell her. I make no move to break out of her hold, relishing the strength of her grip. "It's just that it's you two, all alone out there. People might assume—"

"People don't assume things like that out here."

And now it's my turn to go still. "Like what?"

She exhales, dropping my wrist and swooping up the check all in one motion. "A lotta folk don't take too kindly to the notion of two women bein' . . . together like that. You'd better start watchin' how you speak, or—"

"Or what?" I challenge, leaning closer, wishing the table wasn't a barrier between us. "Genuinely. What's going to happen to me if I keep running my mouth, about *this* specifically? You think I don't know about all the various dangers of being an out and loud lesbian? I've been out since I was thirteen, and we've got plenty of ignorant fucks up north too."

Her lips press together, forming a straight line. "I didn't realize you were . . . like that."

"Like that," I repeat.

"I didn't mean—"

"This gonna be a problem too now?"

Hunter goes silent again, but her gaze never leaves mine. *Is she trying to think of a way to disguise her homophobia as small-town charm, or is she thinking of an apology fitting for what she's said?*

"No," she finally says quietly.

"Well, isn't it good to know there's something about me that doesn't offend you and everyone else in this town?"

Heat rises to her cheeks, turning her face bright red. "Princess, that ain't what I—"

"My name is Quinn," I snap. "The only people who get to call me anything else are the women who have the good fortune of spending the night underneath me. From this conversation it truly seems like pigs will fly before you become one of said women, so you can call me Quinn, or you can stop speaking to me altogether."

I push away from the table, standing and heading toward the exit without another word.

*   *   *

Mercifully, I fall asleep on the drive back, waking just as Hunter pulls into downtown Wonderland.

I blink the sleep from my eyes, straightening. We pass a couple of parks, a gas station, and a mobile home that reads

"Wonderland Branch Library" as she drives through what counts for the heart of town here.

Though the sights are truly astounding, I try to fall back asleep, but to no avail. The truck is particularly uncomfortable, and my neck already aches from how I was resting earlier.

"Look, I didn't mean no harm," she says suddenly, eager to catch me awake. "What I said at the restaurant. You caught me off guard, is all."

"Anyone ever tell you you're shit at apologies?"

"I doubt you're much better at 'em." She rearranges her grip on the steering wheel, tapping her thumb. "You wanna tell me why you're so upset?"

"Perhaps it has to do with the less than hospitable conditions I've been greeted under."

"Hospitable," she repeats.

"Do you need me to define that for you?" I hurl at her. "Did they not give you basic vocabulary lessons all the way out here in the middle of bumfuck nowhere?"

"That's enough."

"Oh, I'm just getting started—"

"I said that's enough."

"You don't get to talk to me like—"

Hunter's jerking the truck to the side of the road, throwing it in park, and getting out before I can even process what's happening.

I'm not idle for long. Anger, still pent up from what happened at the restaurant, sends me out of the truck. She's leaning against the bed of the truck on my side, her head resting so close to the metal that her forehead nearly touches it.

"What in the hell is going—"

"You asked where my family's at."

"What?"

"When I caught you outside. You asked where my family's at." She raises her head, looking me right in the eye. There's so much emotion there, so much that I can't read because I don't understand it. It makes my blood run even hotter, makes me even more jealous, knowing that she can see right through me but I can't even get beneath her surface.

She rights herself, looking at me head-on as she says, "Dead. They're dead. All of 'em." The air is sucked from my lungs. There it is—the thing that's made her like this, all bared teeth and jagged edges. I've been searching for it quietly, trying to coax it out like a trapped animal. Her comment about being the last one standing this morning makes a lot more sense.

"What?"

"Seven years ago, drunk driver," she continues. Her voice is almost robotic, like it's a recording she's playing back. Like she's told this story so many times she could do it backwards, with her eyes closed, while asleep. "Cora was my mom's best friend. She took me in after, let me use the guesthouse. Cora is *all I have*," she spits. "That woman raised me as her own. And now you show back up after all this time, runnin' your mouth and sayin' all these terrible things about her and this place she loves so much, because you're not the one scared out of your mind, wonderin' what's happened to her. As if you know what it's like to have everything and everyone you loved ripped away from you—again."

I want to reply with something just as searing, but my mind's gone blank, and all I can think to say is "I was wrong."

"You'll have to narrow it down for me, Princess."

"About you," I say, stepping right into her face. "I thought you knew me. I thought you understood me. You think I don't know pain? You think I don't know what it's like to lose someone? To have someone who's supposed to love you hate you?" I shake my head. "I'm sorry about your family—truly. But you've got no fucking idea the life I've lived."

"I didn't tell you so you'd feel sorry for me," she retorts, not a shred of regret in her tone. "I told you because I wanted you to know that I've already lived through the worst thing that's ever gonna happen to me. I'm not doin' it again."

"Then we'll find her for you."

She rolls her eyes, and it only drives my rage higher. "Don't do that. Don't act like she doesn't love you," she says.

I go very, very still. "What would you call banishing your only niece from the place she spent every summer nearly her whole life? Especially knowing what she's got waiting back home? Would you call that *love*?"

I think for a moment that I've revealed too much, the words coming out too fast. I feel like my feet have been swept out from under me, and I'm falling, falling, falling, but I never hit the ground.

"Alright," Hunter says almost tentatively, surprising me. "From your side, I can see how you'd feel like that. But that's all you've got here: one side of the story."

"How would you suppose I go about getting the other side, then? Considering Cora has seemingly disappeared from right under your goddamn nose?"

Though I'd thought it impossible, Hunter gets even closer, so that we're sharing the same breath. "You think I don't know that?" she hisses, eyes wide. "You think I don't blame myself every day? Why do you think I called you, of all people? You're right—I don't know anything about you, and I don't want to. What kind of person shows up and says the kind of things that you do—about collectin' money from a dead woman, being so sure she's dead in the first place when you've done piss all to find her?"

"What about you?" I retort. "What exactly have *you* done to find her?"

"I've been talking to the police—"

"Oh, the *police*. I see. No, actually, here's what I see: someone who's so angry with themselves at their own inaction and lack of progress that they're lashing out at the only person actually trying to do something about the situation."

Hunter looks at me, eyes big and wide, like she's shocked I've connected the dots so fast. *Good,* I think. *Now you know what it feels like.*

"Jesus," she breathes, shaking her head. "What . . . what is this? Why do we keep doin' this to each other?"

"Because it's who I am," I tell her. "Maybe it's who you are too."

I can tell she hates it: the idea that she's like me in any way, even though she's already seen proof of it with her own eyes. She doesn't deny it, doesn't try to refute it. We're left standing, staring each other down, nearly nose to nose for God knows how long, neither of us willing to back down, even though I'm quivering inside.

She knew where to hit—maybe not because she knows me, but because she knows *herself.*

"Careful," I taunt, trying to steel my voice. "If you get any closer, you might catch the lesbian from me. Isn't that what they teach y'all around here?"

She finally pulls away, but whip fast throws back, "Can't catch what you've already got."

And I'm so shocked, so stunned, that I fall silent as she storms back to the driver's seat, and I'm that way for the entire trip back to the ranch.

CHAPTER

5

Golden (Then—March 1981)

STARTING AT A new school midyear was as easy as breathing to Holly Prine at this point.

Radley High School was far enough from her house in Wonderland that Lenora had to drive her. Her mother had, of course, made a big deal of having to do so, even though they arrived fifteen minutes late. Holly made a mental note to see if there was a bus anywhere remotely near Wonderland.

She collected her schedule and her late slip from the secretary, a skinny woman with teased-up hair who frowned at her immediately.

"Not the best first impression you're makin', darlin'," she'd told Holly, as if it were her fault her mother hadn't rolled out of bed until well after she was supposed to. Holly had even gone over the schedule with her the night before—what time she needed to be dropped off and picked up. *"I got it, I got it,"* Lenora had assured her.

And now here she was, day one, late slip in hand.

Holly was used to not relying on Lenora for things. Rides to places, dinner on the table, birthday presents. A real home. When Lenora said, *"I got it,"* very rarely did she actually have anything besides a bottle of cheap vodka in her hand, or a hangover the next morning.

The hallway Holly wandered down was tight and smelled strongly of perfume, with lockers on both sides. She wondered if she'd be assigned one or if they were all taken already. At her last school, her locker had been at the very end of the freshman hallway, bottom row, gum covering the bottom of it.

But this was not Castle Valley, Utah. This was Wonderland, Wyoming. Even as hard as she tried to squash any hope that the two would be different, it still flickered through her. No matter what Lenora had done or would do, that hope was what kept Holly going.

Bracing herself, Holly pushed her way inside her first-period class. "English 12—Smith," her schedule read. The teacher, a man who looked to be at least sixty-five, with a small nose and a shirt two sizes too big for him, immediately stopped and stared at Holly's arrival.

"Miss Prine, I presume?" he asked. His voice had a bit of a twang to it, and Holly guessed that was what Wyoming sounded like.

She nodded, handing him her late slip. He narrowed his eyes and gestured to the only open seat, right in the front row. "Don't make this a habit, Miss Prine," he scolded.

Holly sat down. She hunched her shoulders and leaned over her desk, trying to make herself as small as possible. She could feel the eyes on her, hear the whispers. There couldn't have been more than ten students in the small classroom, but it felt as if there were a million people looking at her, talking about her. She hated attention, especially attention like this.

Mr. Smith announced that they would be reading *The Great Gatsby* during the month of March. The entire class, except for Holly, groaned. She was pleased—she'd already read *Gatsby* last year at her school in Nevada. She liked the book well enough, though it couldn't hold a candle to even her least favorite Nancy Drew novel.

"You'll have a project due at the end of the month," Mr. Smith said as he handed out copies of the book. He gave Holly her copy last—the cover was ripped, the pages yellow. "Your partner is the person sitting next to you, and no, I don't want to hear any complaints."

Holly looked over at the same time as the girl sitting next to her did. Their eyes met, and the girl smiled.

She offered a little wave to Holly. "I'm Jessica," she said. "Jessica Coldwater."

Holly just . . . stared. Through all the places she'd been, all the classrooms she'd sat in, she'd never seen a more beautiful person than the girl next to her.

Jessica Coldwater had bright, brilliant, shoulder-length blonde hair. Natural. The kind that her mother always gazed longingly at in magazines, the kind that she always tried to replicate using a bottle, to no avail. Her eyes were an incredibly clear shade of blue, and there was not a pimple in sight anywhere on her face. She had high cheekbones, arched brows, and a perfect jawline.

Holly knew, right in that moment, she was in trouble.

Her tongue stuck to the roof of her mouth as she tried to answer. Jessica smiled at her again, as if urging her on.

"Holly," she managed. "I'm . . . I'm Holly."

Jessica winked. *Oh.* Holly thought she was going to fall out of her chair, to the floor.

"Nice to meet you, partner," Jessica said.

CHAPTER

6

Ain't Gonna Drown (Now)

I THOUGHT IT'D BE quiet out here.

The quiet's only a background that ends up amplifying everything else, all the chirps and rustles and howls.

It's the perfect place to go missing because all the things that makes noise, that cover up what happened, can't say a goddamn thing about what they saw. A million eyes, and not one voice; surrounded by so much life, yet still all alone.

* * *

I go through Cora's closet first.

Hunter goes back to working outside without so much as a *fuck you* as soon as we get back to the house. She, too, seemed to have revealed too much on our little trip into town.

"Can't catch what you've already got."

I exhale, pulling Cora's closet open wide. Summer clothes are hanging, her heavier winter coats and boots stored down below in big gray bins on the floor. Flannels and jeans, probably a nearly identical set to what Hunter's got hanging up in hers. Most of the hangers are full, so she didn't pack a bag, at least not one for a long trip.

Everything looks fine in the bathroom: a bar of soap, a razor, bottles of shampoo and conditioner. There's some moisturizer on the counter, though when I spin open the lid, it's nearly full.

The room itself is immaculate. The bed is made. The desk is tidy. No boots thrown near the bed, no towels slung over the door. Nothing to suggest she left in a hurry, but nothing to suggest she was forced out either.

The surface is telling me nothing. So it's time to go deeper.

I pull out all the drawers from the dresser, drop their contents all over the floor. Nothing of interest falls out among the underwear, the bras, and the socks; and the drawers in her desk and the one in her nightstand are similarly of no help.

There are no compartments in the floor, no lines in the ceiling to signal any paneling. Her closet holds nothing but clothes and shoes. I rip the blankets and the sheets from the bed, to no avail.

The room is spinning when I'm done, my chest heaving from exertion and frustration.

There's . . . nothing. It feels sterile, like you couldn't even tell who was living here. No secrets hidden among the cobwebs and the dead moths. *Nothing.*

I scrub my hands down my face. Another waste of time, like so much of my time spent here has been, and I'm no closer to finding Cora than I was the morning Hunter called. Even though I've been here less than twenty-four hours, I'm already behind the eight ball. I need to find something—anything—that'll send me in the right direction.

I'm standing, moving toward the door, ready to declare this another dead end, when I see it. Perched on the corner of her desk in a tiny black frame: a photo of Cora and me from the last time I was here.

My legs close the distance between the desk and me. I pick up the frame, ignoring the way my hands are shaking just a touch.

Eight years ago, but it seems so much longer. My arms wrapped around her neck, the big smile on her face.

Lies. All of it. Because she ruined it.

I flip it over. On the back, taped to the right-hand corner, is a key.

*   *   *

"You know what this goes to?"

Hunter wipes sweat from her brow, picking up the long barrel of wire next to her. The sun's starting to slip away into the night, the wind brushing by us. It was hot this morning, but the temperature has cooled considerably. "What?" she demands.

I thrust the key in her direction. "This. Do you know what it goes to?"

Her eyes narrow as she stands, studying the key. "Where'd you find that?"

"In Cora's room, taped to the back of a photo of the two of us."

She takes it, and I try to ignore the rough feeling of her gloves against my bare skin. She turns it over, passing it between her hands. "No," she says, giving it back. "I ain't never seen anything like that."

The key is so small it nearly disappears into my hand. It's gold, with a tiny *C* carved into the top of it. Cora, maybe, or Cole. It'd be so easy to lose, to slip through your fingers and be lost out here in the grass and the dirt.

Hunter scratches the back of her neck. "That all you wanted?"

My eyes move to what she's working on. Fixing the barbed-wire fence on the east side of the property, it looks like. The tension between us hasn't dissipated any either. I wonder if she's waiting for me to bring up this afternoon, to acknowledge what she said. At this point, I don't even know the truth about who I am, so how could I possibly try to explain it to Hunter?

"That's all," I tell her as I tuck the key into the back pocket of my jeans.

"Alright," she replies, kneeling back down. "I'm gonna get back to work, if that's alright with you."

"Do you need help?"

We both freeze in disbelief. Why in the hell would I ask that? Why would I offer this woman, of all people, help? I should start looking into what this key could open, not volunteer to help with manual labor. Fixing fences certainly isn't on my list of investigative chores.

Hunter Lemming should mean nothing to me. But she knows my aunt better than I do; she's the one who's gotten all the pieces of Cora that I've missed out on. The pieces I used to get. The pieces I'll never get again if I don't find her.

Hunter is rude and smart and honest. She looks at me like I'm on the top, middle, and bottom of her shit list. She's told me I'm a terrible person, and it only makes me want to ask in earnest, *How do you know?*

Finally, Hunter drops her head toward her lap, letting out a short laugh. "Do you have any sorta idea how to do this?"

Heat rises to my cheeks. I have some memory of this chore, but eight years have damped down the finer points. "Obviously not," I snap. "I'm just a stuck-up city girl, remember?"

She looks up at me from her knees, and a shiver goes down my spine. "Go back inside," she says, her mind obviously not in the same place as mine.

"You give me shit for not knowing how to do any countryfolk things, and now when I'm trying to help you out, you want to send me away? Seems a bit hypocritical of you."

She rises, takes off her worn gloves, then hands them over. "Have at it."

The gloves are still warm from her hands as I slip them on, then take a spot in front of the fence. I stare at the hole, then the bundle of wire next to my right knee.

"Alright," she says. When I look over, Hunter's kneeling, one arm extended as she points toward the fence. "I already took the barbs off for you, and the first sleeve's on there right." She reaches back and around me to grab for something else. Her now-bare hand brushes against my side, and I pretend I don't notice the contact. *Can't catch what you've already got.*

"Clamp this down around the sleeve," she says, handing me a large, jawed tool that looks a bit like a pair of pliers. "This is the crimper."

I do as she says, clamping the tool over the small, bead-like fixture on the line of wire. I press the handles together, and the sleeve wraps tighter around the wire. A memory comes into focus, of Cora's hands wrapped around mine when I was too small and weak to do this by myself. Every time we'd finish a section, she'd stand, wipe the sweat from her brow, and smile at me, her stamp of approval.

Now, I can do this and everything else by myself. And the days of wanting approval are long gone—just, it seems, like the woman whose approval I used to crave the most.

"Harder than that," Hunter instructs, dragging me out of my head.

Please. I blow out a breath, then bring the handles together once again.

"Good," she says. "Now you're gonna separate the wires there and wrap 'em around the sleeve."

Pulling the wires apart is easy, but it's slower going trying to get them all wrapped back together. While I'm trying to finish, Hunter clears her throat. "You gonna tell me why you've taken a sudden interest in ranch chores?"

Shaking my head, I focus on wrapping the wire. "It's a good idea for me to get into Cora's headspace, do the things she would do, put myself in her shoes. Plus it's a good distraction."

"What do you need a distraction from?"

My missing aunt. What you said in the truck. The way I want to trail my mouth after the drops of sweat that are rolling down your neck. "Oh, I don't know. It's not like anything traumatizing has happened within the past couple of days."

She presses her lips together. "Harder" is all she says.

I exhale. "Alright. If you were Cora, where would you have disappeared to?"

"Nowhere," she replies almost before I've even gotten the entirety of the question out. "I already told you that Cora wouldn't have left without tellin' anyone. She doesn't own any other property, doesn't have any family that she visits. She's here every single day of the year."

"So you're assuming she was taken, then?"

"Yes."

"She drive a car?"

"A truck, yeah."

"Where is it?"

". . . Not here."

I raise my eyebrows. "Okay, strike against the kidnapping theory."

"I knew her," she growls. "I *know* her better than anyone else. When I say she didn't run away, I mean it."

A beat. Then I add, "Better than I did."

Her eyebrows pull down. "What?"

"What you meant to say is you know her better than I did."

She blinks, then opens her mouth to say something, but I don't let her. "Who in her life would've wanted to hurt her?"

Hunter hesitates, then tries to make it seem like she didn't. The action is small, but I've been trained in this language. The way people hide and dip and shirk away when you ask the wrong question or, rather, the right one. "No one," she says.

"Lie."

"No one," she repeats, shifting away from me.

"Do you want to find her or not?"

"Stop askin' me that."

"Then stop giving me reasons to."

"God, you think . . ." She trails off, shakes her head.

"Say it, Cowgirl."

"You think you know everything!" she exclaims. "You think everything is so small and simple here—that you're gonna snap your fingers and find Cora hidin' in some corner. I already answered these questions from the police two weeks ago, and they've come up with nothin'. What makes you think—"

"The police are idiots."

"Oh, here we go—"

"And in a town this size, severely ill-equipped to deal with a missing persons case. Me, on the other hand? I've been assisting a private investigator for the past six years in one of the biggest cities in the Pacific Northwest. I've seen all kinds of crimes and people and motives and have far more experience at twenty-two with this type of case than whatever idiot is running the police force in town. I hate to break it to you, but our best bet of bringing my aunt home is *me*. It's only gonna work if you start being honest with me and tell me what I need to know.

"That's not me knowing everything," I continue before she can accuse me of being overconfident or arrogant. "That's me being incredibly capable and good at what I've been taught to do."

The silence stretches between us as I finish my task, my hands cramping and aching, but I don't complain. After a few moments, Hunter hands over a small pair of shears. "Clip the ends. Then we'll move on to the next one."

"What happened to the fence?" I ask.

"Storm probably knocked it down; happens. Gotta fix it quick or else the cows'll get out."

"Cows?"

"You do know this is a cattle ranch, right?"

"Of course," I reply, not completely truthful.

She looks at me with clear distain. "We've got twenty-seven of 'em right now. Right before Cora went missing, some gal named Lindsay, from the bank, came down and counted 'em all up for us."

"She *counted your cows*? Is that a Wyoming-style euphemism?"

"I don't know what you mean."

I rub at my forehead with the back of my gloved hand. "Of course not."

We keep moving down the fence line, patching holes, me doing the work, Hunter only speaking to offer instructions or advice. Sweat starts to drip down the back of my neck as I work, the time ticking by as the sun starts to fade entirely.

"Alright," Hunter says eventually, my mind too lost in the monotony of fence fixing to register how many hours have gone by. "That'll be enough for today. Time for dinner."

We gather all the tools and supplies. I follow her back toward the main house, to the tool shed that's set off to the side.

There's some strange, tentative part of me that likes this: working outside, seeing the instant results of my energy, the dust clinging to my palms and under my nails. That part of me isn't new; it's just been lying dormant for the past eight years. I loved coming out here and seeing Cora, but I also loved helping her with chores, working alongside the sun as it gave way to the moon. It was in those moments that I understood my aunt the most: why she gave up something she was so passionate about to run a ranch that was barely earning enough money to break even.

"If there were people who wanted to hurt her—and I'm not sayin' there were—she had it under control," Hunter suddenly offers as we step into the shed. It's small but crammed full, yet still somehow remarkably organized: tools hang on metal shelves above a small workbench, which is covered in neat stacks of paper on one side, and larger power tools on the other.

I hand my items to her, one at a time, watching as Hunter meticulously puts them away. The line of her body is strong and hard, but smooth. She's a well-oiled machine moving cohesively, every twitch of every muscle purposeful.

"And what if she didn't?" I ask carefully, even as alarm bells are going off in my head.

"She did," Hunter replies. "I know that for a fact. This isn't even worth talkin' about."

I hand her the last of the tools. "Why don't you tell me and then let me decide if it's important or not?"

Something incredibly odd happens after that: Hunter smiles. It's so unexpected I nearly lose my balance. But what a sight it is: white teeth against tan skin streaked with dirt and dust and sweat.

For a moment, I consider closing the distance between us, backing her up until she has no choice but to perch her ass on the workbench. That wouldn't work, though—she wouldn't give up ground so easily. Or maybe she would if she knew what I'd do to her in exchange for her giving me an inch to run with.

Hunter clears her throat, her eyes dropping to the floor as she rocks back on her heels. I wonder if, in the safety and privacy of this tiny shed on this sprawling ranch, similar thoughts had found their way into her head too. "Good work today, Princess."

"Good enough to get me one of those little hats for my own?"

As if on instinct, she reaches up to touch her hat, then stops halfway. "No," she replies, not even considering it. "You gotta earn one of these."

I take a step closer. "What'd you do to get yours, then?"

There's warning in her gaze when she looks up at me. This too must be personal—something connected to Cora or her family. "I earned it" is all she says, voice gruff.

With one more step, I'm standing nearly on her toes, sharing the same air. I was right: she gives no ground, makes no concessions. I raise my hand, aiming to skim the brim of her hat with the tips of my fingers, but she moves so fast it makes me dizzy. My hand is snared in her grip, hovering near her cheek, the heat from our palms searing into my knuckles.

"You don't touch another woman's hat," she all but growls.

Her grip doesn't loosen any, and I don't mind. "What can I touch, then?" I ask.

A muscle in her jaw jumps. "You can keep your hands to yourself is what you can do."

"That doesn't sound fun at all."

"You're not here for *fun*," she snaps. "You're here to find Cora."

"Did it occur to you I could do both?"

She finally lets go of my hand. "I ain't an idiot," she says brusquely, her cheeks starting to redden. "I know what you're suggestin'. And I ain't interested."

My eyes widen in mock surprise. "I was thinking that we could go get ice cream and paint our nails. But please, do tell: What are you so uninterested in?"

She says nothing, but her body betrays her. Hunter's cheeks have turned a shade of red I didn't even know existed. I wonder if it has a name or if I will forever remember it as *Hunter Lemming Arousal.*

I turn, walking back the way I came, letting the question sit with her. "Dinnertime."

*   *   *

I am drunk. Resoundingly so.

The vodka bottle next to me is half empty—*half full*, the few brain cells still hanging in there urge. I found it stowed beneath the sink when I went looking for alcohol again, Hunter retiring to the guesthouse instead of eating with me. Again.

Music is blasting through my phone, my attempt to drown out the thoughts that the vodka isn't adequately silencing.

Even though everything around me has changed so much, it's mind-bending how much hasn't. It's driving me up the fucking walls, wondering how both can be true—wondering if it's true of Cora too. If her hair is longer or if she ever thinks about me; what kind of person she's become.

I stagger to my feet, the room spinning slightly around the edges, not bothering with shoes or a coat or even a glance at the time before I'm out the door. My feet eat up the ground quickly, the crickets chirping incessantly, the world humming with life I can't see, and then I'm at Hunter's door.

I knock three times. "You up?" I yell . . . to no answer.

I scrub my hands over my face. The light from the porch is plenty to illuminate the space around me, so when I hear a rustle, I spin and can clearly see the giant wolf staring back.

I jump right back into the door. Wait, no—it's not a wolf. Just a huge, feral white cat.

I've seen feral cats scurrying around the more rural parts of Spokane before, but they were always much smaller, and there was always a three-thousand-ton vehicle in between the two of us.

The cat stares, as if transfixed, its fur a bright white, its eyes solid black orbs. It seems to be alone, but God knows what else is out here. I remember Cora's warnings, from so long ago, about the animals that roamed freely around here, especially at night: wild turkeys, raccoons, deer, bears, cougars. Though she probably wasn't speaking about pudgy feral cats when she issued those warnings.

The cat keeps staring but doesn't advance. I tip my head to the side, studying it as it studies me. I'm the one out of place here, I realize—the intruder. The one who doesn't belong.

Not for the first time and I'm sure not for the last.

Suddenly I'm falling backward, the air leaving my lungs as I land flat on my back. And then I'm staring up at the wide-eyed, bed-headed Hunter Lemming, whom I have very clearly woken up from sleep.

"What is wrong with you?" she exclaims. "It's three in the morning, and you're out here stargazing again?"

"There was a cat."

She rips her angered gaze upward, and mine follows the same path. "Nothing there, Princess," she says as we stare at the empty space.

"I swear to God, there was this huge fuck—"

"Have you been drinking?"

My brows pull together. "What, you don't drink?"

"No," she says sharply. "I don't drink."

The line of her jaw is locked down hard and—*oh*. She is not wearing any pants. Only a red flannel that hangs below her ass, the buttons done up except for the top one, baring the hollow of her throat.

"Why are you out here in the first place?" she asks, ripping me from my less than godly thoughts.

I exhale slowly. "I needed to talk to you."

"It couldn't wait until the sun was up?"

"No. I wanna know who she is."

"Who *who* is?"

"Cora," I snap. "I want to know who Cora is. And you're probably the only person left on Earth who knows the answer, so here I am, drunk and lying on my ass and screaming at a cat on your doorstep."

She says nothing for a moment, as if she's trying to process everything I've told her. "Why?"

"Why what?"

"Why do you want to know who she is? You haven't even spoken to her in eight years. You didn't even know she was missing until I called."

Because I need answers. Because I need to know what makes me so unlovable. Because I want to finally be able to leave this place in the past.

"That's why," I reply, so quietly I don't even know if she hears me.

I'm expecting her to shove me out the doorway and slam the door in my face. But all she does is sigh, long and loud, and say, "Alright."

*　*　*

The guesthouse is a sight.

It looks like a ranch-inspired Pinterest board, somehow even more beautiful than the main house. The walls are a bright and brilliant brown, as are the floors. There's a large, intricate woolen rug in the middle of it all. The room is completely open except for the bathroom, which is enclosed and set off toward the right side. Kitchen to the left, a small table and two chairs next to it, desk in the corner, Hunter's bed pushed under the window across the room. Everything is neat and tidy but the bed, which is empty and unmade. I try not to let my gaze linger on that particular piece of furniture.

I unceremoniously flop down onto one of the chairs. Hunter rolls her eyes but brings me a glass of water and a blanket. I make a big show of not staring at her bare legs as she moves around, then ends up in the chair across from me.

"You do this a lot?" she asks.

"Get drunk? Yes."

She watches me, gaze edged in caution. I down half the water without pausing for breath, then slam the glass down harder than I meant to. "Tell me what she'd gotten herself into," I say, eager to change the subject.

"Ranching," she replies without missing a beat. "Fixing fences. Book club with her friends in town once a month."

"And . . .?"

"And nothing else pertinent."

"Let me get this straight," I say, leaning back in my chair. "She'd gotten herself into something that ended up causing people to want to hurt her, and now she's missing, and you don't want to tell me anything about said activities?"

"Cora . . . she rubbed some people the wrong way. Nothing more sinister than that."

"How so?"

She presses her lips together, says nothing for a moment. Just when I think I've lost her, the woman across the table asks, "Have you ever heard of the Parker Mountain case?"

Of course I've heard of the Parker Mountain case. It's only the most notorious coldish case in the state of Wyoming. Forty years ago, the body of a seventeen-year-old girl, Jessica Coldwater, was found at the base of Parker Mountain, forty-five minutes outside of Wonderland. Jessica was the daughter of Wonderland's mayor and was found brutally murdered. A couple of days into the investigation, they discovered that Jessica's best friend, Holly Prine, was also missing. Police quickly concluded that Holly killed Jessica and fled the scene, but the case was never officially closed. Hence, coldish.

I've never bought that it was Holly. When Cora used to talk about it, she'd said that the motive was practically nonexistent—something about the girls fighting over a boy, hardly something to kill your best friend over. And they never had any leads on where Holly disappeared to after the murder either. I didn't do any sort of real investigating because I was a thousand miles away, and anything associated with Wonderland—or Wyoming in general—I've attempted to steer clear of.

"Of course," I reply. "That was the case that first got me interested in being a PI." Which isn't quite the truth, but it's not a whole lie either.

"Cora's become obsessed with the case over the past couple of years," Hunter explains. "She was trying to solve it. A lot of the folks in town didn't take too kindly to that."

"Why not?"

"Most people are convinced that Holly did it," she continues. "Cora gave up on it a few months back. Which is why," she says, her voice growing sharper, "I told you it wasn't worth mentioning."

"What if she didn't?"

"What?"

"What if she didn't stop investigating?"

"Of course she did," Hunter insists.

I pick up my water, throw back the rest of it. "Maybe she stopped investigating," I reply. "Or maybe that's just what she told you."

Hunter has no response to that. It probably never occurred to her that Cora would lie; that Cora would betray her trust; that Cora would, one day, suddenly become an entirely different person.

"Exactly," I say, leaning back, trying to stop the ceiling from circling so violently. "Such a good thing that you called me down here. Truly."

She tips her head to the side, studying me. "What'd you leave behind?"

The abrupt change in topic only makes the room spin more. "What?"

"In Spokane," she continues. "Family, friends? Who's missing you right now?"

"Who's missing you right now?" What a question to ask. "Well, certainly the women whose beds I would've been warming for the past few evenings."

It's another half-truth—or maybe the whole truth and I don't want to accept it. I don't know if Carson is missing me or not. As their assistant, almost certainly. I'm good at my job, an asset to their operation, and we both know it. But as a person? As Quinn Cuthridge? Not the private investigator in training, but the twenty-two-year-old who's looking for something to keep her holding on just a little bit longer? I could not answer that question, and maybe that in and of itself is the answer.

Two dots of red appear on Hunter's cheeks, which makes me think about earlier, in the shed. "What about your family?" she asks.

That goddamn question again. "Only family I have is currently missing right now."

"Your parents?"

"I already told you not to ask about my family," I snarl.

"I told you the same thing," she replies. "Yet, I told you about mine. Only seems fair you return the favor."

Oh, there are all kinds of favors I'd like to do for you. "I have no idea who my father is," comes tumbling out of my mouth.

She holds my gaze. I know what question she's going to ask before she even poses it. I could stop her, shove the question back between her lips before it ever has a chance of escaping. I've given her what she asked for. I've already warned her. Still, I let her ask: "Your mom?"

I grin so wide I'm sure it looks like I need to be institutionalized. "I do not speak about my mother."

Elain. Elain Cuthridge, who would change her last name at the drop of a hat just so we wouldn't have the same one, so there'd be nothing but the blood in our veins tying us to each other. Elain, who never attended an open house in elementary school or chaperoned a field trip or came to my high school graduation. Elain, who every Christmas would give me twenty dollars and disappear for a night or two or ten, and I'd watch the snowflakes fall through our tiny, fingerprint-smudged window, boiling with a jealousy so intense I'm surprised it didn't burn down our entire shitty apartment complex. Jealous of *snowflakes* because there were so many of them. Snowflakes never fell by themselves; they fell in groups, in packs and bunches. Snowflakes were never alone. Even when they melted, they slipped away in solidarity.

"I do not speak of her," I say again, wondering who I'm trying to convince of that.

Hunter nods once. Slow and methodical, as if she somehow understands this too. As if she can see a flicker of the truth and knows the rest of it belongs only to me.

I stand, nearly toppling back over. "Thanks for the water."

"Quinn, I'm—"

"Oh, don't pity me," I snap, wheeling around. "Don't feel sad for me because of something you think you know, something you think you've figured out. Don't look at the alcohol and assume it's any more than me liking the burn down my throat. Don't feel bad for me, because there's nothing to feel bad about."

"What I said earlier, on the side of the road," Hunter continues, as if she hadn't even heard me. "I didn't mean it. I shouldn't have said it. I'm sorry."

The words, the apology, shake something loose in me. Whether that's a good thing or a bad thing, I've got no idea. "Don't apologize," I tell her. "You were probably right anyway."

"That really how you think about yourself?"

I give her no answer, just hold on to her gaze from across the table.

Hunter is something else. Impossible to get a handle on— prickly on the outside, soft on the inside. And that's just the beginning. As much as I fight it, I want to find out the middle and the ending too.

CHAPTER

7

Silver Lining (Then—March 1981)

NINETY MINUTES HAD passed by the time Holly decided
that her mother wasn't picking her up.

Maybe her mom had forgotten. Maybe she was running
late—but out here, where was there to even run late *from*?
There were no malls to wander around, no theaters to take in
a movie. There was just free, open land covered by animals,
windmills, and irrigation systems. Plenty of room to get lost
in plain sight, but not to do much else.

Holly sat back against the brick wall of the school, considering her options. Her first day had carried on in similar
fashion to the way her first class did: teachers eyeing her suspi-
ciously, as if they knew already she didn't belong. She doubted
any of them would give her a ride home, and the single bus
was long gone. It was way too far to walk, and most of it
would be on the highway's narrow shoulder.

So. She would have to wait. Praying that at some point her
mother would stumble home and realize her daughter wasn't
there. It would be entirely like Lenora to assume Holly was
locked up in her room, though—Holly might be stuck there
at school until it opened the next day.

It was her own fault, really. *"I got it, I got it."* She should've gotten on the bus. The school was so small, there was only the one. Logic reasoned that there had to be a stop along the route somewhere near Wonderland. And even if it dropped her off a mile or two or six from Wonderland, it would've been fine. Holly had certainly walked farther than six miles by herself before.

A lesson learned for the final time, she promised herself. She had to stop trusting people. She had to stop trusting that her mother was going to take care of her. Holly had seventeen years' worth of evidence to prove Lenora was never going to change, and she needed to start believing what her own eyes had been telling her for so long.

The idea of bouncing around aimlessly for the rest of her life, with no end in sight, made Holly's stomach ache. Subjecting a child to that kind of life—it made her stomach hurt even worse.

Not that Holly had ever deeply considered her future family, let alone children. It was expected of her, surely—Lenora mentioned it from time to time: finding a good man to put a roof over her head and, more importantly, take her off Lenora's hands. Whenever Lenora mentioned her lack of a boyfriend, Holly would always shrug and say, *"All I know how to do is microwave a TV dinner. How am I supposed to hold down a man?"*

That was enough of an explanation for Lenora, one that probably made her feel better about her own relationship situation. And it allowed Holly to ignore the real reason she never had a boyfriend.

The sound of a door slamming jolted Holly from her thoughts. When she turned, she saw Jessica Coldwater in her cheerleading uniform, leaving the far side of the building.

And she was walking toward Holly.

Jessica was shaking, but that could've been from the chill in the air. It was mid-March, cold enough that you still needed to wear a coat. A coat that Holly didn't have.

Finally, Jessica looked up, stopping dead in her tracks when she saw Holly sitting by the front door. "What are you doing here?" Jessica asked, surprise peppering her tone. "Only cheerleaders are supposed to be here this late."

Holly shrugged. "Waiting on my ride."

"It's almost five."

More time had passed than Holly had realized. "Oh."

Jessica sighed, then walked closer to Holly and sat down next to her. Holly tried not to stare at Jessica's legs, all the smooth white skin her short skirt exposed. Jessica began digging around in her backpack—probably new from the past August, Holly guessed, by the lack of wear it showed—and pulled out a pack of cigarettes and a lighter.

Lighting hers up, she then offered one to Holly. "You smoke?"

Holly shook her head but took one anyway. Jessica gestured for her to put it between her lips. The lighter flashed bright in front of Holly's eyes as Jessica brought it to the cigarette in her mouth. A tingling sensation skittered down her spine at Jessica's bare skin being so close to hers.

"So," Jessica breathed as she took a long drag, staring out at the nearly vacant parking lot. "Where're you from?"

"Everywhere," Holly answered truthfully, exhaling a puff of smoke. She liked the taste of the cigarette. She'd had a couple before that had tasted burnt and sour, but not this one.

Jessica nodded like that made all the sense in the world. "Cool. Where're you living now?"

"Wonderland."

"Really?" Jessica exclaimed, eyes widening. "I'm out in Wonderland too. My dad's the mayor. And so was my grandfather and my great-grandfather and my great-great-grandfather."

Holly nodded, tapping ash onto the walkway. It wasn't the first time she'd wondered what that was like, to be tied to a place so solidly and for so long that you could trace your roots back for several generations. To be someone, not just another stranger, another body passing through. To belong, not just exist.

"Are you good at English?" Jessica asked. "No offense. I've grown up with everyone in my classes, and I know what kinda work I'm gonna have to put into group projects with them. And that's gonna be all of it."

"So you're the nerdy girl?" Holly asked before she could think better of it.

Jessica grinned. "Sure am. And the cheerleader. And the QB's girlfriend. And the mayor's daughter. And the girl who smokes only when no one else can see."

Holly's eyes traced Jessica's face. She wanted to know what was lurking beneath the surface of those blue eyes, that blonde hair. She wanted to know very, very badly.

"'*So we beat on, boats against the current, borne back ceaselessly into the past,*'" Holly quoted.

Gatsby itself hadn't been Holly's cup of tea, but she loved the image of the green light. It resonated with her so deeply, it was as if Fitzgerald had been talking to her, specifically, when he'd written it. The idea that there was hope, salvation, just beyond the water—yeah, Holly could relate to that.

It was the same idea Holly clung to on the longest, darkest nights. The notion that one day she'd be done with the motels and the stolen books and the loneliness. The possibility that she'd have a house of her own, stuffed to the gills not just with Nancy Drew books, but any book she could get her hands on, *Gatsby* included.

Jessica stared for a moment, then asked, "You've already read the book?"

"Yeah."

"You like to read?"

"Yeah."

"Me too," Jessica said. Then she paused, as if considering something, and took a long drag of her cigarette. In that moment Holly felt so much older, so much wiser than she ever had. "I've read it four times already," Jessica continued. "I like trying to find out what the author's really trying to tell you with the writing. What's hidden beneath."

"Yeah," Holly said again.

"I'm sorry," Jessica said quickly, as if she had done something that warranted such a hasty apology. "I don't . . . I don't really have anyone to talk to about stuff like this," she confessed. "My boyfriend's not into school. He's so focused on football all the time, trying to get an athletic scholarship, and my friends don't really like to read."

Holly didn't know what to say to that. *I could be your friend,* she wanted to say, but she was afraid. Afraid that beautiful, popular Jessica Coldwater wouldn't want anything to do with her. Especially after she learned what was really running through Holly's head most of the time and what she thought about the girl next to her.

"I like mysteries best, though," Jessica said. "You read any Nancy Drew books?"

It was like Holly was taking her first breath, hearing Jessica ask her that. *"Yeah,"* she said once more, but this time with more emphasis.

Jessica smiled, and it sent a warm, fluttery feeling through Holly's chest. "Tell me which one's your favorite then, partner."

CHAPTER

8

Old Gods (Now)

BRIGHT AND EARLY the next morning, Hunter drags my hungover ass an hour west to the Sweetwater County Sheriff's Department.

It's the same way that we drove back from the airport out in Rock Springs, so I've seen this area before. Still, every time we set out somewhere, I dare to let myself hope I'll see something more geologically stimulating than gold and brown fields.

Spokane's on the eastern side of Washington, and even though it's the second-largest city in the state, it's still surrounded by land that looks a lot like this. Yet there are hills that give the illusion of something better lying beyond what you can see. Here? You know exactly what's up ahead at all times: more of what you've just passed.

The drive is silent, no mention of last night, and my pounding head is relieved for that. No music, no talking, just more of the same landscape that paints this entire state.

The department is both nicer and newer than I'd imagined. It's a new build, all glass and metal, sleek lines that give it far more of a city vibe than any other structure I've seen out here. The sun is high and blazing, bouncing off the walls of the building, even though it's not even nine in the morning yet.

Hunter pushes the door open but doesn't bother to hold it for me. It hits me in the shoulder, and I let out a sound, half grunt, half moan, that has her turning and staring.

"Are you alive?" she asks impatiently.

"Barely," I manage.

She shakes her head and continues forward. She's in a flannel, jeans, boots, and that ridiculous hat of hers again.

"Morning," Hunter says to the woman at the front desk. She's probably in her mid-forties, with light brown hair that's been flat ironed so straight it hardly moves an inch.

She offers Hunter a big smile but doesn't acknowledge me. "Howdy," the woman replies. "What can we do for you today?"

"Hopin' to speak with Sheriff Bridgers, if it ain't too much trouble."

The woman pulls back a bit. "What's this concerning?"

"Cora Cole, who's been missin' for over two weeks now."

"Oh, yes. Out in Wonderland, isn't that right?"

"Yes, ma'am."

"Terrible business," the woman says, shaking her head. I was right about her hair: not a piece of it moves. "Lemme see if Sheriff Bridgers is available to talk with y'all."

"Appreciate it."

We wait for fifteen minutes before a short blonde woman materializes before us. Her hair is pulled back into a ponytail, and there's no makeup on her face. Her white blouse is ironed, crisply tucked into her dark dress slacks.

She extends her hand toward Hunter, big smile on her face. "Lem, good to see you. Was hopin' you'd give me a callback soon, but this works too."

Lem? A callback?

"Sheriff," Hunter replies, shaking her hand. She hooks the thumb on her other hand toward me. "This is Quinn, Cora's niece. She works as a private investigator in Spokane."

The sheriff shifts her attention. Big blue eyes; high, perfect cheekbones; sculpted, full brows. Her features make her look more like a model than a sheriff, and she can't be much older than Hunter or me.

"Cora's niece," she repeats. She does not offer to shake my hand.

"The one and only."

"Yeah, I remember you," she says. "You used to spend the summers here, right? When you were younger?"

It seems like she already has the answer to her question, which makes me wonder why she posed it in the first place. "Yep," I tell her.

"Well, welcome back," she says, turning her attention back to Hunter as if dismissing me. "Y'all gonna be at the fundraiser tomorrow night?"

My eyebrows shoot up as I glance at Hunter, a million questions forming: *What fundraiser? When? Where? For who? Why didn't you bring this up earlier?* "Will we be, *Lem*?"

Hunter exhales through her nose. "Yeah, we'll be there."

"Good, good." Bridgers clears her throat, readjusting the belt at her hips. She talks and acts like a woman who's used to having to prove herself to men. She stands a little straighter, talks a little deeper. It tells me more about the fine folks working here than any introductory tour ever could. "Well, Lem, there's not much in the way of updates, I'm afraid. Sorry you drove all the way out here to hear the same thing I've been tellin' you on the phone all week."

"Quinn had some questions for you."

"You know this is an open investigation, and I can't—"

"Just some simple stuff," I say, jumping in. "Hunter told me you don't think there's any foul play involved?"

Bridgers is still looking at Hunter. It's like I'm invisible to these people, like my presence doesn't even register.

"Correct," she replies.

"What makes you think that?"

Now she cuts her gaze to me. "No sign of a struggle at the ranch. Her vehicle is gone. She has no known enemies. We have not received a ransom note. There is no—"

"The enemies part—how do you know that?"

"Because we investigated," she replies, irritation running into her tone. "This may not be Spokane, but we do know how to—"

"It's not you specifically," I tell her. "It's the police in general that I have no faith in. Have you listened to an episode of any true crime podcast lately? Most cases are unsolved because the police botched something, or their implicit bias got in the way, or they were incompetent. And don't even get me started on the impunity that you all have—it's impossible to count all the times the police have gotten away with actual, literal murder."

I hate working with the police. Most of them are guilty of the same crimes they're arresting people for, hiding behind their badges and blue lines and qualified immunity. The times I've seen the Spokane police interact with Carson—my nonbinary Black boss—have been horrifying, from the purposeful misgendering to the rampant microaggressions. It's why, when we have to tangle with the cops, I'm the one who goes to the precinct or fills out the forms or makes the calls. Not because Carson can't do it, but because the worst thing that's gonna happen to me is getting called *sweetheart* and turned away. I don't need to wonder about what would happen to Carson if they put even a toe out of line—I've seen it on the news, on social media, on the street.

Bridgers blinks, in a state of shock. I figure Hunter is going to drag me out of here in about thirteen seconds, so I continue. "Did you know she was investigating the Parker Mountain case?"

That jerks her out of her daze. Hunter's fingers wrap around my wrist, tugging slightly. *"Enough."* My question even draws the gaze of the woman working behind the computer, her eyes wide.

Bridgers stares at me like she's seeing me for the first time. She might've underestimated the hungover woman at Hunter's side upon first glance, but not anymore. "That case has long been closed," she tells me.

"Closed-ish," I reply to her nonanswer. "Even when I first heard about it as a girl, I didn't buy it. And neither did Cora, who, after investigating on her own for years, suddenly gave up on it a few months back."

"Then it's not even relevant," Bridgers counters. "Cora went missin' two weeks ago, not months ago."

"Or," I continue, "she found the real killer, decided to do something with that information, and is now missing because of it."

It's a leap, but a possibility. I'm fishing for information more than anything, and when Bridgers widens her eyes once more, I know I'm on the right track.

Next to me, Hunter clears her throat. *My thirteen seconds are up.* "Is there somewhere private—"

"Your aunt was not investigatin' the Parker Mountain case, because there is nothin' *to* investigate," Bridgers says, cutting Hunter off. "She likely got tired of keepin' up with that monstrosity of a ranch and left, as she did when she was eighteen. Sad, but not criminal. When I called the state police, that's what they thought as well. There is nothin' here for you to investigate, nothin' sinister afoot. I suggest you get on the first plane back to Spokane and stop stirrin' up trouble for God knows what reason."

"Finding my aunt," I reply dryly. "That would be the reason."

"If your aunt wanted to be found, she would've come back by now."

"And you knew Cora well enough to make that deduction?"

"I knew her better than you did."

Next to me, Hunter sucks in a breath. But I don't react; it'd give Bridgers exactly what she wants. She's badgering me, looking for a reaction, anything to give her a reason to throw me out of here and stop me from asking questions.

So confident, this woman, with so little information at her fingertips. So eager to stamp "CLOSED" on this folder and tuck it away in the back, like they seemingly had with the Parker Mountain case forty years ago.

"When I solve this," I tell her, already stepping away, "I'll be sure to tell the podcasters and the reporters that it was your idiocy that fucked this case."

Bridgers's face goes red; she is clearly not as good at keeping a poker face as I am. She opens her mouth to say something, but then Hunter is shoving me toward the exit, and *end scene*.

* * *

"You can't talk to people like that—"

"Who was Cora last seen with?"

The doors of the truck aren't even fully closed before we're at it again, questions and insults like knives at each other's throats.

Hunter blinks at me in shock. "That's all you've got to say for yourself?"

"I'm here to solve this case, as you so astutely pointed out yesterday in the shed," I reply. "So, can you tell me: Who was Cora last seen with?"

"Do you have no emotions at all? No respect for authority or—"

"Those are two entirely different questions, and neither are pertinent to finding Cora."

"How are we gonna get help from the police now that you've said all those terrible things and—"

"Why are you so worried about getting their help when they've done *nothing* thus far? And what terrible things did I say?"

"About how they're incompetent and biased and—"

"Sorry to burst your little Republican Wyoming bubble, but they absolutely are."

"Jesus," she blusters, shaking her head. "Is this how people treat one another in the city? All these assumptions and names—"

"They're not assumptions when you have decades' worth of data and—"

"There you go again."

The cabin falls silent. I don't know if she's waiting for me to apologize—I'm not going to—or start talking again. Finally, she exhales, then scrubs a hand over her face. "The last person to see Cora was one of her book club friends, Irene. We'll drive past her house on the way back to the ranch. We can stop and see if she's home, if you want."

"Absolutely."

She puts the key in the ignition, and the truck rumbles to life. "Fine."

I seemingly can't get enough of this bickering, because I ask, "Why did the sheriff call you *Lem*? And what was all that about calling her back? Do you know her outside of work, or—"

"She was a senior in high school when I was a freshman," she replies, voice clipped. "We played on the same basketball team. Lem was what my friends called me."

Friends. With the older girl who I'm sure was just as pretty then as she is now. "She made sheriff fast," I remark.

To that Hunter says nothing.

"If y'all are such good *friends*, you'd think she'd want to help you solve this case," I comment.

"She does."

"Doesn't fuckin' seem like it."

No reply again.

"Does she have something against Cora?"

"You shouldn't have brought up the Parker Mountain case."

"Why not?"

Hunter exhales loudly through her nose, her grip on the steering wheel tightening. "The mayor whose daughter was killed? Maddie is his granddaughter. And he's still mayor, FYI."

"Maddie?"

Her cheeks go red, all the indication that I need that there's most definitely a story here. "Sheriff Bridgers," she amends, but oh, it is far too late for that.

"You played on the same basketball team? Pretty gay of y'all."

"She is married," she snaps. "Happily. To a *man*."

"Bisexuals exist, you know."

"She's not . . . we didn't . . . it's nothin'. *Nothin'.*" She's shaking her head so hard I'm surprised her hat hasn't come flying off yet.

"Protesting a bit much, aren't we?"

Hunter wipes a hand across her mouth, eyes straight ahead. "We really were just friends on the team, alright? She knew I really didn't have anyone else 'cept Cora, so sometimes we'd stay after practice, and she'd give me some tips and . . ."

"And?"

"And none of your goddamn *business*."

"Well, I'll just have to fill in the missing pieces, then."

Why am I pushing so hard on this? It doesn't matter whether Hunter used to hook up with her basketball buddy after practice. It doesn't matter that said basketball buddy clearly hasn't forgotten.

"Fine," I relent when she lets the silence draw out. "So she got her job with her last name, but it doesn't explain the rest of it. Her aunt was killed—she should want answers more than anyone."

Unless she's convinced of the original findings: that Holly Prine killed her best friend that August night forty years ago and disappeared into the wind. Or she has the answers, and she doesn't like what she found. That's the option I'm leaning toward. The mayor's office, the cops, and God knows who else all commanded by the same family, seemingly for generations. It's a perfect pyramid of power and simple enough to pull off in a town this size.

"What's this fundraiser we're going to tomorrow?" I ask.

"They're throwin' a big memorial fundraiser for Jessica Coldwater up in Radley. She has her own scholarship fund for in-state kids who want to go to UW. Buncha big, important people comin' from all over."

"So people who might know something about the Parker Mountain case? About where Cora is?"

"Suppose so," she replies after a moment. "I . . . wasn't plannin' on going. Not until Mad—the sheriff brought it up."

"Why not?"

She shifts on the bench seat, in obvious discomfort. "I keep to myself."

"Yeah, I gathered that." It's hard to tell what she's deliberately keeping from me, for reasons I haven't yet deciphered, and what she fails to mention out of pure ignorance that it might be helpful. "What's the dress code?"

"The what?"

"Dress code," I repeat. "Formal, semiformal?"

"It's . . . your good jeans and a nice shirt."

Goddamn Wyoming. "Of course it is."

* * *

Irene's Richards's house is small, neat, and unassuming.

Which is true of several of the houses on her street, each one accompanied by fresh-cut grass and small plots of flowers still in full color this deep into August. The exterior of Irene's house is robin's-egg blue; the one next to it, a faded pink; and the one next to *it*, deep olive. Houses that have roots nearly as old as the trees in their yards; houses that have withstood the Wyoming heat and snow, the wind and the lightning, year after year, dutifully cared for by their residents.

I've lived in the same small, cramped, two-bedroom Spokane apartment all my life. Elain never had the money or the desire to decorate much, a tradition I've kept up with since.

Affordability was all she was looking for when she moved in twenty-two years ago, and it's all I've been able to continue affording with the money Carson pays me. Even though I hate it, knowing a part of her is still there, in the furniture and the kitchen and her bedroom. Even though I wish I could burn it all to the ground and throw the ashes away into the worst possible place I can think of.

I knock on Irene Richards's door now, clearing my throat, ready to meet another person in this town who has had the privilege of *knowing* their entire life. I've always thought that people that complain about the mundane don't realize how good they have it—what I would trade for a doting mother and a handsome father and beautiful flowers in the yard. They take it all for granted, all the luxuries I've never been privileged to have.

The door opens slowly, revealing an elderly woman. She is slight, bent over a bit, hair graying and thin. Seventy, if I had to guess. She's already frowning, and I haven't even said anything yet.

The door isn't open completely, just enough for the woman to glare at me through. "Whatever you're sellin', I ain't interested."

"Not selling anything," I reply. "Hoping to speak with Irene Richards."

The woman's eyes narrow further. "You're doin' that right now."

"About my missing aunt."

She straightens a bit, her demeanor changing completely. She meets my eyes, blinking a couple of times, as if she can't quite believe the sight before her. "Well, fuck," she remarks. "You must be Quinn, then."

"Unfortunately."

Irene shakes her head, then jerks her chin over my shoulder. "Shoulda figured, you showin' up with Cora's shadow."

I raise my eyebrows but don't turn toward Hunter. "Can me and the shadow come in? Ask you about Cora?"

"Reckon that'd be fine," Irene says, opening the door wider. "Nothin' on the fuckin' agenda today anyway."

* * *

I'm slow to like people, but I like Irene Richards right off the bat.

Maybe it's the way her house smells fresh and open, like Wyoming clambered inside and took hold of the walls and the floorboards. Maybe it's the decor, sparse but precise: a vase of fresh flowers on the glass coffee table; family photos hung perfectly equidistant from one another; the books on the bookshelf faced and ordered like they'd be in a store. Maybe it's Irene herself, all spit and ire.

Irene leads us to the kitchen, gestures for us to sit around the table. She takes the seat farthest from the door, the seat I would've taken, given the choice: clear line of sight toward the exit, ability to see everyone who enters or leaves the room.

"Whaddya wanna know about Cora?" Irene asks, all business.

"Hunter mentioned you were in a book club together," I say.

Irene's eyes—cloudy with age but still sharp, still able to see everything—dart to Hunter. "She did, did she?"

"Yes, ma'am," Hunter says. She's seated next to me, her knee bouncing up and down, so unlike her. *Nervous.*

Irene grumbles something I don't catch. I'm not even sure if it was words or not. "Sure," she says. "We were in a book club."

"What was the last book you read?"

"Thought you were here about your missing aunt," Irene grumbles.

Book club isn't real, and she's going to no real lengths to hide that. So why were they meeting and felt the need to cover it up?

"When was the last time you saw her?" I ask instead.

Irene exhales, clearly more comfortable with this line of questioning. "Day before she went missing."

"Where did you see her?"

"Here—she drove over because she wanted to talk to me."

"About what?"

"Ranch equipment," Irene replies. "She was sellin' me some of her old stuff."

I believe it, almost—sounds innocuous enough—until Hunter's knee stops bouncing, and I remember that was the exact thing she'd told me earlier, the reason for the silence and the gun and the trip to Casper.

Lies. Both of them, lying to me.

"What piece of equipment?" I push.

Irene's eyes narrow once more. "Nothin' you'd know about, city girl."

"I may be a city girl," I say, voice dropping as I lean closer to the woman across from me, "but I know when I'm being lied to. By you and by the shadow. I can't find Cora unless you both start telling the truth. I know that you and Cora don't meet for book club, and I know that she wasn't selling you ranch equipment. So tell me: What the hell was she up to?"

Irene doesn't move an inch, doesn't flinch, doesn't draw a breath. She keeps her gaze trained on me, not giving anything away, almost identical to the look Hunter is so fond of throwing my way. I wonder if that's something they teach in the schools around here: how to stare right through someone, constantly make them feel like they're on defense and you've got the upper hand.

"You ain't got no idea what it's like out here," the woman finally says, her voice a whip that cracks through the room, solid and harsh. "Generations of my family have been here. Generations of *yours*, not that you care much, I'd reckon. Ranchin' and farmin'—that's how folks used to make a livin'. A good livin'—nothin' outstandin', but enough to keep food on the table and buy a new tractor should the old one break down. And now?" Irene scoffs, shaking her head. "Seems like another family farm's goin' down every other day around here. They're havin' to give up the only thing they know, the only *home* they've known, thanks to the banks and the factory farms and the politicians, who are all in business together, mind you. No, it's up to us to save ourselves—as usual."

"What does that have to do with Cora?" I ask carefully.

"Cora left, but then she came back to run the ranch. When she did, she was a little smarter, a little harder. She did a hell of a job fixin' up the ranch after what your granddaddy let it fall into. But it still . . . it wasn't enough."

I don't correct her that Cora's father isn't my grandfather—not by blood or in any of the other ways that count. "What are you saying?" I ask instead.

"You know how cattle ranchers make money, girl?"

"I . . . no."

"Figured as much. Well, they buy calves, feed 'em and care for 'em until they're the proper weight, then they sell 'em off. Problems come when the price of beef's too low, or the price of hay's too high. A little fluctuation's normal, but eight years ago—"

Eight years ago, my aunt banished me from this place and told me never to come back.

"—it was even worse than it is right now," Irene continues. "Only three of the ranches in the area made it through intact. One because his daddy sent him a boatload of cash, and the other because he took out a loan with some . . . unsavory figures in California."

"And Cora?" I push. "What did Cora do to save her ranch?"

"Nothin'," Hunter snaps, jarring me. Locked in the stare-down with Irene, I'd forgotten entirely that Hunter was still very much present.

The smirk on Irene's lips says it all.

"What did she do?" I repeat.

Finally, Irene takes her gaze from me. She looks around the room, as if she's searching for answers, trying to scrape secrets from their hiding places where her gaze lands: where the ceiling meets the walls; out from behind the stove; stuck between the fruit-themed magnets and the refrigerator.

If that's true, then the greatest secret of all must be where she looks last and longest: at Hunter. "Isn't that the question we'd all like the answer to?"

* * *

I could fill an entire room with the things that Irene Richards does not know.

She has no idea what the key I found behind the picture frame goes to or what (likely illegal thing) Cora did eight years ago to keep the ranch running, or—the biggest mystery of all—where Cora is.

It wasn't a complete waste of time, though. Because now I have a real, legitimate reason to turn my ire on Hunter.

"You fucking lied to me. Again," I say hotly as soon as Irene closes the door behind us.

Hunter is on a mission it seems, already halfway to the truck before I can get the words out.

I do not get angry. Not like this. I've spent years training myself to stay calm, to hide my feelings at all times. To be the perfect, detached investigator; to be neutral and unbiased; to see nothing but the truth, unbidden by the gray in a black and white world. People can't find the holes in your armor if you're standing still.

All that work, all that time and effort, so easily undone by this one incredibly infuriating woman.

She doesn't turn around. I walk faster to catch up with her so that when she opens the driver's side door, I'm there to slam it shut.

"What is wrong with you?" I demand.

She shakes her head, staring back toward Irene's house. "I knew this was a mistake."

"Knew what was a mistake? Coming here or going to the cops or flying me out here—"

"All of it!" she yells. "All of it's a mistake, because it's *all my fault*!"

I let a beat go by, vainly trying not to read into what she means by *it's all my fault*, even though the gears in my head are already spinning.

I foolishly had not considered Hunter a suspect. Hunter, who talks about my aunt with more love than I ever have. Hunter, who knows Cora better than anyone, who had all the access in the world to her, who knows this area well, who has a gun in the truck next to her—

"Did you kill her?" I ask.

All the air leaves her body. I watch it happen, watch the woman in front of me deflate, slumping forward, knees swaying.

Yes, I think, at the same time I breathe, *No.*

"I didn't protect her," she whispers. "She's all I've got left in this world, and I didn't . . . someone . . . something happened to her, and I didn't stop it."

"How do you know that?"

"Because she wouldn't leave me!"

The desperation in her voice is so visceral it's leaking into the air around us. It makes my heart pound, makes the world tilt around the edges, so familiar and naive—it's the same thing I used to believe, and finding out it wasn't true— twice—nearly killed me. It ripped away everything that kept the demons at bay. It made me look myself in the eye, see the monster so clearly, and decide who was going to rule whom.

It is the hardest thing in the world to endure: getting a taste of love, then having it taken from you without warning, without reason.

"What do you know?" I ask, moving closer. "Tell me. Tell me so we can bring her home."

She shakes her head, as close to hysterical as I've seen her. Worse than she was when she pulled the truck over and spilled all the secrets about her family history, worse than she was inside Irene's house. *She's breaking. Something inside of her is breaking.* "I can't," she manages. "I can't. She told me . . ."

"What?" I ask, unable to keep the plea out of my voice. I'm practically choking on it. Being so close to some semblance of an answer but also seeing her like this, so upset and so un-Hunter-like . . . it makes my chest go tight.

I don't like it. I want it to stop.

"Cora told me not to tell anyone. Ever. That the past is in the past, that no good comes from digging up old ghosts."

Oh, how I wish she were right. If the past had truly been laid to rest, I wouldn't be here, and Hunter wouldn't be unspooling like this.

"The past is here, Cowgirl," I tell her, only inches away now. "And it's staring us right in our goddamn faces. So break whatever pinky promises you made to Cora and start talking, before you make any more new ghosts."

War flickers across her face. A pledge to one woman, an alliance with another.

Promises, breaking and bowing—does she play the martyr or the savior?

"I haven't given you a reason to trust me," I continue, "so I'll give you one now. The same way you're feeling? Like your stomach's trying to crawl its way out of your throat? Like you've got a Cora Cole–shaped knife digging into your spine? Like your hands are pinned behind your back while everything you thought you knew slips out from beneath your feet? I've been there. I've been there for eight fucking years, and I still came back. I'm still standing here, by your side, in the place I hate more than anywhere else on Earth, looking for her. I can't do it without you, though."

Hunter closes her eyes, then lets out a long, long breath. "Every few weeks," she says softly, making the choice, "Cora gives me a name, a date, and an address. Always a man's name and always somewhere public. I pick up an envelope of money and drive home. The trip we made on Sunday—that was the last name she gave me before she disappeared."

"What's the money for?"

"Ranch equipment."

"Are you out of your—"

"That's what Cora told me," she says, eyes opening. "At the beginning, I believed her. Then there stopped being equipment to sell."

"What's the money actually for, then?"

"She never told me."

"Bullshit."

"It's the truth."

"I should believe you because . . .?"

"Because I'm breaking a promise to the one person I swore I'd never break a promise to," she barks. "Because I thought they would've already found her by now. Because . . ." She trails off, then swallows, my eyes tracking the movement down her throat. "We have to find her. *I* have to find her."

The fury is still there, in my bones. I can feel it rushing through me from head to toe. Anger and frustration from how little I've been told, how much has been kept from me; but I know the kind of hold a promise like the one Hunter made to Cora can have. As if the world will fall right off its axis if you break it, if you tell.

"Thank you for trusting me," I tell her softly. "I know it's not easy, especially for people like us."

People like us. Damaged, but still managing to patch ourselves up. So burned by the past that the flames of the future don't phase us. So desperate for love, or even something that vaguely resembles it, that we're willing to do almost anything for it—come back to Wonderland, Wyoming; put trust in a woman who doesn't deserve it; leap off the cliff without looking.

I reach out, grab Hunter by the forearm. She jumps a bit at the contact, but once I squeeze lightly, she relaxes. Friend, not foe. A line drawn, at least for now.

"And we will," I say, another promise I don't know if I will keep or break. "We'll find her."

9

Ribs (Then—March 1981)

"YOU WANNA GO ride bikes?"

Holly looked up from her science textbook. Science, which she hated almost as much as math. If there were numbers anywhere near a subject, Holly was already running in the opposite direction.

She and Jessica were sitting at the Coldwater dining room table, Mrs. Coldwater going in and out, constantly busy with something: dusting or cooking or fixing her hair and makeup. She was perfect always, and so was her house—spacious, immaculately cleaned, and decorated tastefully to fit the season. Fresh flowers sat in the center of the table, submerged in an antique vase Jessica had explained was older than the town of Wonderland itself.

The Coldwaters' house was the nicest in town. It was up on a big hill, far away from where Holly's house was. They even had a freshly manicured lawn and pretty pink flowers along the porch. Jessica had her own room, painted a light lilac, filled to the brim with clothes and toys and books. She even had her own *television*.

Holly was jealous sometimes, sure, but it always passed quickly. It was hard to be jealous of Jessica for very long.

After that first day, they'd become inseparable—some sort of bond forming between them that neither quite understood the entirety of. It was a pull, a connection; one that couldn't be severed by the strange glances they got in the hallways or the way teachers, thinking Holly was out of earshot, assured Jessica she didn't have to befriend *that kind of girl*. Jessica always smiled politely, the teachers not even realizing she *was* one of those girls they were warning her to steer clear of.

Jessica had given Holly a ride home after their cigarettes had turned to ash, and then she showed up bright and early the next morning. It became their routine. After school, Holly would sit in the bleachers in the gym, waiting for Jessica to finish cheerleading practice, trying to keep her eyes on her book and not on Jessica's flipping form.

Holly was amazed by Jessica. The way she threw herself so majestically into the air, spinning and rotating, landing perfectly. Her arms and her legs, always in perfect sync with each other. And when her skirt flew up and exposed her thighs, or her top showed off her toned stomach, Holly couldn't help but flush as she hastily tried to avert her eyes. She was unsuccessful most times.

Jessica's boyfriend, Troy, never made an appearance at her practices. Jessica explained that he was busy with his football friends, that he hardly had any time for her. That was music to Holly's ears. The times that she had to see them together—like in the cafeteria, Jessica so close to Troy that she was practically on his lap, his arms wrapped around her in a way that could only be described as possessive—she felt as if she were going to be sick.

But the drives to school, the long talks she and Jessica had, the time they spent together—it all made up for it. For the fact that Holly knew she wouldn't ever be able to touch Jessica like that, be seen with her like that.

She thought about it sometimes late at night, long after Jessica had dropped her off. Sometimes Lenora was home, making noise in the tiny kitchen, and sometimes she wasn't. Holly thought about being with Jessica in the way that Ned Nickerson and Nancy Drew were. She thought about them being together in . . . other ways. Ways she'd read about in the books she'd read in secret from the adult section of the library. There were never two girls, of course—at least, not in the books in the towns Holly lived in. She didn't know at first if two girls could even be together like that. Holly had never made any friends—before Jessica. Life seemed to be divided up into *before Jessica* and *after Jessica*—but Holly had over-heard girls talking about their boyfriends, about losing their virginity to them. Mean things were written about some of those girls on bathroom stalls too.

Could girls lose their virginity to each other? If there was no . . . *thing* going in *there*? And if so, then what counted?

So many questions. And no one to turn to for answers.

It was wrong, two girls being together like that. Or two boys. Unnatural; a sin. Holly had been told that, at least—especially at the two schools she'd attended in Utah. But weren't there lots of things that were wrong, that were sinful, that went on anyway? Wasn't it *wrong* that Holly didn't know if there would be food in the fridge when she came home, or where Lenora was, or if she was even alive? Once, Lenora didn't come home for *four days*, and Holly was sure her mother had died.

What gave Troy the right to be with Jessica, especially the way he treated her? Ignoring her, letting other girls hang onto him at games, not showing her much affection. Holly knew that if *she* were Jessica's girlfriend, she'd never treat her like that. She would treat her *right*. She'd give her flowers every morning, right when Jessica picked her up. She'd remind Jessica how smart she was, how athletic, how beautiful. She'd never look at another girl again the way she looked at Jessica.

It was lonely but also consuming. It brought heat to Holly's cheeks as she lay in her bed, mulling it all over. The way she wanted to touch Jessica. The way she *did* touch herself.

There were some mornings that she could barely stand to look at Jessica, knowing the things that were running through her own mind. But if Jessica was onto her, she never showed any indication. They talked in the car and hung out at Jessica's house, Mrs. Coldwater always there after school with cookies fresh from the oven. It was all so normal—so right.

* * *

"Sure," she told Jessica now. "Bikes sound like fun." They headed out to the garage, Jessica pulling two bikes from the rack along the far wall.

It seemed there was every kind of machinery one could ever dream of in the giant Coldwater garage: bikes and motorcycles and scooters; giant contraptions Holly didn't even know what to call.

"Here," Jessica said, giving Holly a pink bike. "This one's Sarah's."

Sarah was Jessica's older sister, who was away at college in Colorado, studying to be a doctor.

Jessica pulled out a blue bike, and the girls put on matching black helmets. The garage door rose, and they were on their way.

There wasn't very far to go in Wonderland—the highway wasn't an option, and the little side roads that led in and out of town were filled with potholes and animals Holly didn't care to run into.

They went down the hill from the Coldwater house and into town. It was overcast, but warm enough that they didn't need jackets. They drove in single file, Holly behind Jessica. A couple of cars passed by, people waving out the windows, likely at Jessica; the only person in this state who would wave at Holly was currently riding up ahead of her.

When they wound their way down the hill and into what passed for downtown Wonderland, Jessica steered toward the two streets of houses. "Which one's yours?" she called to Holly.

A reply got stuck in Holly's throat. There was a lot she had told Jessica—the places she'd been, the things she'd seen—but there was also a lot she hadn't. The fact that it would probably take Lenora a year to save up for a bike like the one she was riding on right now was one of them.

Jessica looked back, blonde hair blowing behind her. It made Holly go speechless for an entirely different reason.

Holly pointed to the house on the very end, and Jessica nodded. They stopped across the street from it. There was no car in the driveway, no indication that anyone was home. No indication that anyone lived there at all, really. It wasn't a *home*, no matter how many times Lenora proclaimed otherwise. It was a house, and someone else's at that.

There was no stopping the flush of embarrassment that ran through Holly's entire body. Here was Jessica Coldwater, town *royalty*, seeing her house. The place her mother had dragged her to, another map dot Holly hadn't ever wanted to be a part of.

And Jessica—Jessica, who would run this town one day; Jessica, who lived in a house fit for a queen; Jessica, who could choose anyone at all to spend time with. Jessica, who was sure to bolt now that she'd seen who Holly truly was.

"It's just you and your mom, right?" Jessica asked, breaking the silence.

Holly nodded, her eyes on the ground in front of her. Lenora had come up in their conversations frequently, Jessica listening intently as Holly recounted tale after tale of her mother. Nothing too unsavory, but certainly enough to paint the picture.

Jessica didn't say anything else. She started riding again, back up the hill and to the Coldwater house.

This is it, Holly thought as she got off the bike, helping Jessica put it away without a word. They were both flushed from the uphill terrain. *This is the part where she dumps me.*

Holly had never had a friend before, and certainly not one that meant something to her in the way Jessica did. Her chest ached just thinking about not getting to spend time with her anymore, no more drives to school and back, no more snacks from Mrs. Coldwater, no more time spent in the bleachers.

"It's okay if you don't want to be my friend anymore," Holly said in a rush.

Jessica's back was to her, and she straightened as she turned around. "What?"

"I know I'm . . ." Holly trailed off. There were so many ways that she could finish that sentence: *not rich, not right, not good enough.* "Different," she decided on, the sanitized version of her thoughts, the version she was so used to giving.

Jessica's eyes narrowed in confusion. "What are you talking about?" she asked. "Is this because I saw where you live?"

Holly shrugged, avoiding Jessica's gaze. *It'll hurt less this way, if I convince myself that it was my idea to stop being friends. If I give her an out.*

"Hey," Jessica said, drawing Holly's gaze back up to hers. They were suddenly so close, close enough that Holly could reach out and touch any part of her. "I don't care about any of that. I don't care how you dress or where you live. I don't care what people at school say about you, or me. I care about the fact that you're nice and funny, that you tell me these amazing stories of all the different places you've seen. I care that you're willing to help me with math, even though you hate it, and ride bikes with me and show me your house. I care that you're *real*, Holly. I care about *you.*"

Holly recognized all the words that Jessica was saying, but they weren't computing. How could . . . how could someone like Jessica Coldwater think those things about *her*, Holly Prine, who wore thrift store clothes and had lived most of her life making company with her own shadow?

"I care about you too," Holly said softly, though she meant it in a very different way from how she knew Jessica did.

Regardless, a smile lit up Jessica's face. *Beautiful.* "Good," Jessica said emphatically. "Then let's go back inside. I'm starving."

10

Don't Blame Me (Now)

"Was wondering when I'd hear from you."

I scoff into the phone, sandwiched between my ear and shoulder. "It's been what, two days?"

Carson responds with a laugh. I can picture them in their office, spacious and open and airy, shaking their head, cold Diet Coke within reach. It's always a pattern with Carson—all repetition, everything scheduled and planned to the tee, not even a speck of dust out of place. It's been that way since we met six years ago: me fresh off what I thought would be the experience that finally killed me, Carson looking for someone to answer phones and respond to emails at their PI firm. They'd noted the ink smudges on my fingers and the deep, bruise-colored bags under my eyes immediately. They'd noted the look in my eyes too—desperate for something more than a desk job.

"Doesn't time pass slower out there?" Carson asks now.

I get down on the floor, looking under Cora's bed, searching for the box or case or whatever it is that the key I found earlier opens. "I guess you could say that."

"No luck finding your aunt yet?"

Sitting back on my haunches, I let the bed skirt fall back down. "None."

"Police any help?"

"What do you think?"

Carson lets out a long breath. "Well, it's good to know that they're useless in every part of the country. You think she took off, or . . .?"

They trail off, letting me fill in the blank. I stand, rubbing a hand across my forehead. I've been at this for over an hour, since Hunter and I got home and she once again disappeared—whether it was outside or back into the guesthouse, I have no idea. She was silent on the drive back to the ranch, but it was different from her usual silences: not like she'd chosen it this time, but like she was scared to say anything.

What was Cora hiding? It's the question that's making me want to pull the hair out of my head. It's the question that's the key to this whole thing. It's the question that seemingly only a missing woman knows the answer to.

"I don't know. The ranch hand thinks that she was taken, but the cops seem to want to close up shop fast."

"What else is new there?"

"Point taken." Standing close to the bed, my eyes snag on Cora's knitted blanket atop her comforter. One of Cora's own, made in whatever downtime she could scrape together. Likely, it took her months. Sometimes I used to watch her knitting long stretches of colorful yarn into works of art, when I was still allowed to set foot on this property. Her hands, rough with callouses from her day job, so adept and proficient in the more delicate work she did at night. Cora had tried to teach me how to knit, but I hadn't had the patience then—another thing that hasn't changed. My hands itch to touch the blanket, to hold one of the few things that still connect us, but I stop myself.

"Everyone's lying, though," I continue. "Apparently Cora was investigating a decades-old murder, but she stopped abruptly a handful of months ago, if you believe the ranch hand."

"And you don't?"

"I don't know," I reply. "I don't think so. She took me on a 'chore' earlier that included a gun and a very large envelope of money."

"Jesus," Carson snorts. "Sounds like something I'd get up to."

"I talked to one of Cora's friends too," I continue. "They'd been meeting monthly, and the friend was skittish about telling me why. She told me that almost all the farms around here closed eight years ago except for a couple that stayed afloat illegally."

It's hard to imagine Cora breaking the law. Cora was always by the book; I remember watching her late into the night, the summer heat still raging even at those hours, bent over various books and ledgers, keeping meticulous notes and—

Oh.

"Carson, I gotta go," I say in a rush.

"Alright, well make sure you—"

I'm off the phone before Carson can finish their sentence.

* * *

I find Cora's collection of books easily enough.

They're in the right bottom drawer of her desk, little black composition notebooks stacked neatly, their spines pointed outward. They're not much larger than a standard paperback book, maybe a hundred pages or so. On the cover, each is embossed with gold lettering, *CC*, followed by the year it tracks. Custom-made, important. I grab them by the handful, dumping them out onto the desk.

I start with the ones from nine and eight years ago, setting them side by side. The year before Irene said that everyone's ranches went under and the year during. They're both detailed: dates, names, addresses, whether the transaction was a sale or a purchase. Her writing is painstaking and precise, nothing crossed out, no lines skipped. This was a system that she had thought out from beginning to end. Toward the end of the book from nine years ago, the entries got sparser and sparser: fewer sales and smaller purchases.

She was hurting for money, I think, turning my attention to the other book: 2013. The early months are the same as those in its predecessor, but then . . . *there,* in August. The same month that Cora banished me eight years ago. The same month that Jessica Coldwater died forty years ago. The same month Cora Cole has gone missing now.

I wonder if it's another coincidence or something more sinister. The month that separates summer from fall, that unleashes the last gasps of heat into the Wyoming landscape. The month before everything starts to get a little darker a little earlier, when everything seemingly slips away into a moment in time. The month that all these terrible things in Wonderland's history have taken place.

Now, beneath my palms, is Cora's record of August 2013. There are sales. Lots of them. Many more than the year before. When other ranches were falling to pieces, Cora's was flourishing. Horses and cows and—*ranch equipment.*

The names have disappeared too; in their place are only numbers. Some have a letter next to them, but a lot of them don't. Whatever she was selling, she had to conceal the identity of the buyers. Which means not only did something change, but it became a hell of a lot more dangerous than just raising cows.

I flip through the next few books, all of them revealing the same thing: lots of sales made to lots of numbers, some with letters. All of them repeat throughout the years, but the amount of money Cora was making off them varies, anywhere from five hundred to five thousand dollars.

Opening this year's ledger, I skip ahead to August. There's only one entry, dated from the first of the month: *4T, ranch equipment, $10,000.*

* * *

I'm doing something I rarely do: I'm worrying.

I can't find Hunter. Not in the guesthouse, not in the main house, and not anywhere I've looked outside.

I've been waiting for her for hours now. It's long gone dark, the Wyoming sky pitch-black and star scattered. My body's thrumming with the need to grill her about the ledger entries, to find out what she knows about them, to find out where in the hell Cora stashed the ten thousand dollars she got just before she went missing, and what *4T* means. At least that's what I tell myself—that's the reason I'm so desperate to lay my eyes on her, to make sure she's alright.

I shouldn't worry. Hunter's lived out here her whole life, knows this place better than I could ever hope to. She's competent and strong and able, and she probably got tied up with the cows and the fences and the hay.

But.

Cora's missing.

And now I can't find Hunter.

Twenty minutes pass, and I'm about to do something *really* stupid, like go out and look for her by myself in the dark, when I hear the truck rumble up the path. I go to the window, stare out the glass, wait for her to get out of the cab.

Then I see the agony on her face, and I'm moving.

The night air hits me, cool and crisp, as I rush toward her. "What's wrong?" I ask immediately.

She looks up, eyes open wide, jaw locked down tight. "Nothin'," she grunts out. The driver's side door is still open behind her, and her right arm is wrapped around her left, grabbing at her elbow.

"Your arm?" I ask, moving closer. She doesn't withdraw, doesn't flinch back from my attention and concern—and that's when I realize something must be *really* wrong.

"I'm fi—" She takes a step forward, but something moves, shifts in a bad way, because her eyes flare wider, and she gasps in pain.

The sound spurs me forward, and I shut the door to the truck and repeat, "What's *wrong*?"

"Shoulder," she bites out. "It's happened before. It'll be fine in the mornin'. I'll take care of it—"

"Move."

She still manages to narrow her eyes. "What?"

"You heard me," I say sharply. "Get inside the house so I can help you."

"I don't need your help."

"And people in hell don't need ice water." I stretch my arm out, pointing toward the house. "Move."

The pain must truly be getting to her, because she goes without another word of protest. I hold the door open for her, and she doesn't even stop to kick off her boots.

"Where should I go, since you're in charge?" she grunts.

"Bathroom."

She moves slower than usual, all the sureness in her step long gone as we make our way to the back of the house. I push the door open for her once more.

"What now?"

"How'd you hurt yourself?"

"I ain't hurt," she insists. "Hefted a bale wrong and messed up my shoulder, that's all."

"What do you usually do when this happens?"

She exhales through her nose, like I'm wasting her time. "Take a hot shower, throw back a couple pain pills, and sleep it off."

I reach toward the tub, turning the water on nearly as hot as it'll go, then give Hunter a once-over. *She says she's fine, I should leave her.* Patching her up certainly isn't on the list of things I need to do to find Cora.

And still I'm saying, "I'll run over to the guesthouse and get you some clothes."

"Why don't I just shower in my own—"

"So you can fall over and hurt yourself further, and I won't have any way of knowing about it?" I raise my eyebrows. "Not happening."

She says nothing for a long moment. I think she's about to shove me out of the way and storm back to the guesthouse, but then she blows out another long breath and nods. "You gonna leave anytime today?"

"You're welcome," I say as she turns, shutting the door behind me.

Quickly, I make my way to the guesthouse, grabbing a pair of sleep shorts and an oversized T-shirt, along with a pair of underwear. Plain white cotton briefs—the first pair I find, the temptation to linger overshadowed by the reason I'm here in the first place.

Not even three minutes later, I knock on the bathroom door. "Clothes are here, Cowgirl."

No reply. She's big, bad Hunter Lemming—a lone wolf, abandoned and solitary, teeth bared, and ready to snap at any moment.

"Whatever," I mumble. I knock one more time. "I'll leave your clothes here."

Silence greets me once more, and my irritation rises. This is what I get for trying to be nice, trying to show some sort of feeling besides anger and annoyance toward this woman. *Stupid*, and I'm the only one to blame.

I step away from the door, ready to go back to the couch and never talk to Hunter ever again, but then I hear, *"Quinn."*

I spin around, throwing the bathroom door back open.

She's sitting on the toilet seat, clad in her bra and underwear, chest heaving, grabbing at her shoulder like it's about to fall off.

"Jesus Christ," I breathe, scrambling forward. "What happen—"

"I can't get the hooks," she says, pain etched into every syllable. "I got the shirt and the pants, but the goddamn hooks on the goddamn bra—"

"Okay, okay," I say. "It's okay. It's fine—I'm here, I'll help you."

The look of relief on her face is so visceral I think that I've imagined it. And I remember, probably for the first time since I've gotten here, just how young she is. Twenty-one. Not even as old as me. Out here, with all this pain and loss and grief, alone now, and shouldering it all with so little experience under her belt.

"Can you stand?" I ask.

She nods, but the motion's jerky, and she winces. She rises, her shoulders slumping so drastically that we're basically the same height right now.

"Turn around," I say softly.

She does. Her hair, probably the least of her worries, is a mess in the back, tangled and wild. I reach up on my tiptoes to run my fingers through it.

"My hair'll be fine. I need to—"

"It's gonna be a wreck in the morning if you don't let me take care of it now," I say. "Just . . . let me, alright?"

Her arguments fall silent as I continue, untangling the knots I can get. Her hair is warm and smooth, thin, with pieces of hay and small clumps of dirt scattered throughout, but with these imperfect streaks of gold from the sun.

I pluck a few pieces of hay out, letting them fall to the ground. Her breathing has calmed, returning to somewhere near normal. I let my fingers trail from the top of her head to the base of her skull, massaging gently.

"Princess," she breathes, and it makes the blood in my veins run a little quicker.

I keep rubbing small circles into Hunter's skin, dropping down the length of the back of her neck, making my way to her other shoulder. I apply more pressure once I get there, and she lets out a small gasp.

Immediately, I still. "Are you okay?"

"Yeah, I—sorry. It . . . feels nice."

It's not until right then that I notice all the tan, muscled skin that's on display in front of me. I was too focused on making sure she was okay to take it all in before, but now that she's relaxing back into my touch and making these small noises of pleasure—

My hand moves back to her bad shoulder, and immediately she tenses. "Would it help if I massaged it?" I ask, trying to keep the hoarseness out of my voice.

"Maybe," she replies, her voice higher in tone than I've ever heard it. "You could try, but not real hard."

Softly, taking every cue from her body and how she reacts, I use my thumb to apply pressure. Almost imperceptibly she starts to loosen up, but I notice. Every soft groan she makes seems to embed itself under my skin, heating my blood and sending sparks right between my legs.

After a few minutes, I finally reach for the clasp on her bra. I slide the hooks through without a word, carefully helping guide her arms through the straps. The bra drops to the floor, and then I'm left to stare at the bare expanse of her back, muscled and smooth.

Hunter clears her throat, and my mind stills. The air around us has started to turn humid from how hot the shower water is, even with the door open. "Thank you," she says softly.

My hand lands on her hip, the band that rests there, and I hear her take a shaky breath. "And these?" I ask, and this time I can't keep the hoarseness out of my voice. I hear it, and I know she must too.

Her hand comes down on top of mine. "I got it."

I stare at the line of her spine, the way her back has started to heave. "You shouldn't have told me," I whisper.

She turns her head to the side, but not all the way. Not enough that I can see her eyes and all that they remind me of. "Told you what?"

"'Can't catch what you've already got.'"

Her grip on my hand tightens. "I—"

"Because now I've seen you like *this*," I continue, lifting my hand from under hers only to drag the tips of my fingers down the length of her spine, watching goose bumps appear. "And I was already having a hard time keeping you out of my head. Now it'll be impossible."

I take a step back before I do anything more. "I'll be in the living room," I tell her, eyes on the floor. "When you get out. If you need anything else."

I'm halfway out the door, hand already on the doorknob, when she says my name again.

This time when I turn back, she's looking at me over her shoulder, eyes as wide as they were when she first stepped out of the truck. But there's no pain there now—no, there's something else staring back at me. The same thing I saw in the shed. The same thing that I'm sure she can see in my gaze now, plain as day.

There's a reason I've always done casual, why I refuse to even consider a relationship, and it's because of this. Because I know I'd fall—fast and hard and wholly—and then turn around and get burned once more. I've stood in the flames for so long, I'm not sure I'd survive another trip to hell.

There've been girls who understood that, who were like me, looking for an escape, for a distraction, but none like Hunter, who's got me practically all figured out after two days—and that's what makes her so dangerous: her burns match mine.

"Thank you," she says again.

"No problem," I choke out.

11

All the Pretty Girls (Then—April 1981)

O NE RAINY FRIDAY night in the middle of April, Jessica asked Holly if she wanted to spend the night.

Holly had never been to a sleepover—what did she need to bring? How should she act? Was there something she was expected to do? She was nervous, but she accepted Jessica's offer readily. She was never able to deny Jessica anything.

Mrs. Coldwater made dinner from scratch, a big, steaming chicken pot pie filled with fresh vegetables. Holly had never had something like that. Even on Thanksgiving or Christmas, the most Lenora did was buy a premade pie from the store. There were some holidays when she hadn't been around at all or had slept all day.

"What side of the bed do you want?" Jessica asked after they'd put on their pajamas and washed up.

Holly's eyes went wide. "What?"

"The bed," Jessica repeated. She wore a tight pale pink tank top and matching shorts. Everywhere Holly's eyes landed seemed to be dangerous territory.

Realization dawned on her. They were sleeping in the same bed tonight. She was sleeping next to Jessica Coldwater.

"Either's fine," Holly said at last, trying not to let her nerves, the fluttering in her stomach, show.

Jessica threw back the covers on the far side of the bed, climbing in as Holly tentatively did the same. She closed her eyes as Jessica turned out the lights except for the one on her side table. Holly tried to calm her racing heartbeat. *I got it, I got it,* she found herself thinking. She focused on the cool sheets below her, the soft blanket above her. She could do this. She could—

"Troy wants me to give myself to him."

Jessica's confession cut through the dark room like an arrow, landing true, right in the center of Holly's heart.

"Oh," Holly breathed.

Holly knew many things about Troy: he was a year older; he had a full-ride football scholarship to the University of Wyoming next fall; he was a terrible boyfriend; he was All-American handsome, with thick brown hair and bright blue eyes; and he was absolutely, unequivocally not in love with Jessica Coldwater. The last thing was her opinion, Holly supposed, but she believed it to be the truth, so she counted it in her lists of absolutes.

"Yeah," Jessica replied on an exhale. "You know how worried I've been about losing him, especially with school next year. Laramie's so far away, and there are going to be so many prettier girls. Maybe . . . maybe this is the only way to keep him."

Laramie's not that far, Holly wanted to say; as well as, *He doesn't deserve you. And there's no other girl as pretty as you.*

Holly had traversed miles and miles of this country throughout the years; and she'd do it all again, travel any distance for the girl next to her.

"Do you want to?" Holly asked softly.

"I don't know," Jessica said again. "I love him. But I don't think I'm ready for . . . *that.*"

Holly wondered why Jessica had chosen this moment, lying here in the near-complete darkness together, to bring this up. She could've mentioned it at school, in the car, or even earlier that day.

"Then don't," Holly said.

"It's not that simple," Jessica replied, shifting on the bed. "Sometimes you have to do things that are hard, right? Things you don't want to do? For the greater good? And you know how boys are about this stuff."

Jessica wanted Holly to talk her into it, Holly realized. Convince her that giving herself to someone—to *Troy*—when she didn't really want to was the right thing to do.

Heat rushed through Holly's body, from her head to her toes, but not in a good way. She looked over at Jessica, who met her gaze, backlit by the lamp behind her. "No," Holly said, with more force than she'd ever used to say anything in her life before. "It's not right. If he really loved you, if he really wanted to be with you, he'd never even ask you in the first place. He'd know you weren't ready. He'd *never* pressure you. He'd take whatever you gave him and feel like the luckiest person in the world, because he is. So if he's going to break up with you because you won't have sex with him, then good riddance. Then you'd be able to be with someone who sees how perfect and beautiful and smart and worthy you are *exactly the way you are.*"

Holly couldn't catch her breath, couldn't get enough air into her lungs. She stared at Jessica, her chest heaving. Her heart was thumping so fast and so hard that she could hear it in her head and was sure that Jessica could hear it too.

"And you know what?" Holly continued, on a roll now. "Boys aren't the only ones who want to have sex. It's okay for girls to want it too. Even if we're not supposed to or we're supposed to wait until marriage or whatever. Still, I'd never pressure someone to do it with me who wasn't ready. So no. I don't know how boys are, because they shouldn't be like that. Any of them. It's terrible they get to act like that because of how they're born."

It was a huge, tremendous mistake, saying all of that, her intentions so blatantly clear they burned her tongue. She'd ruined the only friendship she'd ever had in the span of a few seconds. But she knew that this moment had been building—there was only so long that she could keep the barriers up, keep the storm from cascading through, keep everything she felt for Jessica bottled up.

Jessica whispered, "No one's ever said something like that to me."

Holly whispered back, "I meant it."

The moment pushed and pulled between them like a live, tangible thing. As real as the air they shared. As real as Holly's feelings for Jessica.

And then, Jessica moved closer, only a fraction of an inch. "You're my best friend," Jessica told her.

"And you're mine."

Jessica inhaled sharply, like she was surprised. *How could she not know?* Holly wondered.

The words kept coming, dangerous in their truth and sincerity: "Of all the towns I've visited," Holly began, "and all the people I've ever met, you're my favorite. Of all the houses I've lived in, being with you is the closest I've ever come to being home."

A tear slipped down Jessica's cheek. "That sounds like something from a romance novel," she said.

Holly fell silent. *Please,* she thought, maybe even praying to anyone or anything that was listening. *Please let her understand, let her feel the same, let her—*

"That sounds like something Troy should be saying to me," Jessica continued.

"But," Holly breathed, "*I'm* saying it to you."

Jessica gasped again, but softer this time, before she pressed her lips to Holly's.

It was so sudden that Holly had no idea how to react at first. This very scenario—Jessica kissing her, her kissing

Jessica—had played out so many times in her head she'd lost count. She should've been prepared, should've been ready. But the pure shock of it, of *Jessica Coldwater* kissing her, made her tense up.

Jessica pulled back as quickly as she had moved in, her hand flying up to cover her mouth. "Oh gosh," she said, horrified. "I—what was I *thinking*? Holly, I'm so—"

Everything hit Holly in that moment when Jessica pulled back and started apologizing. *Apologizing.* For the very thing Holly had been wishing for during every moment of the past month.

Holly kissed her again, cutting Jessica off. Holly wrapped a hand around the back of Jessica's neck, pulling her closer. And then there was no more apologizing—no more talking at all.

CHAPTER

12

Happier Than Ever (Now)

B RIGHT AND EARLY, I find Hunter out in the barn the next morning.

She's throwing around bales of hay as if they're weightless, all concern for her injured shoulder clearly forgotten. The barn is vast and open, hay on the floor, the only sound her grunting and the horses moving around. Cora owns three of them—all brown, and all I am more than happy to keep my distance from. When I was younger, Cora tried to get me to ride them, coaxing me closer until the animal turned its nose a bit too sharply toward me, and I flinched away. I didn't understand—still don't—how anyone could see a thousand-pound animal and not see anything besides warning signs. One wrong move, one awry kick . . .

I clear my throat. "Your shoulder alright?"

Hunter hefts a bale especially high. She wears a black tank top that clings tightly to her figure, her chest heaving as she turns around to acknowledge me for the first time. "What?"

"Your shoulder," I repeat, trying vainly to keep my eyes above her neck. "The one you couldn't even move last night."

"It's fine," she says, sounding annoyed at my show of concern. "I told you, it happens all the time. Stiffens up on me if I don't get it movin'."

That sounds like the direct opposite of what a doctor would be telling her, but I know that I'm useless to stop her. "Okay. Well, I need a ride to the library."

"Why?"

"I want to research the Parker Mountain case."

"You still think that's got something to do with Cora goin' missin'?"

"I found ledgers in Cora's room," I say, stepping forward. "Lots of sales of ranch equipment, with only numbers and some letters listed. You wouldn't happen to know anything about that, would you?"

It is of course that moment that she chooses to grab the bottom of her tank top and pull it up to her forehead, wiping the sweat there and exposing her black sports bra in the process. *Damn, way to deflect!* She clearly knows more about the ledgers than she's letting on.

"No clue," she replies before turning back toward the hay, movements full of grace and purpose. Sweat starts to drip down her neck, rolling under the upper edge of her tank top.

"Well, until you decide to start being helpful to my investigation, I figured I better explore my only other lead."

"I already told you that we got a computer here."

"It crashed three times just trying to open the internet home page." There's no Wi-Fi here—the computer in Cora's guest room is connected to a fucking *modem*—so my laptop is useless.

Boom. She throws another bale, the muscles in her arms flexing. "Until I get all these taken care of, neither one of us is goin' anywhere."

"How long is it gonna take for these to be taken care of?"

She looks down at the numerous bales that lie near her, unstacked. "A little while."

I close my eyes against a wave of annoyance. "I suppose it would go faster if I helped?"

"Pair of gloves with your name on 'em, sittin' right there."

Opening my eyes, I look to my right, where, sitting next to a couple bottles of water and some bolt cutters, is said pair of gloves. I exhale, slipping them on. Yet more manual labor I absolutely did not sign up for.

"We're stackin' them four high," she instructs, gesturing toward the pile she's already assembled before I can call her on her bullshit. "Lift with your legs, not your back. And when you throw one, use your knee to propel it up."

I bend to start on my first bale. I cannot believe how difficult it is and how easy Hunter makes it look. I'm three bales in before I'm gasping for breath, as if I've run two miles. I keep working, though I know it's barely helping.

When we finish, my muscles are screaming, and I'm drenched in sweat. Hunter hands me the bottle of water we've been sharing. "Good work," she says, throwing a flannel on over her tank top.

"I barely did anything," I say dismissively.

"Doesn't matter. You still did it and didn't complain the entire time."

My eyes shoot up my forehead. "Was that a *compliment*?"

She steps closer, so close I can smell the sweat on her skin. It mixes with something else, something rich and earthy and entirely Hunter. She reaches out and tucks a stray piece of hair behind my ear, fingers brushing across my cheek. The feel of her calloused fingertips against my skin makes my breath catch in the back of my throat.

"Don't get used to it," she says.

I have suddenly become a live wire, and Hunter is about two seconds from igniting me. "I won't."

"And thank you," she says, soft but firm. "For last night. Helping me."

"You still think I'm a terrible person?" I ask. I shouldn't because if she answers yes, it'd prove me right again.

"No," she replies, softer than I've heard her speak since I've gotten here.

I open my mouth, but then one of the horses startles, sending Hunter jerking away from me.

"Shower," she says abruptly, turning to leave. "Then I'll drive you to the library."

"Wait—"

"I'll be ready in fifteen minutes," she replies. Then she's gone.

*   *   *

There are two computers located inside the Wonderland Branch Library, and they operate even slower than I'd imagined they would.

I have two hours to research before Hunter is scheduled to pick me up. I'd originally thought that would be plenty of time, but that was before I saw the state of the computers. They are crammed inside of what I strongly believe is a renovated double-wide trailer. The monitors are big and boxy, the type that I thought had gone obsolete.

The old woman staffing the front desk grudgingly gave me the guest log-in information, watching me skeptically, as if I'm here to look up how to make a bomb or something. *Although,* I think as I open the browser, *this might be its own kind of bomb.*

My first task is researching the Parker Mountain case. I know the broad strokes, but I need to go deeper. I need to go as deep as Cora went, get inside of her head—a place I have absolutely zero interest in lingering in. The librarian paces particularly close to me, and I know she's trying to get a glimpse at my screen. I hunch over as best I can to block her view.

There's not much—the folks around here seemed to make certain of that—but there's one article from the *Casper Star-Tribune*, and it's recent—from this year—commemorating the thirtieth anniversary of the killing.

FORTY YEARS LATER, STILL NO ANSWERS: THE PARKER MOUNTAIN CASE

by Tricia Clark

The sleepy, quaint town of Wonderland, Wyoming, rests along I-80. Home to a population of under 200, there's not much of note to the town except for one of the most notorious unsolved murders in Wyoming.

In August 1981, 17-year-old Jessica Coldwater, daughter of the town's mayor, Todd Coldwater, and his wife, Rebecca Coldwater, was found murdered at the base of Parker Mountain, located near Wonderland. Jessica was killed by a gunshot wound, with little evidence for police to go on. She was last seen heading toward the mountain with her best friend, 17-year-old Holly Prine.

Jessica and Holly, on paper, couldn't have been more opposite. Jessica was a Wonderland local from a long line of Coldwaters who were also born and raised in the town. She was a three-sport star athlete, the president of the Radley High School branch of the National Honor Society, and a shoo-in for valedictorian.

Holly, on the other hand, had moved to Wonderland only months prior. Her peers described her as a "loner" who "didn't have any friends" except for Jessica. Raised by a single mother, Holly was not involved with any extracurriculars, though she too excelled in her classes, particularly in English.

"I tried to convince Jessica not to befriend Holly," said Rhett Smith, an English teacher at Radley High School, who taught both Holly and Jessica before retiring this past fall, after 43 years. "But Jessica was such a kindhearted girl; when she saw Holly, who was new to town, she immediately reached out. It was Jessica's big heart that ultimately cost her in the end."

Smith is referencing the belief held by police, and many familiar with the case, that Holly Prine killed Jessica before fleeing the scene of the crime.

"They didn't find evidence of anyone else at the scene," said current Sweetwater County Sheriff Madison Bridgers, granddaughter of Mayor Coldwater and niece of Jessica Coldwater. "They concluded that Jessica did not kill herself, because of the angle of the bullet and that it came from a shotgun, but the weapon was not recovered at the scene, so they rightfully started hunting for Holly. Involved the state and everything. There's still an arrest warrant out for her to this day. But there wasn't enough evidence to charge her, so they closed the case."

How could a 17-year-old girl with seemingly no resources evade capture when the entire state of Wyoming was trying to track her down?

"If you've got an answer, I'd love to hear it," said Sheriff Bridgers when asked.

With not enough evidence to resolutely confirm that Holly Prine killed Jessica Coldwater, it stands to reason that, 30 years later, folks in the area would still want answers. But that's not the case in Wonderland; many locals decided 30 years ago that Holly was guilty, and don't take kindly to questions that suggest any other possibility.

"Holly Prine killed beautiful Jessie Coldwater, and we all know it," said lifetime Wonderland resident Sawyer Clawson. "That angel was taken from us by that horrible girl. You know she was a Satanist, don't ya? Probably killed Jessie in some kind of anti-Christian ritual."

The sentiment that Holly Prine was an outsider, a hellraiser, and a bad kid was echoed by many in the town, making it an easy conviction in the court of public opinion.

Still, 30 years later, there has been no official answer as to who killed Jessica Coldwater. That seems to sit fine with the citizens of Wonderland, who believe they already have all the answers they need.

* * *

I read through a couple of other articles, but there's no new information.

There are reasons, so many reasons, to think that Holly *didn't* kill Jessica: she had no motive; the murder weapon was never recovered; and the surviving girl disappeared into thin air that very night.

There are questions—notably the biggest one: If Holly Prine didn't kill Jessica Coldwater, then who did? The article mentioned that police couldn't find evidence that anyone else was present at the scene where Jessica died—but what does that mean? How much investigating was actually conducted, especially when they had the perfect suspect in Holly Prine?

If she's still alive, Holly Prine would be fifty-seven. A new name, a new home, probably a new hair color, maybe even colored contacts to give her a new eye color too. A murderer, but . . . maybe not.

I sit back in my chair, closing my eyes. If this is the reason Cora's gone missing, then she solved the case, or at least came close to it. She either resolutely found out that Holly Prine killed Jessica Coldwater or that someone else did. Finding evidence of the latter would've been far more dangerous for Cora. If the answer was Holly, the town would've rejoiced, making Cora a hero.

One theory: Cora solved the case, and the murderer wasn't Holly. If she had evidence, she would've gone to the police. *Well, maybe not,* I think, remembering my interaction with Sheriff Bridgers. Only one way to find out.

I pull out my phone, searching for the Sheriff Department's number. I find it, clicking through the link.

"Sweetwater County Sheriff's Department. How may I direct your call?"

"I'd like to speak with Sheriff Bridgers," I say. "Regarding the Cora Cole case."

"Oh, I'm sorry. The sheriff isn't in the office today. Can I—"

The phone is plucked from my hand before I can reply.

I push away from the computer, turning and standing. "I know I'm breaking library rules, but—"

Sheriff Bridgers holds my phone in one hand, the other one poised on her hip. "Let's take this outside, shall we?"

* * *

"I suppose you were just in the neighborhood?"

Bridgers closes the front door to the library behind her, coming to stand next to me. "I was, actually. I couldn't ignore the librarian's call for help when she phoned the station with concerns about a young woman conducting suspicious research."

"Suspicious?" I repeat.

"Internet searches for Jessica and Parker Mountain tend to trigger that feelin' in folks 'round here."

"I didn't realize researching cold cases was illegal in this part of Wyoming."

"It's not," she replies carefully. "You're free to go back in and keep researchin' to your heart's content. Or you can stand out here and talk with me about the case, and we can shut all this down."

I press my lips together, considering. "Did Cora ever say that she'd found the real killer?"

"*Real killer?* You say that like Holly Prine's innocent."

"Maybe she is."

"Alright," Bridgers replies. "I'll play along. Cora called the department several times over the years, askin' about the case. My predecessor didn't take too kindly to the calls, but I indulged her. I respected her, growin' up—especially the way she came back to run the ranch, and I knew about her PI background. So I figured, what's the harm in lettin' her sniff around?" Bridgers rubs at her jaw. "And now, here we are."

"Hunter told me people didn't like her."

"Lem would know better than anyone," Bridgers says. "Look. Four months ago, Cora called me. Said she had evidence and wanted to meet up privately to give me her ledger, but then at the last minute she called it off."

"Her *ledger*? She said exactly that?"

"Yeah," Bridgers replies. "That mean anything to you?"

"No," I say quickly. A bad lie. I don't miss the way Bridgers narrows her eyes.

"I know we got off on the wrong foot at the station," she begins, "but we're on the same side here. I want to find Cora as much as you do. I've known her my entire life; she's good people. Truly, I don't think anything bad's happened to her. I don't think she found anything new out about Parker Mountain either. I think . . ." She sighs. "I think that she got tired of it all, Quinn. She told me that the ranch was strugglin'. I know she missed investigatin'. It's too bad that Lem got left behind, but she wouldn't be the first one, especially not in this town."

She wants me to trust her. Hunter does, and apparently Cora did. But there's something . . . off.

Maybe it's because she's a cop. Maybe it's because she's been a little too eager to track me down and find out what I know. Maybe it's something I haven't discovered yet. It's there, though—holding me back.

"Well, *Lem* didn't really get left behind, now did she?" I ask. "Not with you still here, right?"

Bridgers tips her head to the side, confusion flickering across her features. Then it clears, she nods, and says, "Oh, I get it. So the three of us have more than just knowin' Cora in common."

"I don't—"

"If it makes you feel better, we haven't been out since before all this happened with Cora," she says.

My thoughts grind to a sudden halt. "Out?"

"Out," she repeats. "Food. Movie. Pretend it's just a work dinner or friends catchin' up so no one gets outed. We call that a date here. Of course, I don't know what all goes on up in your neck of the woods."

Hunter on a date. With another woman. Not just making out behind the bleachers after a little secret practice in high school. Adults having conversation and dinner and a bottle of wine that costs more than six dollars.

I open my mouth to say God knows what, but then Hunter's truck rumbles up next to us. "That's my ride," I bite out. "So sorry to cut this short."

"Sure," Bridgers replies dryly.

I turn toward the truck, gravel crunching under my sneakers, when Bridgers says, "I know more about all this than you think I do, Quinn."

I hesitate at that, hating myself for it. "What's that supposed to mean, Sheriff?"

She looks past me, to the truck, offering Hunter a wave. I don't turn to see if the gesture is returned. "It means I wasn't lyin' when I told you back at the station that I know Cora better than you do," she says.

God, am I getting sick of people saying that.

I can't tell if she's trying to clue me in to something or looking to claw her way further under my skin. "If you knew her so well," I say, turning toward the truck, "then why haven't you found her yet?"

She smiles, and it only puts me further on edge. "Ain't that the million-dollar question?"

* * *

I'm finishing up my makeup when a knock sounds against the front door.

I put down my tube of lipstick, walking out of the bathroom and down the hallway. The guest bathroom, that is—I still can't bring myself to be in Cora's space unless it's related to the case. I see her in everything in this damn place, and it's the worst in her bedroom, the photo of her and me, caught, seemingly, in another life.

Ghosts have never scared me before, but this. . . .this is a different kind of animal entirely.

Hunter's running a hand up and down the back of her neck when I pull open the door, but stops abruptly when she sees me. I'd wanted to grill her about going out with the sheriff before Cora disappeared, but was too annoyed to do it in a way that wouldn't get me immediately shot down.

"What are you wearing?" Hunter demands.

I look down at the black dress I've got on. It's short, but not indecently so, the hem hitting mid-thigh. The neckline is high enough; five buttons secure it down the center, showing off my collarbones, but not much else.

"A dress," I reply dryly, meeting her gaze once again. "Maybe you've never seen one before, but this is pretty typical fare."

The expression on her face makes it seem like she's trying to solve a complicated equation, and she can't even get through the first step. "It's . . . I said jeans and a nice shirt."

I give Hunter, who is currently wearing jeans covered in dirt and dust, and a blue flannel, a dramatic once-over. "I guess *you* didn't get the message either, then."

"I'm not going."

"*What?*" I exclaim. "What are you talking about? You have to—"

"I already told you, I keep to myself."

"So, I'm supposed to go to this barnyard fundraiser alone, then? Solve the case myself?"

She presses her lips together, hat covering most of her face as she dips her head. "It'll be better if I'm not there."

"Why?" I demand. "You've got connections I don't. People know you; people like you—"

"People don't like me," she snaps, head whipping up, blue eyes wide with indignation. "They may know me, but that ain't a good thing. Everybody that you need to talk to'll shut down the second they see me."

"Why?" I ask again, but quieter this time. It's a tender spot for Hunter, clearly—one where I need to tread carefully when pressing on. But what issues could people in this tiny town have with a twenty-one-year-old who's lost all the family she's ever known?

Hunter pauses, as if considering answering, but then her gaze looks off over my shoulder.

There's a story here, a bad one.

"We're leaving in ten minutes," she says finally.

I reach out, trying to grab her arm. "Tell me—"

"Ain't nothin' to tell," she replies, stepping back, away from my grasp. How she can be so close and yet still so far away is beyond me. "Not anymore."

She brushes past me, heading toward Cora's room. *Not anymore.* Because Cora's gone, or because her family's—

"*Quinn!*"

I move so fast I nearly trip over my feet, sprinting down the hall. Hunter's standing in the bathroom, frozen, staring at the mirror.

"What's wr—oh."

The mirror. The mirror is what's wrong. More precisely, the message in all capital letters written there, in bright red: *STOP LOOKING.*

"That wasn't here this morning," I breathe.

"I came back after I dropped you off at the library," Hunter tells me, voice quiet. "I was in here, lookin' for extra towels. The mirror was . . . not like that."

"Someone wrote it when you left to pick me up, then. Would've been a small window, but not impossible."

Which means someone was watching either one or both of us. The idea that someone else is out here, with access to Hunter, to the moments that we've shared—

"Someone broke in," Hunter whispers. "Someone was here. In Cora's room."

I lean forward, pressing my fingers to the glass where the message is written. I touch the letters, and when I pull back, red stains appear on my hand.

I rub my fingers together. "It's not paint," I say. "I think it's . . . lipstick."

"Cora doesn't own any red lipstick."

"Wouldn't have thought so," I reply, wiping the stain off on a towel. I step back into the bedroom, surveying the area. Nothing else seems out of order: the bed is still made, the desk neat, the picture of her and me exactly where I left it.

Only the bathroom. Only the message. At least, that's what I hope.

"Might just be someone trying to scare us," I tell her, trying to assuage her nerves. "Has anything like this happened before? Any threatening messages?"

"No, nothing like that."

I nod. "Well, you said it yourself: people in this town didn't like her, don't like you. Probably a prank."

When I turn back to the bathroom, Hunter is still standing in the same position I found her in. Her gaze hasn't moved from the mirror, as if she can find out who wrote it by staring at it long enough.

Threats are not new to me. As far as how menacing they can be, this one rates pretty low on the chart. But still— someone was *here*, even if it was only a prank.

"Hey," I say softly, reaching out and touching her arm. Her skin is cold, almost clammy. "You alright?"

"Something happened to her," she says in a small voice. "Something bad. This proves it. And the person that did it was here, in her house, and wrote this—"

"Hey," I repeat, turning her toward me. Finally her eyes meet mine, and the fear I see there makes me want to do very, very bad things to whoever did this. "There's no guarantee of that. Like I said, it could just as easily be a prank. Do you have any idea how they would've gotten in here?"

"The front door," she replies. "Cora never locks it. There's never been a reason to. There's never . . ." She shakes her head as she trails off.

"Alright, so we're going to start locking all the doors," I say. "That gun in your truck might actually prove useful."

"No one's gonna hurt you," she says suddenly, fervor embedded in her tone. "Maybe . . . maybe someone got to Cora. They ain't gettin' to you—I swear it."

The certainty with which she speaks shouldn't surprise me, yet it still does. I'm not used to people standing up for me, or even being willing to protect me—and definitely not with such determination.

As if on instinct, I pull her closer by the elbow, tugging her into me so there isn't an inch of space between us. What a picture we must make: me, in a full face of makeup and a nice dress, Hunter in her boots and hat. It's one I'd frame and put up on the wall in a heartbeat.

"If anyone hurts you again," I begin, "they will have me to answer to. I don't care who—even Cora. I may not know how to fix a fence or ride a horse, but I know a thing or two about protection."

The same vow, made two different ways from two very different women. I can see it in her eyes, deep and blue and real, and in her actions before this, that she means it. And God knows I do.

In that moment, I'm more concerned about the way she's been affected by the message than what it means for Cora. I realize the danger in that, the *wrongness* in that, but I don't care.

My cares are very quickly disappearing, whittling down to a handful that all seem to exist in Wonderland, Wyoming.

* * *

Radley is a forty-minute drive east on the highway, and about double the size of Wonderland.

The town has streetlamps lining its downtown, a luxury that Wonderland does not. I watch the shops, all dark and closed at this hour, roll by as Hunter drives past them. There are a few people out and milling around, but still I can't help comparing these tiny towns to where I'm from. Spokane could swallow up all these places and not even blink. The population of Spokane alone probably rivals that of the entire state of Wyoming.

I try to imagine Hunter living in a place like Spokane. Hunter, in her dusty jeans and old cowboy hat, never having to drive more than twenty miles to get where she needed to go, walking through the neighborhoods to downtown. The crowds, the noise, the cars. The coffee shops, the bookstores, the restaurants, the ice rink—all of it new and nice and renovated, with a few leftover structures from the 1974 Expo. The giant tent that was the centerpiece of the Expo is still there, in the middle of everything; that could be the one thing Hunter might actually like.

She pulls into a lot, putting the truck in park. "This is the event center," she says softly. "You head on up and go inside. I'll be back in a couple hours."

The building is small, like everything else in this place. Rust-red bricks cover the outside, lights illuminating the walkway up to the front door.

I sit for a moment, watching couples and families make their way inside. It's a small thing, an unimportant thing, but it still yanks at something in my chest: another reminder of all the things I don't have, all the things that have been taken from me.

Hunter, who knows that feeling better than anyone else I've ever met, clears her throat. "You alright?"

"Yes," I lie. "I'm fine. What about you? With the message and everything."

"Reckon I'm about as fine as you are."

"Fair enough," I reply. "Try not to get into too much trouble while I'm gone."

"That's your area of expertise."

I grin, moving to get out of the truck, but Hunter stops me. "Wait," she says, gently grabbing my bare elbow. Her hand is big, and so warm, my skin heating up on contact. "You have a . . ." She trails off, her hand moving from my arm to my cheek. I've gone still from shock—she's touching me again, like she did in the barn, except this time, she's got nowhere to run.

Her fingers move softly across my cheek, pulling back to reveal what she's holding: "You had an eyelash." She lets it fall between us. "You look so nice tonight, and I didn't want that to ruin it."

My eyes widen, and even in the dim light of the truck, I see her cheeks go red.

"Sorry," she sputters. "I . . . don't know why I said that. I—"

"Don't apologize," I say, my voice dropping. "You've spent enough time apologizing and hiding. Fucking own it, Cowgirl."

Hunter shakes her head, which only draws more attention to the way her cheeks are blazing. "You're . . ."

"I'm . . .?"

"I can't decide if I want to strangle you or . . ." She trails off again, trying to let the words fade into the night between us.

"Or what?" I push. "You can't decide if you hate me or you like me, right? If you want to strangle me or fuck me?"

"God," she chokes out, her eyes in her lap. "The way you talk—"

I cut her off, bringing my fingers to her chin. Lightly, I tilt her face so that she's looking right at me, my grip keeping her gaze from straying. "They're going to hate you no matter what," I tell her. "They'll find a reason. Whether it's who you want or what you want or how you talk, so you might as well do it all on your own terms."

This time, when I move to get out of the truck, she doesn't try and stop me.

* * *

Hunter was dead-on about the dress code.

There are a few women wearing sundresses, but everyone else is in boots, jeans, and cowboy hats. I stick out like a sore thumb, but I suppose that would've been the case even if I'd abided by the yee-haw dress code.

The space is small, sparsely decorated. White walls, cheap wooden floors, harsh overhead lighting. There's a big picture of a girl—Jessica Coldwater, I presume—perched on an easel right next to the refreshment table, which I'm pleased to see is serving alcohol alongside water and lemonade. I've been to a few fundraisers in my life, but none quite like this one.

I make my way across the room, the eyes on me as tangible as if the twenty-five people in the room had reached out and smacked me across the face. Surely, everyone knows everyone else in this room—except for the woman getting a glass of local whiskey in the black dress. For the first time that evening—but certainly not the last—I wish that I had a certain sullen cowgirl by my side.

I survey the room as I take a long sip of my drink. It's expensive—smooth and sharp on my tongue. I truly have no preference when it comes to liquor. Whatever's on hand does the trick. But now I've drunk Wyoming whiskey and hefted barrels of hay and fixed a fence. I can't help but wonder what Cora would think if she could see me here, with all that under my belt. If she'd be proud.

I don't need it, I remind myself, taking another swig of my drink. *I don't need anyone's pride or affirmation or love. I've gone twenty-two years without it.* But the difference between want and need is as deep and wide as the valleys all around this place.

"Quinn Cuthridge," a voice announces, startling me. When I look over, Sheriff Bridgers is settling in next to me like we're old friends, like we've grown up together. Like we played on the same basketball team in high school and called each other by our nicknames and messed around behind the bleachers.

"Sheriff."

"You scare Lem off already?"

I let out a distinctly unladylike grunt, thinking about my last words to Hunter in the truck. "The opposite, actually."

The sheriff takes in the glass in my hand, my attire. She's dressed as everyone else is, but there's an intensity in her eyes that sets her apart from the other guests.

"Well," Bridgers says, "send my regards, then."

"I'm sure you're capable of sending them yourself, Sherriff."

Bridgers grins, then pauses as I drain the rest of my glass, as if waiting for me to bring my full attention back to her. "I'm sure she told you we played basketball together," she finally says. "She was quiet, kept to herself. But she had my back on the court, that's for damn sure. There was one time—we were playing a team out of Casper, I think—and one of their girls called me a nasty name. Lem heard, and she used up all five of her fouls tripping and elbowing and pushing that girl around." Bridgers smiles at the memory. A shot of something goes through me, the same feeling that's surfaced every time I've listened to Bridgers talk about Hunter with such familiarity. I recognize what it is immediately, though I don't want to admit it to myself: that I'm jealous of this woman who has these pieces and memories of Hunter that I'll never get.

"Lem mentioned you were married?" I continue, the whiskey starting to settle in my bones. "Is he here? I'd love to meet him."

Bridgers smiles again, but it's slow this time, something sinister behind it that I don't like. "I'm divorced, actually," she says. "Paperwork went through about a month ago. He moved to Arizona. Lem wouldn't have agreed to go out with me otherwise, of course."

LONG TIME GONE 129

"Of course," I repeat, digging my fingernails into the side of my leg through my dress. "Oh, you're Jessica's niece, right?" I ask abruptly, feigning ignorance. This, after all, is what I came here to do: find answers. Not worry about who may or may not be interested in the same woman I may or may not be interested in.

The smile, the mischief, drops from the sheriff's face. "Yes," she replies. "She was killed before I was born. But still. Family's family."

"Have you tried investigating what happened to her on your own at all?"

Bridgers leans a bit closer. "It's one thing to run your mouth outside a library with no one around, but here? As far as this room is concerned, Holly did it."

"Not Cora," I counter. "And not me. And not even the law, officially. So not everyone."

The sheriff shifts uneasily on her feet, like she wants to say something but is holding back. A terrible poker face. *What does she know? What's she not telling me?*

"The ledger, then," Bridgers says. "I know you found it. Or know what's in it. Tell me, and I'll return the favor."

Tit for tat. Fair, maybe, but still too much of an ask. Bridgers isn't someone I can trust, largely because she's given me no reason to trust her. She's related to the Coldwaters; she hasn't found Cora; she's here at this fundraiser for her dead aunt, relishing memories of old basketball games with *Lem*.

"Like I told you before," I reply, "I don't know anything about a ledger."

That brings the smile back to Bridgers's face. "Alright," she says. "Though, tell me, because I've been trying to put my finger on it: Why such a disdain for the police?"

I throw back the rest of my whiskey, feeling the burn down my throat as I place my empty glass on a passing tray. "I think the better question is why the police have such a disdain for everyone without money or power or privilege."

"That's not me," she replies, an edge to her tone. "That's not my department."

"How many excessive use of force complaints have been filed against you and your department, Sheriff?" I counter. "How many allegations of racism? How many sexual assault reports taken seriously? How many missing Black and Indigenous women on your watch?"

"I was elected to this office to *help* people—"

"People like your grandfather, who handles the politics side of things." I pause, taking a long look around the room. "But not anyone else. You're a pawn in this, and a willing one by the looks of it. Consider me this: What if someone in this room is responsible for Jessica Coldwater's death—someone with the same last name as you? What does the young, connected, well-read sheriff do then? Would she arrest her own kin? Would she admit that the police force she oversees has been standing in the way of justice for forty years? Or maybe that a certain missing persons case is somehow connected to all of this, and that's why my aunt hasn't been found yet?"

"That's a lot of *what ifs*."

"Maybe," I tell her. "Maybe not."

Madison Bridgers wants to pretend she's above it all, that corruption and bias and familial ties have no room in her department, that she's not complicit in an unjust system. But most of us are: me, Hunter, Cora, and most definitely the sheriff in a map-dot Wyoming county.

"Consider it," I offer when the conversation grows quiet. "Think, for a moment, that I might be right about even some of it."

"I—"

"And that *maybe*," I continue, on a whiskey-fueled roll now, "you had your chance with Hunter. And you didn't choose her, and she deserves far more than to be anyone's second choice."

The words are out before I even fully realize I mean them. That it shouldn't have taken all these years and a divorce for

Bridgers to see what I so clearly do, even after only a few days of existing in the same universe as Hunter Lemming.

Bridgers opens her mouth, cheeks flushed, but is interrupted by another woman approaching us. She's older, but in an entirely elegant and poised way. She wears a dress of midnight blue, a scarf draped around her shoulders. Her steps are measured, confident—she owns this room, and she knows it. Her demeanor gives so much away, so much more than any string of words could.

"Quinn," Bridgers says, her tone falling stoic, "this is my grandmother, Rebecca Coldwater. Grandmother, this is Quinn Cuthridge, Cora Cole's niece."

The woman looks me square in the eye, like she's searching for something. The reason I'm here, maybe; or perhaps which parts of Cora I inherited. If I got her intuition, her cunning, her need to pick and pick until the truth is revealed, bloody and unseemly as it may be.

"Yes, I remember you," she says, a small smile on her face. I can't tell if it's fake or not, but I'm leaning toward the former. "You used to visit Cora's ranch each summer—gave the Lemming girl someone to occupy her time with."

Lovely—another woman who wants to talk about Hunter.

I do not remember ever meeting or seeing the matriarch of the Coldwater family before this moment. Certainly, a figure such as herself would've stuck out, would've held a memory or two. But there's . . . nothing. Either she's lying or I'm forgetting; again, I know which option I favor.

"Speaking of which," Mrs. Coldwater continues, "where is that girl? I thought that maybe she'd make an appearance, even after last year."

"What happened last year?" I ask.

"She and your aunt showed up," Mrs. Coldwater says. Although her tone remains calm and perfectly amicable, her vowels have turned harder, the consonants bending in on themselves with how much emphasis she's putting on them.

"They usually keep to themselves out on that ranch, doing God knows what. If I were one to gossip, I might even mention the rumors of illegal activity going on out there."

"Grandmother," Bridgers warns before I can interject. Hunter wouldn't even leave the safety of the parking lot, and here she is, her name on the lips of all these people I want to drag it from.

"Of course, my granddaughter assures me there's nothing of the sort," she continues, patting Bridgers on the shoulder. The gesture might've appeared loving, but the way Mrs. Coldwater's fingers wrap around her granddaughter's bones, lingering a beat too long, suggest otherwise. *Remember your place,* she's saying, only without the words. "Be a dear and get me some lemonade, Madison."

It's not a request, and Bridgers hears it the same as I do. She rolls her eyes, Mrs. Coldwater oblivious to the gesture as she keeps staring at me, but it's then that I notice they've got the same blue eyes. Before I can linger too much on the detail, Bridgers steps away, leaving Mrs. Coldwater and me alone.

"Cora's been asking ugly questions about my daughter's murder for far too long," she continues. "Last year, she thought it appropriate to bring those questions *here*, on this night. Finally I'd had enough and had her and the Lemming girl escorted out."

"And what exactly do you have against Hunter?"

"I had nothing against her until she showed up with your aunt that night."

"Do you remember what they were asking about?"

"Why?" Mrs. Coldwater says in a tight voice, her polite facade slipping. "Don't tell me you've picked up where your aunt left off."

"No," I reassure her. "Simply looking for anything that might help me locate her. I'm not looking to reopen old wounds, especially when the case is clearly closed."

If she sees through my lie, Mrs. Coldwater doesn't mention it. "Well, she was asking my husband, the mayor—he's sick as a dog tonight; otherwise he would be here—about some cover-up. He was the mayor when Jessica was . . . when she died, and his brother was the sheriff. Your aunt thought . . . well, I don't know exactly what she thought. I had her thrown out before she was through with her interrogation."

A cover-up. It makes sense, with the power and the positions that the Coldwaters have in this town. What was Cora onto? How someone was hiding the identity of the real killer and pinning it on Holly Prine, maybe? That's the only thing I can think of, the only thing that would make sense, but that doesn't mean it's the right answer. It just means there might be something else for me to uncover here, a section of the puzzle I haven't seen yet, a lens I haven't examined this all through.

The lights dim, the music dropping. "That's my cue," Mrs. Coldwater says, extending her hand toward mine. "I wish you better choices than your aunt and her ranch hand have made, Quinn."

I shake her hand, even though it's the last thing I want to do. Being at all friendly with this woman feels wrong somehow, like I'm betraying Cora and Hunter.

As if she can hear my thoughts, Mrs. Coldwater's gaze drops to our hands. Suddenly, her grip goes tight, holding me in place. "Your wrist," she says sharply. "Is that a scar?"

"Birthmark," I reply.

She drops my hand as if it's burned her, stepping back in the same motion. She is silent for so long I begin to worry that something's wrong.

"Are you—" I begin.

"Cora's niece," she interrupts. "On your mother or father's side?"

"Why do you ask?"

"Oh," she says, waving her hand dismissively, as if this discussion hasn't very suddenly taken a very strange turn. "Just family things, dear."

She's off without any further explanation, the crowd parting like the Red Sea as she makes her way to the stage, the center of this town for the past forty years, beaming and shining on the night of her murdered daughter's fundraiser.

*   *   *

I down two more whiskeys before deciding to take a lap around the room.

People glance at me as I circle, wondering who in the hell these people are. *Hunter would know.* I almost consider asking Bridgers, but even if I were that stupid, the sheriff's seemingly disappeared, probably at the behest of her grandmother.

Carson wouldn't stop without getting the answers they came for. Carson wouldn't let some newfound crush mess with their head like this. Carson would put on a big smile and introduce themselves to everyone in the room until they found their target. I was not taught to be weak, not taught to be a fool—so I refuse to act like one. Even if coming here, to this fundraiser, to Wonderland, makes me very likely both of those things.

I step back toward the refreshment table, taking in the massive photo of Jessica. She was pretty in the same way that all white girls and women who go missing and gain notoriety are: thin and perky, blonde hair and blue eyes. If she'd lived, I imagine she would've looked a hell of a lot like her sheriff niece.

If Jessica had been from another town or had a different last name or a deeper skin tone, this entire fundraiser wouldn't even be taking place right now. There would've been no search for her, at least no real one. There would be no pretty picture of her. There would just be a name, forgotten and tossed aside, as if her life didn't matter.

And still. Jessica Coldwater had it all going for her: the look, the name, the power, the privilege. They all do. Every single soul in this room. They haven't had to endure the kind of suffering that I have—the kind Hunter has. Hunter, who wouldn't even show up tonight because of these people. If the way they feel about Cora and Hunter is any indication, I'm sure they have less than kind inklings about me.

They haven't found Jessica Coldwater's murderer in forty years. This is the best they can do: throw on jeans and meet up in a building only slightly larger than a barn and blame it all on her best friend.

Her best friend, who might also be dead—or who might still be out there somewhere, living with the truth of what happened that night. But why wouldn't she come forward? Why wouldn't she want Jessica's murderer to be brought to justice? Maybe she did do it, after all. Or maybe—

She's scared. I can see it so clearly, looking around this room, suddenly collapsing in on me, filled with people who've never been strangers for a day in their lives. They watch out for one another; they protect one another. But the poor, out-cast girl who had just moved to town? They had no loyalty to her. No reason to lie for her.

And she had every reason to run if she'd seen something she shouldn't have.

* * *

I'm a little more than tipsy as I walk through Cora's front door.

I know that, at least. What I don't know is why Hunter is putting steaming plates of food down on the table, which is set for two.

Hunter arrived right when she said she would. The ride back was mostly silent, the world swirling too violently in front of my eyes for me to make much conversation. Then she'd walked back into the house, hung her hat by the door, and headed right for the kitchen.

Now Hunter barely even looks up before saying, "Dinner's ready."

Dinner. At close to ten o'clock. "Is this another Cora–Hunter ritual that I'm not picking up on?" I ask as I kick my shoes off.

She puts down a heaping bowl of mashed potatoes in front of my plate, then sits down. "I was hungry. I made dinner. There are extras. Eat or don't—I couldn't care less."

The fact that she set a place for me makes it seems like she does in fact care, but I don't push. I make my way over to the table, settling in as I scan all the food on the table. It's a spread that rivals Thanksgiving: steaks out on a cutting board, green beans and corn to go with the potatoes, practically an entire bucket of dinner rolls, and three—no, four—different sauces in varying colors and viscosities.

"Are you gonna talk to me about the ledgers?" I ask at the same time that Hunter asks, "How did the fundraiser go?"

I raise my eyebrows. "So that's what this is," I reply. "Trying to bribe information out of me."

Color rises to her cheeks. "I told you, I made dinner for myself, and—"

"It was fine," I say, sparing her. "Illuminating, for sure."

"What does that mean?" she asks, spooning herself a giant helping of potatoes.

I watch as she gathers items from around the table, filling her plate all the way to the edges. She looks up only when she's finished, and after a moment, looks back down at her plate and digs in.

I push away from the table, my chair scraping against the wooden floors as I stand, heading straight for the nearly empty vodka bottle atop the fridge.

I spin the cap off, taking a long swig before I hop up on the counter. "Your corrupt little sheriff was more than happy to chat with me about the two of you."

Her eyebrows pull down in confusion. "What're you talking about?"

"Well, she's divorced," I say. "And she went on and on about your high school days. And of course all the dates you were going on before Cora went missing."

Her cheeks begin to redden again. She tries to duck her head, evade my eyes, but it's to no avail. "We're just friends."

"Friends," I repeat, disbelieving. She's killing me here. "I mean, maybe if you'd made an appearance, we could've hashed it out right then and there. But since you didn't, I guess I'll have to take your word for it."

"Anything about—"

"But you," I continue, "*you* touched me in the barn this morning."

Her grip on her fork gets a little tighter. "It was stupid," she replies. "I was . . . I don't know what I was doing."

"All the same things you did with Maddie, I'm guessing."

She snorts, then wipes at her mouth with the napkin tucked in her lap. "Rest assured, whatever sordid things you're thinkin' we did never happened."

My interest only rises as I continue to pry, Hunter's lesbian love life suddenly the most compelling thing in the entire state of Wyoming. "Expand on that."

Hunter rubs at her forehead like she's trying to stave off a giant headache. "Look. In high school, she was older and popular and religious. And I was intimidated by her. And she didn't even know if she liked girls, so nothing much really went down."

I'm off the counter before I can think better of it, prowling back toward the table. "But you two dated more recently."

"Jesus," she says dismissively. "We went to dinner twice. Seems like she just mentioned it to get a rise out of you. Which—" She raises a hand in my direction.

Ignoring that, I ask, "So you've never been in a relationship? Never had se—"

"And why do you wanna know so goddamn bad?" she snaps, cutting me off.

I tip my head to the side, studying her, taking another step closer. "Probably the same reason why you want to tell me."

"I *don't* wanna be having this—"

"Do you like her?" I finally ask. It's the same question I've been dying to know the answer to ever since we set foot in that police station and I heard Bridgers call her *Lem* for the first time.

"Of course I like Maddie," she says.

"You know that's not what I was asking," I reply. I've made it back to my chair now, but I don't sit. I lean my hip against it, using my arm to support most of my weight. I'm trying to look casual, even though that's the furthest thing from how I feel about Hunter and her basketball bestie reconnecting after all these years.

We stare at each other, waiting to see who breaks first. I want my answer, so it's the other woman at this table who blinks and looks away. She lets out a sound of frustration, though I don't know if it's because she lost or because now she has to answer my question.

"No," she says softly, and my grip on the chair loosens. "For a long time I thought so. That's why I agreed to go out with her, and it finally clicked that I was only interested in her . . . like *that* because she was the only other woman like me I thought I'd ever know."

Okay. That was a level of honesty I was not expecting. But I'm also thrown by what she *didn't* say, what she left for me to fill in: *"And then I met you."*

She meets my eyes again, and the words are hanging between us as if she'd written them down on a piece of paper and thrown them at me. Between the alcohol and my interaction with the Sherriff and what Hunter's just said, I am about two seconds from saying something catastrophically stupid.

I've had one foot on a flight back to Spokane the entire time I've been here. I didn't come to Wonderland to stay. I certainly didn't come to fall into some storybook romance with a woman who wouldn't leave this town even if her life depended on it.

I must be silent for an alarming period, because Hunter raises her eyebrows and asks, "You still alive over there?"

That makes me remember where I am, what I'm doing. Why I started this conversation in the first place. "Sorry," I reply. "I got distracted staring at your chest."

She gives me this weird little nod, as if acknowledging that she understands the conversation has shifted, turning to far less panic-inducing topics. "Is your head just always uncontrollably filled with these types of thoughts?" she asks.

"Maybe it's just you who brings this side of me out. Did you consider that?"

"I hadn't, actually."

"Maybe," I continue, this fire we've been dancing around reigniting, "it's not so much a problem that I'm having these thoughts about you, but that you're not having them about me. Maybe I need to try a little harder, and I just needed your girlfriend recounting all the good old times you two have had to motivate me."

"Maybe," she snaps, shifting on a dime, "you should be more focused on finding out where Cora is and less on me."

She makes a good point—a great one. I should have no interest in this woman I've been spending so much time around, sharing so much of the same space with. I can't even remember the last time I spent this much time with someone platonically—not even Carson.

But then I think about how Hunter looked the other night in just her flannel. And the fact that she's twenty-one years old and has never been in a relationship before. And everything that we've just said to each other. And the red-hot itch of jealousy that rears its head every time I have to hear Bridgers talk about Hunter.

So, not platonically.

I take one last sip of the vodka before placing it on the floor next to me. Then I'm moving again, closing the distance between me and the woman at the head of the table.

She tenses as I approach, shoulders back, neck straightening. My feet move silently, and I stop right beside her, leaning back against the table.

"What if they did?" I ask, voice low.

"What?"

"All the sordid things I've been seething about, thinking about them happening between you and Bridgers. What if they happened between you and me instead?"

Before she can respond, my hands move to the buttons at the top of the dress. I thread the first one through its hole, Hunter's eyes falling to my chest as the rest of her goes completely still, her gaze so intense I can practically feel it burning my hands. I undo the next one, letting the material fall open, exposing the top of my cleavage.

"Tell me to stop," I say. She's got all the opportunity in the world to stop this, to turn me down—yet she keeps her eyes on the buttons, as if she can undo them with the power of her stare alone.

Buttons three and four slide through. She swallows, and I want to lean forward, track the movement down her throat with my teeth.

"Tell me," I begin, my finger on the fifth and final button, "how you'd dance with me. Would it be slow and sweet—your hand on my back, guiding me around the dance floor? Or would you pull me up against you until there wasn't an inch of space between us, until I could feel your heart pounding against mine?"

She drops her fork, the sound ringing through the otherwise soundless room. "Princess," she says finally, her voice low in warning. *"Don't push,"* she's saying.

"Tell me how you'd kiss me," I continue, rising from the table. "Would it be shy, a little uncertain, because you hadn't done it before? Or would you grab me by the throat and put your mouth on mine like you had a *right* to do it?"

"Quinn," she exhales, sounding as out of breath as she did after throwing around all those bales of hay.

Now, I couldn't stop even if I wanted to. I bend down, ducking so that we're at eye level, not even an inch of space between us as I say, "Tell me how you would fuck me, Hunter Lemming."

She breaks.

She's moving, out of her chair, sweeping aside the plates and silverware and glasses, all of it crashing to the ground thunderously. Then she's spinning back around, her hands at my hips, picking me up and lifting me onto the table like I weigh nothing, moving with such simultaneous grace and ferocity that it makes my head spin.

Hunter's shoulders are heaving as she cages me in, hands flat on the table, body solid and hard, face inches away. I want her so bad I don't even care if it's right here on my aunt's dining room table.

"Stop *talking* like that," she demands, eyes laser focused, breath hot against my face as the words rush out.

"Why?" I taunt, expectant and relishing this. "Because it's not how the good, proper people of Wyoming talk?"

"Yes," she spits out.

"I don't believe you."

"So now I'm a liar?"

I reach out again, trailing one single finger down the length of her neck—slowly, so, so slowly—then back and forth across her collarbones. It's the boldest I've been, and the thrill of waiting for her to step back, to end this, to keep up the charade that she isn't attracted to this foul-mouthed city girl, only makes me want her more. I press my thumb into the hollow of her throat, feeling her pulse.

For a heartbeat, I think she's going to give us exactly what we both want. But then. *Then.* Something changes, and she tears her gaze from mine, looks over to where I'd left the vodka bottle, ruining the moment completely when she says, "Tell me why you drink so much."

I jerk back as if she slapped me, my hands falling from her body. *Wrong, wrong, wrong.* She holds my gaze, waiting, and now I'm going hot for all the wrong reasons.

"Tell me why you don't drink," I retort.

Her reaction is the same as mine was. Except this time, she was able to brace for the blow. She opened the door and wasn't ready when I slammed it right back in her face.

The edge, the push in both our questions—too much, too far, and we both know it.

We're picking at old wounds, looking for new answers that neither of us are entitled to, that neither of us are willing to give the other, at least not yet. It's a chess match, both players one move away from a stalemate, a perfect game ending in both sides being unsatisfied and upset.

I could tell her that I drink because when I've fried enough brain cells on any given night, I'm gone enough to forget myself. My mother and Carson and Cora and the dead end that my life is spiraling toward. I only finished high school because Carson forced me to, so I certainly don't have the grades to get into college. If it weren't for them, I would've dropped out entirely.

But I can't tell her about any of that. Because then it'll lead to more questions, more answers I'm not ready to unleash. What I *can* do is tuck it all neatly behind glass bottles, the liquor washing the sins of everyone else away.

I push away from the table, nearly stumbling over my own feet and tumbling to the floor. Hunter says nothing, watching silently as I retrieve the bottle and disappear down the hallway.

CHAPTER

13

Dancing With Our Hands Tied (Then—May 1981)

WHEN JESSICA SUGGESTED that they go camping over Memorial Day weekend, Holly thought she'd lost her mind.

Jessica Coldwater, in her pressed pink skirts and freshly curled hair. Jessica Coldwater, who screamed the last time she saw a spider, making Holly take it outside rather than kill it.

That Jessica Coldwater. She wanted to go camping with Holly. For three days, just the two of them.

Jessica had mentioned it one day after school, the girls studying up in Jessica's room, Holly on the bed, Jessica at her desk, textbooks sprawled out in front of them. It had been a little over a month since that night in Jessica's bed. The kiss. Their sleepovers were a lot more frequent now. Holly was practically a permanent fixture in the Coldwater house, neither Mrs. Coldwater or the mayor knowing why the door was always closed, why Jessica's hair was always tousled in the back, why Holly's cheeks were so red when they came down for dinner.

"Camping?" Holly had asked, looking up from her math textbook, the numbers all swirling in front of her. That was another thing they had in common: an extreme distaste for anything related to the study of arithmetic. "Have you even ever gone camping, Jess?"

Jessica turned in her chair, eyes narrowing. "Of course I have," she replied. "When I was little."

"How little?"

"Maybe . . . five?"

Holly couldn't help the laugh that escaped her. "Do you even remember it?"

"Well, no," Jessica allowed. "But this is something I want to do. Flaming Gorge is beautiful this time of year, and we'd be by ourselves, so we wouldn't have to worry about anyone . . . seeing us or anything."

Camping suddenly seemed like a wonderful idea to Holly. While there had been plenty of kissing behind Jessica's closed door the past few weeks, there hadn't been much more than that. A hand daring to venture under a shirt but resting carefully on a stomach; pressing against, but not into. The threat of Mrs. Coldwater neglecting to knock and barging in or one of the girls making a sound she shouldn't was too great.

There was no label on what this was, the time that they spent together, lips locked on lips, hands in each other's hair, rolling around on Jessica's bed. Holly had known the truth about herself for a while, but it had truly cemented two years back, when she'd read about the ten-year anniversary of Stonewall in the paper. She'd been so overcome with emotion that she'd rushed to the library, breathless, reading everything about the riots she could get her hands on. *That's me,* she'd thought, her fingers on a black-and-white photograph printed in one of the national papers. There were two women, each with a brick in one hand and their other hands entwined together. Their bravery, their love on full display for everyone to see. New York had never felt as far away as it did in that moment.

She remembered walking into the women's restroom at the library, making sure no one else was inside, then standing in front of the mirror, straightening her shoulders, and mouthing the word to her reflection. *Lesbian.* And then, because it wasn't quite enough, with her voice church-mouse soft, she said it again. Out loud. She liked the way it sounded to her ears; the way her lips wrapped around all the letters. It was a rush she'd never felt before.

Holly had never met another gay person before Jessica. There was a danger in it, being this way—not knowing whom to trust, whom to confide in, especially out here in Wyoming, Utah, and Nevada. *"Good religious country,"* Lenora had called it once. More land and sky than the eye could see, but no tolerance or understanding to go along with it.

She didn't even know if Jessica thought of herself as a lesbian yet; they hadn't talked about it. She could be bisexual too—Holly had read about bisexuality in the Stonewall articles. God, there were so many questions that Holly wanted to ask her. Maybe this camping trip would be the chance to do that, when it was just the two of them and the land and the sky, and they didn't have to worry about anyone.

That was how they ended up piling their things into the back of Jessica's car after school had gotten out during the final weekend in May, as June was about to break, the heat already starting to settle into the Wyoming landscape around them—as so many other things were about to break open too, Holly hoped.

Wyoming had grown on Holly. Maybe it was because of the company, of how she was spending her days: tangled in Jessica's arms and staring at her in the halls or in classes, when no one else was looking, instead of wondering and worrying about Lenora. She'd forgotten how many days it had been since she'd even seen her mother, let alone heard from her. A town ago, that would've seemed incomprehensible. Each was all the other had. But things were so different now. Wonderland, Wyoming, it seemed, had lived up to its name.

Jessica finished putting the tent in her trunk, then slammed it shut. "Alright," she said. "Let's get this show on the road, shall we?"

Holly smiled, visions of everything this weekend would hold already running wild through her mind.

"You girls all ready?" a voice called from the porch.

It was Mayor Coldwater. He was dressed in a dark suit, but his tie was loosened around his neck.

"Yes, Dad," Jessica replied, making her way to the front of the car. "Since you already checked the tires and the engine and whatever, can we go now?"

The mayor laughed, coming toward them. He stopped in front of Jessica, studying her for a moment, then looked over at Holly. "Good to see you again, Molly."

"*Holly*, Dad."

Holly smiled tightly. "You too, Mr. Mayor." She'd run into the mayor once or twice before, though he wasn't home nearly as much as Mrs. Coldwater was. But he was always *in* the house, by way of his portrait in the foyer. It was his official mayoral portrait. Once he retired from the position, it would be moved to Town Hall to hang on the wall with all the other past mayors. It was a beautiful painting—strong, authoritative—done by an artist from Cheyenne who had traveled to Wonderland for the occasion. But there was something about it that left Holly uneasy. Sometimes she thought it was his eyes, a bit too dark; sometimes it was his posture that bothered her—too forward, as if the portrait had the ability to move, and at any moment the mayor would jump through the golden frame.

Now, the mayor was corporeal, not just oil on canvas. He looked nothing like his portrait, really. He was always distracted, and his shoulders were always slumped. There was nothing strong or prestigious about the man in front of them.

Mrs. Coldwater, it seemed, was always stealing the show, always one step ahead of her husband, and he was none the wiser.

"Girls?" Mrs. Coldwater called, materializing behind her husband. She rested a hand on his arm. "Remember to drive safe! And don't have too much fun out there."

Mrs. Coldwater's words were jovial, easygoing, like always. But there was something . . . off. The way she was standing seemed defensive, her grip on her husband's arm a bit too tight.

And then she looked at Holly in a way she never had before. It was as if she was trying to find out all Holly's secrets; as if she was trying to determine why, exactly, her perfect daughter was so caught up with the new girl in town. The one who had no family of her own to speak of, standing in this picturesque driveway, dressed in an old Beatles T-shirt and ripped jean shorts.

Something had changed, almost imperceptibly. Maybe it was the fact that Jessica had finally broken up with Troy, publicly and resolutely. Holly had overheard them arguing about it, Mrs. Coldwater urging Jessica to reconsider, to give Troy another chance. *"He's such a good boy,"* she'd cooed. *"Such a good family too. And what about all your friends? You spend so much time with—"*

"Holly is the only friend I need," Jessica had told her mother, a surge of pride rushing through Holly as she stood above them, leaning over the railing along the stairs.

Holly had gotten good at noticing the small things, at knowing when something was wrong. Most importantly, she knew when it was time to run. She tried to shake off that feeling now, but it was to no avail.

"Well," Mr. Coldwater said at last, giving Jessica a kiss on the cheek, then opening the driver's side door for her. "Like your mother said, be safe. Never know what could be living out there."

"Yes, Dad, we'll be sure to watch out for bears," Jessica remarked.

Holly dropped her eyes to ground, then got in the car. She kept her gaze on the dashboard as she buckled her seatbelt, as Jessica turned the car over.

When Jessica put her hand on the stick, Holly looked up. The mayor was staring off somewhere over the top of the car, but Mrs. Coldwater was looking right at her through the windshield, unblinking.

It's nothing, Holly assured herself. *She's just being friendly.*

But then she thought, suddenly freezing in her shirt and shorts, *What if she knows?*

14

To Hell and Back (Now)

A DOOR SLAMMING WAKES me bright and early.
      Groggily, I sit up on the couch, rolling out my neck, pushing off the blanket. It gets cold here at night, but by morning the heat always comes roaring back. I can feel sweat already pooling on the back of my neck as I rise, looking out the window.

And see Hunter throwing a pillow and small bag into her truck.

Where in the hell is she going?

That very question drives me out the door. *Don't think about last night, don't think about last night, don't—*

Hunter turns at the sound of the door opening, her gaze going right to my legs, bare all the way up to mid-thigh thanks to the fact that I'm not wearing pants.

I clear my throat, and her eyes move to my face. "Going somewhere?"

"I'm heading out," she replies, voice gruff. "Got an errand to run."

My eyebrows rise. "The same kind of errand we ran in Casper?"

She says nothing, and that's all the answer I need.

"I'm coming with you."

"Like hell you are."

"The last thing I need is you getting *shot* because you went God knows where doing God knows what," I tell her. "There's something you're still not telling me about Cora. So until you do that, you're stuck with me."

She is staring at me like I have three heads.

"I mean if you really hate me that much, I'll sit in the house and stare at the walls and get drunk and eat dinner by my—"

"It ain't you," she says, taking a step closer. "It's . . . what I gotta do. Every month. Not dangerous, but a lot worse than exchangin' a little money."

A little money. I think of all the very large sums I saw in Cora's ledger, and almost start questioning her on the spot. But no—I need to be patient. The last trip to Casper was over two hours. If this one's even close to that, I'll have plenty of time to ask her all the questions I need to.

"Do you have a bag?" she asks.

"What?"

"A bag," she repeats. "We won't be back until t'morrow."

I stand there for a moment, shocked that I've changed her mind so quickly. "Not one packed, but I can go and pack one—"

She nods. "We're leaving in ten minutes."

*   *   *

"Where are we going?"

We've been driving for thirty minutes, the ride silent except for the radio—which is a blessing because it breaks up the silence, but also a curse because it's blasting old-timey country music.

I'd rushed out of the house with my hastily packed suitcase, Hunter already in the truck, engine running, hat perched on top of her head. She'd said nothing as I threw my bag in the bed, then clambered into the front seat.

"Boise," she replies now.

"Boise, *Idaho*?"

The line of her jaw goes even tighter than usual. "You shouldn't've agreed to come if you didn't—"

"It's fine," I say to assuage her. "I didn't realize. How long of a trip is it?"

"Seven hours."

"Oh." A seven-hour road trip in a truck that I'm not even completely convinced is going to be able to carry us that far.

The route takes us back toward the airport, but we keep going, all the way over the Utah border. By the time we pass Salt Lake City, I am nearly one hundred percent sure that the silence is going to force me to lose any ounce of sanity I have left.

I clear my throat. "I was out of line last night," I offer. It's not as if I can make things any worse. "I shouldn't have . . . pushed things so far."

Hunter doesn't look over at me, doesn't even acknowledge that she's heard me. She can't be so offended that she's decided to stop talking to me.

"Sorry I ruined your delicious, home-cooked meal," I continue. "With my tits."

"Jesus, here we go," she huffs out. "I'm not doin' this again."

"Not doing—"

"You," she says forcefully.

"You're not gonna do me? This is certainly an unfortunate turn of events."

"No, I meant . . ." She blows out a breath. "Just . . . sit there and be quiet, and keep your clothes on."

"You're just gonna ignore me?" I ask. "That's not any fun."

Her hand grips the wheel harder, her knuckles going white. She's gritting her jaw down so hard I'm surprised her top teeth haven't barreled through her bottom ones.

"Alright," I relent. "You can at least clue me into where we're going."

"I already told you we're goin' to Boise."

"*Where* in Boise?"

She pauses, the silence dragging between us once more. "A place."

"And you think *I'm* the upsetting one?"

"Quinn," she says, her voice falling softer as she says my name, "I am askin' you to do one thing here, and then I promise I won't ask anything of you ever again: stop askin' me questions about Boise."

The tone of her voice, like she's pleading with me almost, shuts me up. Suddenly, I am very concerned about what's waiting for us in Idaho.

* * *

Just after two thirty, Hunter pulls into the parking lot of the Inland Northwest Rehabilitation and Care Center.

"You can wait here, if you want," she says gruffly, the first thing she's said in hours.

"I didn't drive seven silent hours with you to stay behind," I reply, already getting out of the truck. My legs have gone nearly numb from sitting for so long, making me regret not stretching when Hunter stopped for gas somewhere near the Idaho state line.

The facility's lobby is open and spacious, fake trees spaced out around the entryway. The air-conditioning hits me immediately, making me wish I'd brought a jacket in. Hunter takes off her hat as we step inside, tucking it alongside her leg.

What kind of business could Cora have possibly been doing at a care facility in Idaho?

"Good afternoon!" a bubbly blonde woman working the front desk says. "How can I help you?"

"We're here to see a resident in N103?"

The woman looks down at her computer, eyes scanning across the screen before she nods and smiles at Hunter. "Yep, got you right here! Do you need help finding the room or—"

"No," Hunter says, voice low. "Thank you."

The woman offers another smile as Hunter starts down the hallway to our left. She walks quickly, as if this is a place she does not want to linger. The hallway's carpeted in dark green material with small gold swooshes. We pass by numerous rooms, each one with a small light attached to the wall next to it.

Finally, Hunter comes to a stop. She reaches for the door, then stops, opening and closing her fist right in front of the knob.

"You really ain't gotta come in," she says softly.

"Kind of seems like I should."

She puts her hand on the doorknob but doesn't turn it. She inhales, long and deep, then lets it out, the movement ricocheting through her entire body. It's similar to how she acted back in the truck in Casper, gun tucked into the band of her jeans, readying herself. Though she has no gun now, she seems even more nervous, even more unsteady.

She nods, just once, and pushes inside.

The first thing I hear is the beeping of machines, a steady pulse that thrums unerringly through the room. Then I take in the rest of the space: a TV affixed to the wall, two chairs and a small table, a vase of fake flowers resting atop it. The air is stale, like no one's spent considerable time in here for a while.

In the middle of it all, there is the man lying in bed, his eyes closed, skin deathly pale, a giant tube coming out of his mouth.

We drove seven hours to visit a man who doesn't even know we're here, and Hunter makes this drive every month. I'm trying to deduce why exactly, when my gaze lands on the giant whiteboard hanging on the wall:

"PATIENT NAME: Michael Lemming"

I wrack my memory for that name but come up empty. She's never mentioned any family members, never even alluded to any.

Hunter clears her throat and steps forward, making her way toward the bed. She tosses her hat onto the table, next to the flowers. I'm frozen in the doorway, watching the scene unfold.

"Dad," she whispers. "Still truckin', I see."

It takes a moment for the words to sink in, for my brain to process exactly what's unraveling, exactly who this man is.

Her father, the man she's never spoken of. Her father, alive, here, in this bed, only seven hours away from her. Why hasn't she mentioned him before this? And why couldn't she just tell me she was visiting him?

"Ranch is alright," she continues. "Cora's niece is down visitin', so we've got an extra set of hands. Though she's a city girl, so you can imagine how much help she's been. And I turned twenty-one last month. Remember how you always said we'd go to Seattle for my twenty-first?" She stops again, looking up at the ceiling, at the lights. "That's gone now, ain't it? Like Mom and Jack? You made sure of that."

It's then that the final piece falls into place. The reason Hunter doesn't talk about him, the reason he's here and not closer to Wonderland, the reason she was so desperate not to talk about this in the truck: the drunk driver who killed her family was *her father*.

Yet she's still here. She walks into this room and relives that trauma, that pain, every single month by herself— because the only family she has left is the reason that's true in the first place.

Reaching down, Hunter covers one of his hands with hers. "I'll see you next month, Dad."

Then she turns away from him, picks up her hat, puts it on. She looks at me for what feels like the very first time and says, "Let's go."

I follow Hunter out of the care center without a word.

She climbs in but doesn't turn the truck on, just sits with her hands gripping the top of the steering wheel. Her grasp is so tight I'm worried something in her hands or her wrists is going to give way, a tendon or a bone she's exerting too much pressure on.

"Fuck!" Hunter screams, releasing her grip on the steering wheel to slap at it with her open palms. She says the word again, hitting the steering wheel, getting the horn this time.

"Hey—"

"I'm sorry," she says immediately, chest heaving. "I'm . . . I shouldn't have brought you with me. I do this by myself every month—drive up, see him, spend the night in my truck, then drive back the next morning, and I'll have it all together by the time I get back to the ranch. I should've thought about that before I let you—"

"Hunter," I say slowly, trying to catch her gaze, "it's fine. You don't have to apologize, I promise."

"That's gone now, ain't it? Like Mom and Jack?"

"Was Jack . . . was he—"

"My brother." She nearly chokes on the words as they crawl out of her throat. "He woulda been twelve next month. Our birthdays are exactly two months apart, you know that? Or were, I guess. Does a person's birthday still exist if they don't?"

It's not a question for me to answer; and even if it were, I don't know what I'd tell her.

She shakes her head, her eyes still focused on something out the windshield. "You must think I'm outta my mind, comin' to see him. After what he did."

"Grief doesn't care about reason. He's still your dad."

"Yeah," she replies after a moment. "Most days I don't know whether I hate that fact or I'm appreciative of it." She laughs, but there's no humor behind it, only pain. "His parents are the ones who pay for that facility. He's brain-dead, so technically he's not even alive. *Technically*, he killed three people that night."

"I didn't realize you had grandparents."

"I don't," she says curtly. "They don't acknowledge my existence. Never did."

"What?"

"They're real religious. I was born before my parents were married, so it's the good Christian thing not to acknowledge your only living grandchild but keep your brain-dead son alive with a buncha tubes and machines."

My eyes widen, shocked yet again today. There's trauma, there's tragedy, and then there's . . . *this*.

"Don't," she commands, looking over at me. "Don't look at me like that. I don't want your pity."

The same words I'd spoken to her, the same warning I'd given that night in the guesthouse when she'd asked about the woman who raised me.

There are some stories that hurt to tell, that have no business being repeated. There are some stories that you wish with everything in you were fairy tales, lies and untruths spun into stories that never actually happened, because the truth seems so illogical that no one would dare to believe you.

There are so many reasons I keep my story tucked away into the darkest corners of myself, but it's mostly because it explains so much about me, and once you have an explanation, you can start to change things. Hunter seems exactly like the kind of person to try and change things. Change me.

Here I am, giving her the exact ammunition she needs to do so.

"My mother . . ." I clear my throat, pushing back the tightness that tries to stifle my words.

Not even Carson, the one person I've let myself trust fractionally, knows all of this. "Her name is Elain. She never wanted me. And not even in a 'you stood in the way of my career' way. It was in a 'you've ruined my life and I'll never forgive you' kind of way. I don't know why—one mystery I'll probably never solve.

"It's one of the reasons I've hated Cora for the past eight years," I tell her. I'm staring down at my hands, folded in my lap so they won't shake and completely give me away, show Hunter exactly how much this story is costing me. "Because she knew. Probably not all of it, but enough. At the end of each summer, when I'd beg to stay with her for the rest of the year, she'd always shake her head and say, *You wouldn't survive a Wyoming winter, Q. You gotta go back north.*'

"So at the end of every August, I went back to the woman who could barely even look at me most of the time. The only thing that kept me going was knowing that each summer I'd get to come back here. I'd get to see Cora and the horses and this shitty state, until one day she told me it was all over."

I still remember that last day as if it were only a few weeks ago, the memory fresh and searing. It's like an old wound that never heals because I keep picking at the scab, keep letting the pain resurface.

We'd come home from Cheyenne near the beginning of August. I still had most of the month to spend here, but I was already dreading going back to Spokane, to Elain. Cora had driven the two and half hours to Cheyenne for me so that we could get sundaes and burgers and cheese curds from my favorite restaurant in the world, one they didn't have in Washington.

Someone had called her, but not on her cheap, pay-by-the-minute cell phone—it was on the landline in the guesthouse. She'd only heard it ringing because we were outside, unloading the truck. Another mystery I could never quell my suspicions about: who was on the other end of that phone call, and what they said.

Because after she was done, Cora came back to the truck where I was waiting, tension stretching her face in a way I'd never seen, and said, "You gotta go, Q."

"Go where?" I asked.

She looked me right in the eye as she said, "Back to Spokane. Permanently."

I tried arguing, tried asking what the problem was, why I couldn't stay and couldn't come back. She gave me nothing, just started packing my things, booked a plane ticket for later that day. I begged her, even on the ride to the airport, the landscape I'd grown to love rolling by for what I thought would be the final time.

Still, she was silent. Even as she took my bags from the bed of her truck, placing them on the sidewalk. It was only when I stood crying outside of the Southwest Wyoming Regional Airport, that she exhaled, turned to me, and said, "I'm sorry, Q. This is the way it's gotta be."

That was the last time I'd cried. Eight years ago, as I watched my aunt drive away from me for the last time.

I tell this all to Hunter, who doesn't interrupt me once. She lets me spill this story I'd sworn I'd never tell again.

"I was fourteen, and I had no one," I continue, my voice dropping. I hate the way I'm withering away, the way this has all eaten away at me, taken up so much space inside my chest for so long. "I was fifteen when I met Carson, when they let me start shadowing them. They saved me in a lot of ways—ways I probably haven't even realized yet. I think that's the reason I didn't completely fall apart when Elain left a year later."

"Left?" she prompts.

"Left," I repeat. "Took her clothes and her money and left me to fend for myself, at sixteen, in our little apartment. That's how much she hated me." I turn to her then, because if I let this breathe for any longer, I'm sure it's going to kill me. "So. No, I don't pity you—I think you're the strongest goddamn person I've ever met. Because I know all too well what it's like to have no one, to never get love or attention, to seem insane to everyone else around you. Me and you? We're the same, Hunter."

They're perhaps the most dangerous words I've ever spoken, even more than the story that's just preceded them. She knows now how I feel, how I think of her. More importantly, how I think of her in relation to *me*. I'm giving her the knife and turning around, my bare back to her, open and exposed, daring her to sink the blade into skin and muscle and nerves and bone. She could break me in half right now, and I wouldn't even feel it.

"Thank you," she whispers instead, handing the knife back to me. "For telling me."

Silence fills the space between us for a long, long time. I don't know if it's because neither of us knows what to say or because we're too emotionally spent to say anything.

"It's only five," I finally say. "What do you usually do . . . after your visit?"

"Drive around," she replies. "Try to get my head on right. Then I eat somethin' and fall asleep in the Walmart parkin' lot down the street."

"We're not staying in a parking lot," I tell her. "This truck doesn't have enough room anyway."

"You got a better idea? Because I don't think you're volunteerin' to drive us back to Wonderland."

I nod. "I do, actually."

* * *

Hunter emerges from the bathroom, hair wet from her shower. "All yours."

I rise from my side of the bed, gathering my overnight bag. "Thanks."

I move past her, closing the door to the bathroom. I stare at my reflection in the mirror, trying not to think too hard about the fact that I'm sharing a bed with Hunter tonight. Or the fact that I bared my soul to her a little over an hour ago.

Hunter had stiffened at my side when the man at the front desk said they only had single-bed rooms still available, but I'd pulled out my credit card and ID, plastering a smile on my face. That was one of the very first things Carson had ever taught me: how to lie convincingly. Once you could do that without breaking your stride, the world became your oyster.

Unbidden, the memory of last night surfaces. Hunter, breathing like she'd just run a marathon. Hunter, lifting me up onto the dining room table. Hunter, leaning toward me as if by magnetism.

"Me and you? We're the same, Hunter."

I exhale, trying to shake it all from my mind. After the day we've both had, it's absolutely not the time for any possible . . . extracurriculars.

Then I look down at my bag, and think, *Oh fuck.*

In my haste to pack a bag this morning, half convinced Hunter would take off without me, I'd forgotten to pack pants. I could sleep in the jeans I'm wearing right now, but that seems like an even worse thing to wear to bed than nothing.

It's fine, I tell myself as I strip down to my underwear, then pull on an oversized T-shirt. It barely covers my ass—one wrong move and the tiny purple polka dots on my one-size-too-small underwear will be on full display.

Don't be ridiculous—it's fine.

I throw my dirty clothes back in my bag, then pull open the door. Hunter's already getting under the covers, but she stops moving when she sees me. The room is dark except for the light from the bathroom and the one turned on next to her.

She's frozen, the blanket half covering her fully clad legs. Her gaze lands on my bare ones for what seems like an unbearably long amount of time that does nothing to quell the thoughts circling in my head.

"I forgot to pack any pants to sleep in," I explain hastily, gesturing to my legs, as if it isn't already painfully obvious what the situation is. "I . . . sorry. If it makes you uncomfortable, I can—"

"Get in" is all she says.

I pad quickly over to my side of the bed. I get in, lying on my back, heart beating far too fast as I stare up at the ceiling.

Want and need and desire, all hitting me so hard and fast it makes the room spin. Hunter is gorgeous, obviously—the hard lines of her body, muscled and tanned from all the days working out in the sun, coupled with the smaller things, the softer things that she tries to disguise: her smile, her laugh, the Wyoming-midnight sky-blue of her eyes, the way her hands look when they're unfurled from their usual defensive fists. I would be lying if I said that the evasiveness, the skittishness, the way she's so obviously hiding something didn't do something for me too. Twisted, maybe, but between the two of us, what isn't?

"You wanna tell me what you're thinking on so hard?"

I press my tongue to the backs of my top teeth. "Pondering how much of a bastard I am."

"Well, you helped me with the fence. And the hay. And . . . today. So I'd say not that big of one."

I turn, but just my head. She's still staring at the ceiling, her hands folded and lying against her chest on top of the blanket. "Was that the *second* compliment you've issued me?"

Some semblance of a grin tugs at her lips. "Don't get used to it."

"I won't." I press my own lips together. "What about you?"

"I'm fine."

"Still lying to me, I see."

Her head whips over on the pillow. We're so close suddenly, all the freckles on Hunter's cheeks and nose so near I could count them.

"Say it again," she says, her words hot against my face. "Tell me my business again. Tell me what I'm thinking, what I'm feeling."

"You heard me the first time."

"You think you've got me all figured out, then?"

"No, I don't," I retort. "That's why I'm *asking*. Tell me how you're feeling. Tell me what you need from me."

"What I need?" she repeats. "I need . . . I need for my dad to wake up. So I can tell him how much I hate him. And how much I've missed him. So I can finally be with someone who knows what it's like to live with all this *hurt* every day."

She lifts on her forearm slightly so that she's leaning over me. "I need you to leave me alone," she says, her voice dipping to that low tone again, making goose bumps pop up on my arms. "I need you to go back to Spokane and never talk to me again. I need you to never stand in the damn doorway, half naked and blushing like the Virgin Mary when you're about to get into bed with me."

My breath catches in my throat. She's never spoken to me like this before, and goddamn if it doesn't send a shot of heat right through me. "Cowgirl—"

"I need you to not call me that anymore," she says. "And definitely . . . *definitely* not like that."

"Like what?"

She most certainly looks down at my mouth this time, and I suddenly can't remember how to get air into my lungs. "Like the way you were talkin' last night."

"I wouldn't have stopped," I rasp after a moment. "If you hadn't . . . if we'd kept going. I wouldn't have stopped."

She swallows, and I track the movement down her throat. "I . . . that part of me's complicated."

"The lesbian part, you mean."

Her lips press together in a thin line. "Yeah. That."

"It's not a dirty word, you know."

"I know that," she says shortly. "I've spent so long thinkin' bein' like this was wrong or immoral or whatever. And I know it's not, I know that now—but things are different here. People are different here. I'm supposed to be with a man, right? The idea of that . . ." A shudder goes through her. "I've known for a while that's not how I'm made. What I want. *Who* I want. Don't make it any less scary or hard tryin' to accept that this is who I am, that I can't go and change it. I'd already decided a long time ago I'd never find a gal who would feel that way about me—definitely not once she got to know me."

"And now?"

Her eyes meet mine again. "And now, here you are."

I go up on my forearms, pressing into Hunter, so that our chests are aligned, our faces inches apart. "Here I am."

The moment seems to stretch on and on, infinite and never ending. For so long that I think we'll be locked like this until my arms give out. But then she pulls back, slowly returning to her side of the bed. She turns off the lamp next to her, plunging us into complete darkness before she reaches over, takes my hand in hers. Gently, like she's scared I'm going to break; like I'm something to be beholden for, something to treasure.

"I don't understand this, Princess," she says, quiet.

I squeeze her hand. "Neither do I, Cowgirl."

She's silent for a long time—so long that I almost slip into sleep. But then I hear her, barely, as she whispers, my hand still in hers, "Call me Lem from now on."

"I thought that's what your friends called you."

"Yeah," she says. "It is."

*　*　*

My phone is ringing, and when I open my eyes, the room is still dark.

Hunter's arm is wrapped around my waist, my back to her front, which I barely even have time to appreciate before

I reach for my phone. I squint against the brightness of the screen, my eyes reading "Unknown caller" when they finally adjust.

Probably just a telemarketer; I should let it go to message and crawl back to Hunter. But then I remember where I am, and that message on the mirror in Cora's bathroom.

"Hello?" I answer quietly, trying not to wake Hunter.

"I know who you are," the voice on the other end says. It's garbled, disguised by a voice modulator. This used to happen in Spokane pretty frequently—people Carson and I were after, calling and threatening us, using software to mask their real voice. The only exception is that those calls only came to the office, never to our personal phones.

"Stop looking," the voice says.

I swallow back the dryness in my throat. The same words that were scrawled across Cora's mirror now reaching me via phone. Any notion I had that it was a harmless prank has squarely been thrown out the window. "Tell me where Cora is and I will," I reply.

The line goes dead. My hand shakes as I put my phone back on the nightstand, letting out an equally shaky breath. My heartbeat pounds in my ears, but beside me Hunter's breathing is even, steady.

I lie back, staring at the ceiling. They called me—not the police or Cora's house or even Hunter. And Hunter said that threats are new: they didn't start until I got to town.

The new target is clear—but they're gonna have to pull the trigger, not just take aim, to get me to *stop looking*.

CHAPTER

15

Work Song (Then—July 1981)

THE ANNUAL WONDERLAND Town Gala was held in Radley, which Holly thought was strange.

She'd told Jessica as much when she'd first invited her. A fundraiser for one town, held forty minutes away in a completely different one? But Jessica had explained that there wasn't a space big enough in Wonderland to accommodate all the people who showed up—politicians and business owners and even celebrities, some years. Holly could hardly believe it, so many important people coming all the way out to the middle of nowhere to raise money for an even more middle-of-nowhere town. But then again, that was the power of the Coldwater name.

Coldwaters had been running Wonderland since its inception. Over the weeks they'd spent together, Jessica had explained the history of her family, tracing her roots back through the decades. It was mesmerizing to Holly, listening to Jessica recite name after name, generation after generation, from memory. The simple luxury of being able to know where you came from, who came before you, how they made their mark on the world. It was another small jealousy that Holly tried desperately to fight but that nonetheless still crept in on her on occasion.

Jessica had loaned her a beautiful dress—light pink, with beading on the bodice and a full skirt—and as she'd gotten into Jessica's car earlier, Holly had to use both of her hands to gather the skirt. Of course, Jessica looked even more stunning in a bright orange gown, her hair in a bun atop her head. It was the same one she'd worn to prom, back when she was still spinning in Troy's arms.

But not tonight. Tonight, everything would be different.

Jessica exhaled as she ran her hands down the steering wheel, staring out the windshield. "Do you ever think about what it'd be like to be someone else?"

Holly looked over at her. "All the time."

Jessica nodded, like she knew what Holly's answer would be before she'd even posed the question. "Sometimes I wish that I could run away from all of this. That I could move somewhere else, be someone that didn't have so much to live up to."

"What about your sister?"

"She's going to be a *doctor*," Jessica said. "Which means I'm going to have to be something like that, something impressive. Something that makes my family proud. I already know I'm not cut out for something like that. It's never going to be enough for them."

Holly tried to understand, though it was the exact opposite for her. She yearned to be someone, to have something to live up to, so badly that sometimes it was a physical ache. To be more than a face in a yearbook her classmates sort of recognized, more than a collection of motel keys, more than the person her mother had set her up to become.

"Where would you go?" Holly asked, half serious.

"Anywhere," Jessica replied. "As long as no one there knows the name *Coldwater*."

For a minute, Holly hesitated. Didn't Jessica know how lucky she was to have a family that loved her, supported her? To have college and a future and plans all waiting on her?

There was stress and pressure that came with those things, sure—but at least she had them.

Holly smoothed the skirt of her dress, running her fingers along the silky fabric. "I've been moving my whole life," she said. "Never stopping long enough to settle, never having a home. We're two sides of the same coin, I guess—both wanting the same thing for different reasons."

"You always manage to say things so perfectly," Jessica said with a little laugh. Then she looked over at Holly, entwining their hands. "I'd run. But only if you came with me. Otherwise, none of it would matter."

As the words bloomed warmly inside her chest, and she squeezed Jessica's hand, Holly realized something:

Jessica had it all and still felt like she had nothing.

And Holly had nothing and still felt like she had everything.

* * *

The hall was decorated elaborately, black and white streamers running from the ceilings. White linens covered the tables, the settings already in place, black and white flowers in tall vases as the centerpieces. A long, full buffet station was set off to the side. At the very front was a large dance floor and a live band was getting set up.

Mrs. Coldwater was the first person they spotted as they walked into the building. She oversaw the entire event, as she had done every year since she'd turned eighteen. A modest, dark blue dress with long sleeves was her choice for the evening. Mrs. Coldwater was a commanding figure, but not overpowering—a tightrope she had clearly spent years mastering. The same line that she no doubt expected Jessica to learn to walk as well, even if her daughter had no intention of doing so—another late-night, sleepover secret that she'd confided to Holly.

"Girls!" Mrs. Coldwater exclaimed when she saw them, a smile on her face as she turned away from a woman holding a large disco ball with both hands. "Oh, you both look so beautiful!"

"Can we help with anything?" Holly offered.

"How thoughtful of you, Holly," Mrs. Coldwater replied. "If you girls want to head back to the kitchen and help finish plating the hors d'oeuvres, that would be wonderful."

Holly had no idea what an hors d'oeuvre was, but Jessica seemed to, so she followed her to the kitchen. It was empty except for three men cooking and two women who were running plates of food out to the buffet line.

"Hi," Jessica said to one of the women, a thin blonde who held a tray of potatoes in her hands. "We're here to help plate the—"

The woman jerked her head in the opposite direction. "Station's right there—make them look pretty."

It turned out that hors d'oeuvres was a fancy name for appetizers. Some of the tension left Holly's body when she realized that, though not all of it. Her shoulders were still bunched, her neck still tight with worry. She was so out of her depth—she'd never attended a party, let alone something as extravagant as *this*. It was only her borrowed dress and Jessica's presence that gave her any hope that she wouldn't completely fall apart.

Jessica's hand brushed hers as she reached for a bowl of crumbled bacon, and their eyes met. Jessica smiled, and in that moment Holly forgot where they were. She forgot her worries and the ache in her feet from her shoes—also borrowed from Jessica, a size smaller than her own.

"My mom was right, you know," Jessica whispered.

"About what?" Holly managed. It was hard to focus with Jessica's attention on her—especially now that Holly knew what it felt like to be tangled in her arms, to have her lips pressed against her own.

"You look beautiful in that dress, partner."

A flush started to creep up Holly's neck as she swallowed. "So do you," she croaked.

Jessica leaned even closer, whispering right up against Holly's ear as she said, "It's going to look even better on my floor later, though."

Holly exhaled roughly. Even after all the weeks together, kissing and touching and whispering and laughing, Holly still hadn't gotten used to the way her pulse raced and her heart pounded when she was around Jessica like this. She'd thought that it'd get better after their camping trip, when they'd gone further than ever before—though not *all* the way; they'd both agreed they weren't quite ready for that. But, if anything, Holly's feelings had only intensified, something she hadn't thought possible.

Jessica laughed softly as she pulled back, sprinkling the bacon over tiny potatoes that had already been topped with sour cream and cheese.

They finished plating all the appetizers—in addition to the potatoes, there were meatballs served on toothpicks, deviled eggs, buttery shrimp, cheese and meat plates, and three different kinds of dip—and headed back out to the main hall.

Guests were already starting to arrive, and Mrs. Coldwater was standing at the entrance, ready to greet them. So elegant, so poised. She exchanged a laugh or a smile, even with the guests she seemed not to know. It all seemed to come so easily to her, but Holly knew that was part of Mrs. Coldwater's work too.

"I'm starving," Jessica said, pulling Holly toward the buffet line.

They sat down at an open table in the corner of the room, as secluded a spot as they could've picked. Jessica's hand grazed Holly's thigh more than once under the table. Holly's chest was tight, but in the best possible way. When their plates were empty, they went back for seconds, giggling at nothing at all. It was like they were high on it all: the atmosphere, the dresses, the fancy food, the air of maturity.

It was perfect. This night; the girl next to her; devouring a slice of prime rib in her expensive ball gown without a care in the world. In that moment, Holly realized that she'd go through it all again—the motels, the schools, the constant unknowing—a hundred times if it meant she'd end up here.

I love her, Holly thought, so clearly she knew it was true, that it was real.

"Will you dance with me?" Holly asked.

Jessica looked over at her, fork falling from her hand. It glanced off her plate with a dull thunk. They both knew the risks—they knew the risks of everything they did *together*. But they'd hidden themselves so well for so long, everyone thinking they were nothing more than good friends. And girls who were good friends danced together, didn't they? At least, they could explain it away that way.

It was worth the risk to Holly. There was nothing more in the world that she wanted than to dance with this beautiful, lovely girl that she'd been waiting for her whole life.

It must've been worth it to Jessica too, because she smiled, just a touch, and nodded. "I would love to, partner."

*   *   *

Only one song—they didn't push their luck too much.

It was worth it, though. Seeing Jessica spinning and laughing, having the girl she loved in her arms, even if just for a little over three minutes. Maybe one day they'd get to dance to two songs. Or three. Or an eternity of them.

"Girls," Mrs. Coldwater said, appearing in front of them as they headed back to their table. There was an edge to her tone that Holly had never heard before. "Do you mind if I borrow Holly for a moment?"

"Sure," Jessica replied. "I'll get us some water."

Mrs. Coldwater steered Holly toward the entrance of the hall, then out into the night, so they were away from the rest of the guests. Holly rubbed at her bare arms; the night air had turned frosty during the time they'd been inside.

"Tell me, Holly," Mrs. Coldwater said, no preamble. "Has my daughter told you about my sister-in-law, Kathleen?"

The name wasn't ringing any bells. "No," Holly replied.

Mrs. Coldwater nodded, just once, tight and precise. "I wouldn't have imagined she did. We don't talk about Kathleen because she almost burned down this entire town—our entire family and our reputation and everything the Coldwaters before me have done to survive all these years.

"You see, there is a certain way that Coldwaters are to act. A certain standard that my daughter must live up to—the same one that her daughter will have to live up to as well, one day. Kathleen had no interest in getting anywhere close to that standard. She spit in the face of it. Had it not been for the actions of my mother-in-law, we wouldn't be standing here today."

A knot was forming in the back of Holly's throat. "Okay."

"I didn't marry into this family only to have my daughter . . ." Mrs. Coldwater cleared her throat. "Where are you from, Holly?"

"I'm from . . . a lot of places."

"Yes," Mrs. Coldwater said, confirming what she seemingly already knew. "Jessica told me where you lived. I dropped by your house earlier this week, spoke with your mother. Did you know I used to live there when I was your age? Our mothers . . . I imagine they share quite a bit in common. Yours seemed quite out of it; she had no idea who I was. Had no idea, even, that you've been spending so many nights under my roof and in my daughter's bed."

Holly's pulse was racing even more than it had been when she'd danced with Jessica. "She doesn't care very much about me," Holly said in a small voice.

"I gathered that as well," Mrs. Coldwater continued. "Any mother who doesn't know the whereabouts of her child, who

drags her across the country, who doesn't *raise* her to be—"
She cut herself off. In that moment, Holly wondered if Mrs.
Coldwater was talking about Holly's mother or the woman
who had raised Mrs. Coldwater. Either way, Holly was grateful; she didn't want to hear about the person she was supposed
to be. She really did not want to hear Mrs. Coldwater judging
and critiquing her mother as if she knew her; as if she knew
Holly.

Mrs. Coldwater shook her head. When she looked at Holly
this time, there was a smile on her face—she was so much
more recognizable with it, so much more the woman Holly
had come to know. "I like you, Holly," she said. It sounded
earnest. "You've been dealt an unlucky hand and have come
out holding an alright set of cards. But Jessica? She's been
holding the very best cards since the day she was born. But
refusing to continue seeing Troy, who comes from the second-
best family in this town? Alienating all her old friends, girls
she's known since she was still in a playpen, by spending all
her time with one singular girl? *Slow dancing* with that girl in
such a public place?" Mrs. Coldwater shook her head in obvious disgust. "I won't have her switching your cards with hers.
It's not what good mothers do."

Good mothers. The implication that Lenora was certainly
not one of those was heavy and evident. Even if Holly thought
that too sometimes—more than sometimes, maybe—Mrs.
Coldwater had no right to.

"We're friends," Holly said. It sounded like a weak excuse,
the lie that it so clearly was, even to her own ears.

When Mrs. Coldwater smiled again, there was nothing
kind about it. The gesture was all pity and malice. "That's
what Kathleen said about her Holly too."

16

Drowning (Now)

THE WYOMING WEATHER is its own kind of animal.

The rain comes in downpours that only last twenty minutes, flooding even the flattest of plains. The winds last longer but are as unforgiving, lashing through the trees and howling past the mountains. And the lightning—it slashes through the sky like a lover that's been scorned, seeking and searching for a source to punish. The weather screeches and moans, torments and destroys.

But when the sun is high and the sky is blue, all else is forgotten. The landscape is clear and open—Big Sky Country. No danger. No worries.

*　*　*

"Remind me why we're here again?"

"I need a new flannel," Hunter replies, practically dragging me through the narrow aisle of Boise's finest country-western apparel store.

"You need another flannel shirt in your wardrobe like I need a hole in my head, Lem."

She ignores me, looking at a particularly hideous green number that she mercifully puts back on the rack. The open, vulnerable version of Hunter has been firmly stored away, but now that I've seen her, I know she won't be gone for long.

We grabbed breakfast at a McDonald's by the hotel, and I'd remained silent when Hunter mentioned she needed to make a stop here. I didn't tell her about the phone call because I didn't want to alarm her further. But even if I did tell her another warning's been issued—and it's for sure a warning this time—it wouldn't shake her resolve to find Cora.

Country music plays throughout the store, which is covered wall to wall in what seems to be a million different types, colors, and sizes of cowboy hats. They even have tiny pink ones for kids. There are several aisles just for boots—which Hunter spent fifteen minutes perusing before we made our way over to the yee-haw fashion section.

"Why don't you go look at the hats instead of chomping at my heels?" she says abruptly.

I sigh dramatically but do as she asks. There are so many of them, it's overwhelming at first, but a few catch my eye: a brown one with faux-rope accents, a black one that's angled more in the front. There are a couple of white ones that resemble the one on Hunter's head right now, but no identical matches.

When I reach the end of the shelves, I stop, noticing a deep burgundy hat unlike any of the others. It's creased at the top, soft and supple to the touch, accented with a slim black band.

"Figures you'd pick the flashiest one in the whole place."

I turn, finding Hunter before me, arms crossed. She takes the hat from my hands, placing it atop my head. She tugs it down a bit in the back, but it fits like a glove.

"Yeah," she says softly, appraising me. "That'll work."

"I'm not getting it," I assure her. "I was just looking, like you told me."

It's then that I realize she's not holding any shirts, which she'd said was the entire point of this—

"We didn't come for more flannels, did we?"

She shrugs. "Didn't see anything I liked."

"What about now?"

Hunter takes my hat off, tucking it against her leg. Her hand covers the entirety of the top of it. "Yeah," she says. "Think I might've found something."

I want to take a step closer, but then I remind myself that we are at a country-western store in Boise, Idaho, and it'd be unwise to do anything that I can't explain away as *friendly*. "I thought you had to earn it, though," I say softly.

All Hunter does is nod, already heading for the register. "You did."

* * *

"There's a place on the way back that I wanna go look for Cora."

I straighten on the bench seat, my new hat resting safely beside me. Hunter insisted on paying for it, no matter how hard I argued with her. *"It's tradition,"* she'd said, pulling out a worn leather wallet from her back pocket.

A gift, but so much more than that. She could've gotten me anything in the entire world, but she chose this, the thing she'd vowed that I had to earn first. *"You did"* keeps playing over and over in my head, and I run my fingers along the brim of the hat, everything coming into focus a bit more. Hunter and this place—both slowly unraveling and breaking down everything I thought I knew, thought I felt. It's strange to sit here and not worry, even if for only a few moments, after spending so long constantly having to be on the defensive.

We've been driving for about two hours now, Hunter finally letting me switch the radio station. "Alright," I reply. Truthfully, she could get me to agree to just about anything right now. "Where is it?"

"You'll see."

The hours pass wordlessly, as they usually do. Finally, Hunter exits the highway, hooks a pair of rights, then drives another fifteen minutes down a tiny path, navigating the pothole-filled road with expert precision. There's no lot or signage, just a small area of dead grass where she pulls off.

We get out, shaking the sleep from our legs before Hunter leads us uphill. It's somewhat steep, and sweat starts to bead on the back of my neck as I climb. Finally we come to a stop, and I pretend that my breathing isn't labored as I—

"Oh," I gasp.

She nods. "The Flaming Gorge Reservoir."

The water runs a deep, gorgeous blue, such a stark contrast from the current lightness of the sky. It's surrounded by canyons, dark marble grays and pops of fiery red. It's so wholly different from the plains I've seen everywhere else.

"We used to come up here all the time," she says. "Fishing. Or camping in the summers. Or sitting up here for lunch sometimes. Mom would say *'no school today,'* and me and her and Jack'd drive up here and eat sandwiches. *'Some things can't be taught in schools,'* she'd say."

It's the first time she's talked about her family like this. I can't help but think it has something to do with what I revealed yesterday about Elain and Cora. I'm transfixed, staring at the woman next to me, letting her crack wide open. She looks like such a fixture here, belonging as much as the rock that surrounds us. Strong and unyielding, like her feet are rooted into the ground, as if nothing could ever move her, shake her.

"Everyone was nice right after it happened," she continues, her voice soft, low, almost melodic. "Casseroles and hugs and all that. But I just wanted to be left alone. I wanted not to be reminded of it every time I was trying to keep *going.* I wanted quiet. The kinda quiet like when—" She cuts herself off, lips pressed hard together. "People in town couldn't understand the way I coped, the way I still do. So that meant that I was crazy and out of my mind, rude and selfish and a recluse and worse."

I very suddenly want to have a word with everyone who had ever insulted Hunter Lemming, particularly about this.

"Cora was the only one who understood, who didn't turn on me," she says. "She helped me sell my family's house, then let me move into her guesthouse. She's the closest thing I've got to family anymore. I spend half my time wondering how I'm ever gonna repay her for all she's done for me.

"You gotta stop thinking so much," she whispers, eyes still on the sight before us. "Don't even feel it. Just be. You say you hate this place but . . . it's special because it isn't. Because there's so much of it. Because it's all you can see. Because, yeah, it at looks the same, and there's a peace in knowing that it's always been this way, that it'll always be this way."

So much of Hunter's strength is obvious. The physical things: the cut of her jaw, the muscles of her body, the way she holds herself. But her real strength is underneath all that, in the things she has to trust you enough to show you: the holes in her heart she's patched together time and time again, the aches in her body that have nothing to do with physical exertion. There's so much beauty in the tape and glue of it.

And the fact that she's sharing all of this with me? "Let's go find her," I say softly.

She turns back to me, finally meeting my eyes. If she were anyone else, I would've sworn I saw tears there. "Let's go find her."

*   *   *

The road that we came in on is only one-way, so we have to drive up toward the main lot to turn around.

"All the tourists end up there," Hunter grumbles, hooking a left into the parking lot. It's as she's backing up, looking in the rearview, that she freezes.

"What?" I ask.

She doesn't react, not even when another car trying to get past us honks.

"Hunter, are you alright?"

"That truck," she says, and I spin around on the bench seat, trying to find the truck she's talking about. There's only one in view, an old blue Chevy that's certainly seen better days.

"What about it?"

"It's Cora's," she whispers. "That's Cora's truck."

* * *

I know enough not to touch anything, but as Hunter calls Bridgers and we wait for her to arrive, I pace around the truck.

Nothing looks off from the outside, and when I look in through the window, there's nothing inside that looks obviously wrong either. There's a note on the windshield, tucked under the wipers, which I assume is a parking ticket, but the not knowing is driving me even further up the wall.

Hunter doesn't join me in my pacing. She sits on the curb by the truck, staring at the ground. We don't speak to each other, both of us in our own worlds right now.

An hour later, Bridgers and company finally show up, two marked cars pulling into the lot.

"Why are you two here?" Bridgers asks immediately upon getting out of the car.

"This is one of the spots I told y'all to look," Hunter says suddenly, standing in a rush. "We were coming back from Idaho, and I decided to look myself."

"When did you tell them to look here?" I ask, coming to stand near the back of the truck, where everyone else has begun to congregate.

"A week ago," Hunter replies, her eyes on the sheriff.

"Jesus Christ."

"We've been exploring other leads," Bridgers interjects.

"Bullshit."

When Bridgers meets my gaze again, I know she's remembering our chat at the gala: *Or maybe that a certain missing persons case is somehow connected to all of this, and that's why my aunt hasn't been found yet?*

"You've been standing in the way," I seethe. "You and all these other useless cops too stupid or corrupt to find my aunt. If something's happened to her—"

"Quinn—" Hunter tries.

"Cora Cole's blood is on *your hands*!" I yell, temper rising to a fever pitch. Here Hunter and I are, doing everything we can to bring Cora home, and the people who are supposed to be responsible for it have been sitting on tips, barely even investigating. "You know the worst part?" I say, voice dropping but anger remaining. "You people won't even care. You'll write it off as someone else's fault, probably Cora's. Soon enough she'll be to blame for someone taking her, and you people can't fucking—"

"That's enough," Bridgers barks. "We don't even know if a crime has been committed yet. So why don't you let me do the job you're accusing me of ignoring?"

I step back, dramatically sweeping my arm toward the truck. "There's something on the windshield. Maybe you should start there."

It seems like there's something else Bridgers wants to say, but all she does is exhale—loudly—through her nose and brush by me. Hunter and I stand and watch as the cops start looking through Cora's truck, their gloved hands pulling open doors, roving over the seats, combing the floorboards.

Suddenly, one of the cops on the passenger's side jumps out, then hands Bridgers a note.

She reads it, her eyebrows pulling down in confusion.

"What does it say?" I call.

Bridgers ignores me, then grabs the paper from the windshield. She looks them over, side by side, comparing. The need to know everything, right here and now, is so overwhelming I almost start to shake.

Finally, the doors to the truck are shut, and the cops retreat to their own vehicles. One of them pulls out a phone and starts talking rapidly, but in a voice too low for me to hear.

Bridgers approaches us once more, her eyes set past us, like she has no plan to stop and talk. Hunter takes a step into her path and says, "Maddie, please."

Bridgers turns her attention to the woman standing next to me. The woman as desperate to solve this as I am. The woman who knows more about Cora than anyone. The woman who knows more than she's letting on.

"There was a note in the glovebox," Bridgers relents, her voice dropping. "On a little scrap of paper. Looks like Cora's handwriting. It said, *1 = Natrona.*"

"What does that mean?" I ask. "What's Natrona?"

"It's a county," Hunter replies slowly. "One of the biggest in the state. It's where Casper is."

"One is Natrona's county designation. The license plate code," Bridgers adds. "What that means or how it relates to Cora's disappearance, I have no idea."

"Of course you don't," I scoff.

But I do. Because I know exactly where I've seen a series of numbers I didn't understand.

It makes sense that Cora would've left a clue or two behind in case something ever happened to her—maybe this is one of them.

"But I'll find out," Bridgers continues. "You two being here isn't helping, especially with all this talk about us being corrupt."

"How terrible that you have such an aversion to the truth—"

"Unless"—Bridgers interrupts—"you wanna tell me about Cora's ledger?"

Hunter stiffens next to me, still unable to front any kind of poker face. "I don't know what ledger you're talking about," I say.

"Quinn, I know—"

"What about the note on the windshield?" Hunter asks.

Bridgers keeps staring at me. "You don't want to know, Lem."

"Maddie."

Finally, Bridgers looks over at Hunter, running a palm down the side of her face. Hunter has got this woman all the way wrapped around her finger, and she doesn't even realize it. "Stop looking," she tells us. "Someone wrote *Stop looking* in red."

My body goes hot and cold all at once. On the mirror at Cora's house, on the phone at the hotel—and now here the words are again, a third time, affixed to the windshield of a missing woman's truck.

"The same thing as at the house," Hunter breathes.

I close my eyes just as Bridgers demands, "What?"

"Hunter lacks any sort of tact in these situations, that's what," I reply. I open my eyes, meeting Bridgers's wide ones. "Someone broke into the house. On the mirror in Cora's bathroom, someone wrote *Stop looking* in red lipstick. And then I got a call last night, same message."

"You got a *call*?" Hunter asks.

At the same time Bridgers asks, "Did you recognize the voice?"

"It was being disguised," I tell the sheriff.

"You didn't think any of this would be useful information for me to have?"

"If I had, you'd have just sat on your ass for a week before doing anything about it."

She shakes her head, a few hairs coming free from her ponytail. *She's got the same hair as Jessica,* I think suddenly, remembering the picture at the fundraiser. "If anything else happens, you two need to tell me. It could help us find Cora. I don't suppose you have any idea what the folks who broke in might've been doing there? Besides leaving the message— maybe they were looking for something?"

The ledger. The key. Something else I haven't found yet. "No idea," I tell Bridgers.

"Of course," she replies. She opens her mouth to say something else, but she's pulled away by another officer. By the time she turns back, we're long gone.

*   *   *

An hour later, I'm opening this year's ledger on Cora's desk, pointing out the numbers to Hunter.

"What if the numbers correspond to different counties in the state?" I ask. "The letter is a town in the county. Or a person there."

She takes the ledger, flipping through to the final entry from earlier in the month. "I knew she kept these and they were private, but I didn't realize—" She cuts herself off. "Four-T," she reads aloud. "Four would be Sweetwater County, which is us. There's no town that starts with a *T* here."

"So maybe it's a name," I continue. "Did Cora have you pick up money from anyone in the county whose first name started with *T* this month? Or maybe a last name?"

Hunter stares at the table for a moment, thinking. I have this feeling in my gut, the one I only get when I'm right about something—adrenaline and fire and a resounding *yes.*

She closes the book, staring at the cover for a moment. Her thumb drifts across the letters, golden and slightly raised:

CC. A book of letters and numbers and dates that might be the answer to all of this, if only we can—

And then, it clicks. Hunter looks up, but her face has gone pale.

"What?"

"Right at the beginning of the month, right before Cora went missing," Hunter says. "Cora handled that one. It's the mayor, Todd Coldwater."

17

Favorite Crime (Then—August 1981)

I T WAS A rare evening that Holly and Lenora were both home at the same time.

That was largely due to Holly spending so much time—so many of her nights—at Jessica's house. But since her run-in with Mrs. Coldwater at the dance, that time had dwindled significantly. When she was over at Jessica's house, Mrs. Coldwater was still pleasant, but there was an edge to it. That seemed to be the kind of woman Mrs. Coldwater was, at least when you crossed her: smile on her face while she knifed you in the back.

The first night of August, Holly told Jessica that she couldn't stay over. That she needed to spend some time with her mom. Jessica's eyes had narrowed, but she'd raised no objections.

So when Lenora walked in that night, Holly wasn't surprised to see her mother's eyes widen. "Goddamn, kid," she said. "Didn't know if you even lived here anymore."

Holly flipped a page in the book she was reading. A mystery, from the school library. She'd been at the school long enough that she'd gotten her own card, which meant she hadn't had to steal it for once.

She thought of the long, glorious bookshelves at Jessica's house, stuffed full of books of every genre and time period imaginable, and said nothing to Lenora.

"Well, it's good you're here," her mother said, flopping down next to her on the couch. "Got something to tell you, Holls."

Holly kept her eyes on the book in front of her, trying to focus on the words. If Lenora was about to tell her that they were moving again, that she'd lost her job or kissed another married man, she would—

"I'm pregnant."

The words didn't resonate at first, probably because Holly was already driving herself into a tizzy over the prospect of having to leave Wonderland and Jessica.

But this. This was *so much worse*.

"What?" Holly whispered, still staring at her book. The words were lines of ink now, indecipherable, and there was a faint buzzing in her ears. Maybe she was hallucinating or having a nightmare.

"I'm pregnant, Holls," she repeated, as if Holly simply hadn't heard her the first time. "You're gonna have a little brother. Or maybe a little sister. Honestly, I'm hoping for a boy. That way I'd have one of each, and—"

"You're pregnant," Holly said, the book falling from her lap as she rose. "Who's the father?"

Lenora pressed her lips together. "Well. That's complicated. He's married is the problem. But he's assured me that—"

"That what?" Holly said heatedly, voice rising. "That he'll leave his wife for you? That he'll give you money? That you have ruined yet another good thing for me?"

"Ruined another—Holly, what are you talking about? Mr. Cole owns a ranch on the other end of town. He'll have to take care of us. And he's very rich—"

"So that's what this is about? You got pregnant to get *money*?"

Lenora's eyes narrowed. "You need to watch your tone. I'm still your mother—"

"My mother?" Holly was yelling now, the words pouring out of her. "No. You may have given birth to me, but that's all you've ever done for me. Everything else for the past seventeen years has been for *you*. How many times have we had to switch towns and motels and schools because you got bored or lost your job—or now, got pregnant by a married man?"

Lenora stood, a flush running up her neck. "You will *not* speak to me—"

"If you want to do something good for once, something motherly, then you'll get rid of it. You'll have an abortion and save it from having to endure the same miserable, lonely, terrible existence that I—"

Holly's words were cut off by the impact of her mother's hand smacking across her cheek. She was shocked at first. Lenora had never hit her. Yelled, yes, but she'd never laid a hand on her. And now, all Holly could do was stare at the woman in front of her, cheek stinging, thinking, *I can't do this anymore.*

"I will *not* be spoken to like that," Lenora said, her voice low. "And I will *not* get rid of this baby. Mr. Cole will provide, and—" Lenora shook her head. "I've given you food and a roof over your head, which is more than my mother ever gave me. You know what I've had to do to provide those things? Growing up, I would've *killed* for a life like yours. I've done my best, tried to learn from the mistakes of my mother. I'm not a perfect person, Holly—sue me. But this is a real opportunity for—"

"That's it? That's what this baby is to you—another one of your get-rich-quick schemes?"

"It was . . ." Lenora faltered. "That was how things worked, Holly. You would have understood one day. We needed money, and I got us that. You should have been thanking me. You were always bitching and moaning about having to move—"

"I wanted you to get a *job*—"

"That was a good thing for me, and I wouldn't have had you telling me otherwise!" Lenora shrieked.

"For you," Holly replied softly. "But not for me. Your plan didn't really factor me in, did it? Mr. Cole might have given you money for *his* kid, but not for me."

Lenora's nostrils flared, but she didn't deny her daughter's accusation. Even though Holly knew the words were true before she had spoken them, Lenora's acknowledgment of their honesty stung more than perhaps anything ever had before.

"Do what you want," Holly said. "I'm leaving."

"And going where?" Lenora demanded. "I'm still your mother, no matter how you wish it wasn't true."

Holly grabbed the bike helmet Jessica had given her, perched by the door. She fastened it around her chin, exhaling.

"Home," she told Lenora. "I'm going home."

CHAPTER

18

Cowboy Like Me (Now)

M Y PHONE WAKES me up the next morning.

I groan, rolling over on the couch, groping around and trying to find the source of the ringing. It could be an entirely reasonable hour for Carson, the only person who calls me, to be dialing my number, but I'm already annoyed.

"Hello?" I grumble into the line.

"This is Quinn Cuthridge, right?" they reply. "You're not dead at the hands of some angry cowboy?"

"No, Carson," I say, flopping onto my back and rubbing at my temples. "Unfortunately not."

"Why have you been avoiding my calls, then?"

"I haven't."

"I've been trying to get in touch with you for the past couple of days, Quinn."

I pull the phone away from my ear, then see a big, red five, indicating I've missed five calls from Carson. "Shit," I mutter. "Sorry. Been busy here."

"Uh-huh. You and the ranch hand?"

I exhale, thinking about the hotel room. And the kitchen table. And the shed. "Trying to find my missing aunt, actually."

"Sure," Carson offers, as if they think I'm lying. "Well, that's what I wanted to talk to you about. I'm worried."

"Worried?"

"I know how you feel about that place—"

"I can take care of myself. I've been doing it since I was sixteen."

Silence. I don't know why, because it's the truth. "Alright," they say after a moment. "Well. Any updates in the case?"

I tell them about Cora's truck, about the ledger and the mayor. "The ranch hand and I are going to talk with the mayor today, see what we can get out of him," I finish.

"When are you gonna be back, then?"

I rise to a sitting position, rolling my neck and shoulders. "Soon as Cora turns up, I guess."

"What if you don't find her?

"I will," I say resolutely.

"You know not every case has a happy ending. Or even *has* an ending," they reply, and I hate how patronizing they sound. Carson's prone to this, even though they're only about ten years my senior: treating me with kid gloves like I'm one or two moves away from landing myself in shit so thick I'll never be able to free myself. There's always been a lack of trust between us because of it, because they don't respect me fully. Not as an adult, and certainly not as an investigator. There's a part of them that still sees me as that scared, desperate, sixteen-year-old kid. No matter what I do, no matter how hard I try to prove myself, it never seems to be enough to overcome who I used to be.

"Or," they continue, "what if you *do* find her, and you decide to stick around for a little longer? You told me you were only gonna be down there a week or so."

"So that's what this is really about," I reply. "You want to know when I'm coming back to *work* for you."

A pause. "You know you're the best assistant in the business," they say.

Assistant. Not person or friend or even ally—it's strictly professional. They're not worried about me; they're worried about having to find my replacement.

"I gotta go, Carson," I say, and then I hang up.

* * *

Wonderland's town hall is located on the east end of town, right off the highway.

It's a small, light-green building the size of a single-bedroom home. There's a row of bricks that goes halfway up the building and wraps around to the front, and a ramp that leads to the front door. Cora's ledgers and the key from behind the picture frame are stowed under the bench seat of Hunter's truck. Now that I know that whoever's sending the *Stop looking* messages means business, I figure it's better safe than sorry. Where Hunter and I go, so do the ledgers and the key.

"Howdy, Clara," Hunter says suddenly, her voice loud and booming through the small reception area.

The woman at the counter, who looks to be around thirty, with stick-straight black hair and big blue doe eyes, smiles at us. "Hey, Lem," she says, then looks at me. "And . . .?"

"Quinn."

"Cora's niece," Hunter offers.

"No way," Clara exclaims, leaning closer to the glass that separates us.

"It's true," I deadpan.

"How's the baby?" Hunter asks.

"Oh, he's great," Clara replies, beaming. "Sometimes when I'm working, I'll bring him 'round. He loves the sound the bell on the door makes."

Hunter smiles, genuine and full, such an unfamiliar look on her face I almost do a double take. "I'll bet." She pauses, then shifts her weight. "We're here to talk with the mayor. It's important."

Clara's face suddenly grows somber. "It about Cora?"

"It is," Hunter replies. "They found her truck out at Flaming Gorge."

"Oh *no*," Clara gasps, the gesture so dramatic I'd think it facetious if it didn't fit right into this woman's personality. "Any sign of her?"

"Unfortunately not."

"And . . . you think Mayor Coldwater might know something about it?"

"Maddie just wanted us to give him an update," Hunter assures her. "She asked me to drop by and deliver it in person. The police are so busy nowadays, I figured it was the least I could do. And I know how worried folks in town have been."

I know that can't be true—from how the police have fumbled the bag so completely over the past two weeks, to Hunter herself saying that Cora *"rubbed folks the wrong way,"* but I go along with it.

"Of course," Clara replies, the perfect picture of sympathy. "Y'all go on back. And you're in my prayers, of course."

"Appreciate that, Clara," Hunter says, already leading me down the hall. The air is thicker back here, staler. Six portraits of former mayors—all stiff, formal-looking white men and all Coldwaters per the small nameplates beneath each one—line the walls, staring back stoically at visitors, though I can't imagine there are many of those. They try to capture prestige and power using oil and canvas, but there's only so much a pretty picture can paint.

Hunter comes to a stop in front of the mayor's door, knocking once.

"Come on in!" a voice exclaims from the other side.

Immediately, the smell of cigarette smoke envelops us, thick and overwhelming. I hold back a cough as I take in the rest of the office. It's spacious, windows across the far wall, but crammed full of . . . junk. Boxes with their lids hanging askew, loose papers littering the floor, even a dirty shirt or two. There's barely enough room for three chairs, the mayor's desk, and a pair of standing lamps. The walls are lined with old books, their spines embellished with their titles in gold lettering.

The mayor stands, extending his hand. He's older, but not elderly: hair still showing some color in spots, a combination of black and white; wrinkles down his neck, but not around his eyes. "Hunter Lemming, how the hell are ya?"

The mayor's reception to Hunter is certainly warmer than his wife's. "Given the circumstances, I'm alright," she replies, shaking his hand. Then she gestures to me. "This is Cora's niece, Quinn. She's a private investigator in Washington State; she's here to help find Cora."

Suddenly, the demeanor of the entire room shifts. The mayor's smile vanishes completely as he stares at me, eyes wide. Where Mrs. Coldwater was sharp and cold about my arrival, her husband is nervous and wary.

"Oh," he says, sitting back down. "Washington, you said? Quite the journey."

"Only about a four-hour flight," I reply. "Peanuts compared to the amount of time that my aunt's been missing."

"I see," he says, sitting back down. "Well. How can I help you girls?"

I try not to linger on the usage of the word *girls* to describe two twenty-something women. "It's our understanding that you've been buying something from Cora. For the past eight years, once every couple of months, including this one."

His eyes drop to his desk, hands fidgeting with a stack of papers perched near the edge. "I ain't bought nothin' from Cora Cole," he says, voice quiet, like a child who's being reprimanded. It's a careful answer, as if he's been preparing for this very question and had his answer already formulated.

"Are you sure?" I push. "She has records of you giving her money. Sometimes very *large* sums of money."

He clears his throat, a flush crawling its way up his neck. "Perhaps my wife—"

"Not your wife," I say forcefully. "You."

"I . . . no."

"We're trying to get to the bottom of all of this," Hunter offers.

"Well, don't you girls worry about that now," he assures us. "Maddie's doing a fine job as sheriff, don't you think? I'm sure she's got this all under control."

"Oh, she doesn't," I reply. "I'm almost as curious about how she got her job as how you've kept yours all these years."

"Mayors are Coldwater men," he replies smoothly. "Did you see all the portraits in the hallway? Once or twice someone's challenged me, but nothing serious. Until Maddie has a son and he's ready to take over, I'm happy to serve the good people of Wonderland in my role."

In his role. Like someone's given him a script, what to say and how to act, and he's simply out on stage, smiling in the spotlight. "I didn't realize this town operated like a monarchy," I reply.

He tips his head to the side, his eyebrows pulling down. Either he's one hell of an actor, or he truly has no idea what I'm talking about. "You gals really should be talkin' to my wife about all this; she handles any sort of interviews or newspaper—"

That only spurs me forward more, knowing that the Coldwater guard dog isn't in at the moment. "Did you know that Cora was looking into what happened to your daughter forty years ago?"

He relaxes back into his chair, clearly pleased with the subject change. "Sure I did," he says. "She'd been working on it for some time, even though everyone and their mother knows it's been solved."

"You think Holly Prine killed your daughter?" I prod.

"Of course I do," he says, more solidly than with reference to anything else he's said so far. "Not that you would know, but that's a fact around here."

"So you didn't take too kindly to Cora trying to reopen the investigation?"

"No need to open an investigation when you already know who did the crime."

"Can you tell me the last time you saw my aunt?"

"Why would that matter any?"

"We're trying to establish a timeline of her whereabouts. Standard investigating procedure."

"I'm sure Maddie's got all that covered," he replies. "If you want my opinion, Cora got tired of sticking her nose where it didn't belong and left Wonderland for good this time."

"Did you tell your granddaughter that?" I continue. "Did you pressure her to close the case like you pressured your brother to close your daughter's killing forty years ago?"

His eyes widen in shock. "I would never!" he exclaims, indignant.

His reaction seems genuine, as if no one has ever accused him of anything uncouth; as if no one's thought him capable of masterminding anything. How could this man, wilting so quickly under only a handful of my questions, have ruled over this town and kept up the Coldwater name for so many years? It makes me wonder: If the mayor isn't the one pulling the strings here, which Coldwater is? Could it be his wife, the matriarch who showed up at the gala in his stead? Or maybe his granddaughter, running the police force and in a perfect position to sweep things under the rug?

Todd Coldwater may have his portrait in the hall and his name on every piece of recent Wonderland history, but he's not the one with the power.

Suddenly, he turns to Hunter, anger widening his features. "I knew your parents. They would be ashamed to see you acting like this, associating with the *Coles*, of all people."

"What do you have against the Coles?" I ask.

"Well, the circumstances of Cora's . . . of how she . . . that her father was married to another woman when Cora was—"

"Holding the sins of the father against the daughter, is that it?" Hunter replies.

"Cora was no peach herself," he says. "And there hasn't been a man in that house since her father died. That ain't natural. It was fine when your father was around to help, but now it just . . . it ain't right!"

His words cause the room to fall dangerously silent. He shifts in his chair, as if realizing the mistake he's made. How dare he talk about Hunter's family and about mine when his own has done so much damage to this town? When here he is, sitting on a golden throne gifted to him by sheer luck of genetics?

I open my mouth to reply, but Hunter beats me to it. She takes a small step forward, her hands flat on the mayor's desk as she leans toward him. "My father was a drunk who killed my entire family," she says, her voice eerily quiet. "And my mother was Cora's best friend. She'd want me to do everything possible to find her, come hell or high water. She wouldn't stop just because a Coldwater told her to, and neither will I."

The mayor blinks, shocked again. Anger shoots through me—yet another person with the audacity to run their mouth about shit they so clearly know nothing about. "I . . . I had no idea about your father."

"That was the whole point," Hunter replies. Then she steps back, clears her throat, head high and shoulders back. *She's the one who should be sitting in that chair,* I think. *She's the one that's earned it.*

"I . . . you really should be speaking to my wife," he says again, the anxiety in his tone apparent. "I shouldn't have . . . this has all gotten a bit out of hand—"

"Thank you for your time, sir," Hunter says, then turns on her heel without another word.

*   *   *

"Well, that was a waste of time."

I slam the truck door behind me. "Not completely," I reply. "We learned who's really pulling the strings in Wonderland. And did you notice how he answered my question? He said he hadn't bought anything from Cora, but not that he didn't pay her."

"And that means . . .?"

"He still could've been giving her money for something," I continue. "He could've been paying her, but not getting anything in return. Which would mean . . ." I trail off, thinking, *thinking*, and then—

"Blackmail," I breathe. "She was blackmailing him. All those people in her ledger, when things changed over eight years ago—she's been blackmailing them. That's how she saved the ranch."

This is my favorite part of being a PI: when all the pieces fall into place, when everything comes suddenly into focus. It all makes sense—where the extra income's been coming from, Cora's interest in the Parker Mountain case, the ledgers.

"What if she started blackmailing the wrong person?" I ask, more to myself than Hunter as I work through it all. "Or . . . what if one of her longtime payees decided they were done paying? What if that ten thousand dollars from the mayor was supposed to be a last payment, but Cora asked for more?"

I tear my gaze from the windshield, looking over at Hunter, who looks like she's about to throw up. "What if she found the real killer, and she was blackmailing him about it?"

Hunter starts shaking her head. "Cora? Blackmailing people?"

"You heard Irene," I reply. "Whatever Cora did to save the ranch, whatever she was still doing, wasn't pretty. She was desperate. And it makes sense: she can write off all the blackmail money as sales. Who in this area would ever question that?"

"How do you know it's about Parker Mountain, though?"

She's right. It could just as easily be about an affair or something else the mayor's hiding, but . . . "Ten thousand dollars seems like a steep price to pay for anything that's legal," I reply. "But you're right. We've gotta find proof first."

"So all those people in that ledger, all the people I've been collecting money from and then giving to Cora . . . she was blackmailing them. And I was helping her."

"No, don't do that," I demand. "You had no idea—don't blame yourself for this."

She looks down at her hands folded in her lap, avoiding my gaze. "I bet you say that to all your friends."

"I thought we established I don't have friends."

Hunter's brows pull down. "You don't have any friends? In Spokane?"

"No."

"Why not?"

"Why don't you?"

"I asked you first."

Fair enough. "I . . ." I run my tongue along the backs of my teeth, searching for the right words. How we got here so quickly I'm not entirely sure of. "I've seen what people are capable of. Even people that you'd think could never hurt a fly. People hide, and people lie, and people hurt. It doesn't make me want to jump at the idea of friendship."

"And what about me?"

"And what about you?"

"I've hurt you," she answers, finally looking over at me. "And we're still . . ."

She trails off. I lean in a bit closer, drawing nearer to that steel-cut jawline again. "We're still what, Lem?"

The woman next to me swallows. "I don't know," she says, her voice soft and low.

If all I wanted to do with Hunter was fuck her, I would've done it already. By the flare of her nostrils, the color in her cheeks, the hitch of the pulse in her throat, and what she said in bed at the hotel, she would've let me. If there was no attraction and I just wanted friendship, I could've had that too—especially with Cora gone and Hunter out here all alone, her only company the roar of the wind and the eyes of the animals.

I could step away right now and keep things strictly professional until Cora turns up. Then I could pack my things and fly back to Spokane, and Hunter would be a pressure in the back of my mind, a *what if* that might bother me as I move through my life. But it wouldn't control me, wouldn't own me.

That, I realize, is why I haven't acted sooner, why this has felt so different from anything before. She's staying in Wonderland until the day she dies, which means that to be hers, I'd have to stay too. Everything, it seems, comes back to this place.

We sit, staring. Waiting. For Hunter to move. For me to say something. For Hunter to leave. For me to stay.

"Maybe," she rasps at last, and I draw a breath, bracing, ready, "we ain't gotta know all that yet."

"What do we do in the meantime, then?"

I think of all the silent drives, the fights over the radio, the time spent questioning and wondering and pushing. The differences in Hunter's stares when she's upset or annoyed or shocked. The curve of her nose, the line of her jaw. That first night she found me out under the stars. The fuse box that lives inside her, lighting up or going dark at a moment's notice.

It's Hunter that pushes forward, closing the last few inches between us, and kisses me.

Her lips are soft, but her kiss is not. It's ferocious, claiming. I grab her behind the neck as she grips my waist, crushing us together. Our teeth clack against each other's as we fight to get closer. Her tongue is in my mouth, tentative, mine swiping along the roof of hers, not so tentative, and the moan she unleashes—

It takes my breath away, steals the rhythm of my pulse, rearranges everything I thought I knew.

It is the beginning.

It is the end.

Part 2

The Missing Girl

CHAPTER

19

Stubborn Beast (Now)

"G OOD TO HEAR from you as always, Lem."
I roll my eyes at Bridgers's greeting. *She won't help me*, I'd told Hunter, *but she'll help you*. Hunter hadn't denied it as she dialed Bridgers's number and put the phone to her ear.

"We've got a couple more questions, if you don't mind."

"You know that I can't—"

"Not about the case," I interrupt. "About you and Cora."

A pause. "Why the sudden change of heart, Quinn?"

"Nothing's changed on my end," I respond. It's the truth: Hunter's the reason we dialed Bridgers's number, Hunter convincing me that she has information we need. I hate it. But for Cora, for Hunter . . .

"Well," Bridgers starts, "it's good to know that Lem's still got my back after all these years."

Hunter's cheeks go the faintest shade of red, and I bite back a wave of jealousy. "The ledger," I continue. "We connected the dots."

Another pause. Then the sound of rustling, a door opening and shutting, as if Bridgers is moving to a different room. "You're gonna have to expand on that."

"We figured out that Cora was blackmailing the mayor," Hunter says.

Bridgers is silent for a long moment before she says, "I was pretty sure you'd find the ledger, but I didn't know if you were smart enough to put all the pieces together."

"Do you know what she had on him?" I ask.

"No, Cora never told me that. All I know is that he's been on her list since she first started." Bridgers laughs, but there's no humor in it. "The mayor. He's been presiding over Wonderland since before I was born. As if that means something; as if that kept his daughter safe. The blackmail's the one thing he's been able to keep from my grandmother all these years, so I've got to give him some credit for that, I suppose." She pauses, and I remember the words she'd spoken outside the library, when she'd just *happened* to be in the area: *I know more about all this than you think I do.* A threat—or a hint; maybe even both. "Cora moved back to town when I was ten," she continues. "I liked her instantly—the way she'd march into the mayor's office and issue demands, knowing damn well she was right about whatever it was that she was talking about. She'd come to all our high school games—hardly anyone else did. No one ever cares about girls' basketball, but she did. She'd make signs for all of us, not just Lem, and she'd cheer so loud the refs threatened to throw her out."

For girls she didn't even know, while she was busy ignoring me.

"Eight years ago," Bridgers continues, "I was fresh out of the academy, up in Douglas. Two choices in this family, to make yourself useful: police or politics. My family only lets men hold the mayor's office, so it was the sheriff's department for me. One night I was patrolling near town hall, and I saw Cora storm out of the building, the mayor chasing after her. He grabbed her arm, and I jumped out to break it up. When I talked to her after he left, I told her that I'd always seen her at the games, and she instantly remembered me. *'You took Lem under your wing your senior year,'* she'd said. *'I was real grateful for that.'"*

Bridgers pauses, as if stuck in the memory. Then she clears her throat. "I asked what she and the mayor had been discussing. She said it was the Parker Mountain case, that she'd been investigating the case for a while, and the mayor had warned her off it. Anyway, I knew about her PI background, and we decided to team up that night—see what we could find out about the case. I started looking into the official files and . . ."

"And . . .?" I prompt.

"Look, I'm not saying what you said at Jessica's fundraiser is true."

"Not great for your argument that you have to preface with that."

Bridgers exhales, long and heavy. *"That's not me. That's not my department,"* she'd told me with such certainty that it was as if she'd believed it to be an objective truth rather than just her opinion. I don't know what's made her change her mind now, why she's suddenly able to see the forest for the trees. To be honest, I don't really care.

She said that she had been forced into this position, and maybe that's true. Maybe some Coldwater in this town saw the opportunity in having a *#girlbossfeminism* sheriff leading things, one with a connection to the family. An opportunity that killed two birds with one stone, one simply too good to pass up. But Madison Bridgers has still let it happen. She's still done God knows what, protected by her family and the badge with her name on it. That's why I don't trust her, I realize: the impunity that she operates with. She can do just about anything in this town—probably even commit murder—and get away with it.

"Go on," I urge her.

"The sheriff forty years ago—my great-uncle—and his team . . . they barely even looked for evidence at the scene," she says, voice quiet like it pains her to admit the truth. "No one checked into whether Holly had an alibi or not. They spent all their time trying to find her, and after a couple weeks of looking and coming up empty, she became the most convenient scapegoat around. Case closed. I told Cora all of this when I agreed to help her with her investigation. I dedicated my efforts to finding other suspects, and she spent her time trying to find Holly."

It's all so . . . predictable, falling to pieces exactly as I thought it would. "You said this was eight years ago?" I ask.

"Yes."

"That was the last summer I spent here," I say. "Because Cora told me I couldn't come back. But that's also when all the ranches in the area were going under, and she started the blackmail."

She sent me away to keep me safe. I realize that now. Hunter got to stay only because Hunter didn't have a Spokane. I know that too, but it still doesn't stop me from wondering: If Cora had kept Hunter safe, why couldn't she have kept me safe too? After all, Cora was the reason the danger existed in the first place. She chose the ranch and her life here over me—and kept making that choice every day for the past eight years.

There were a handful of times that I'd almost picked up the phone and called her myself, but every time I went to press the "Call" button, I thought, *What if she rejects you again?* The phone always ended up back on my bedside table or in my pocket or away, because even the idea of her holding her ground, of not wanting me again, was too much.

Hunter was right—I could've fixed things first.

"Her search for Holly came up empty, and I never found any other suspects," Bridgers replies, interrupting my thoughts. "We didn't talk much after that. But then two years ago, she showed up on my doorstep, telling me all about this blackmail scheme she'd devised to save the ranch. She said she needed insurance—someone that would still leak the information should something happen to her. She explained it all to me: how it started small, just following cheating husbands around. But then it became this whole . . . vigilante thing. At that point, Cora was blackmailing people all over the state."

"Did she tell you who?" I ask.

"Some of them. There were some businessmen in Casper who were skirting their taxes; teachers and administrators at the bigger high schools who had been paid off to lie about kids' SAT scores. I think she might've even had something on the governor, or maybe it was one of the senators. Anyway, Cora viewed it as her new job to make the blackmail thing work, so she put most of her time into it. Made it easier because Hunter could handle most of the ranch chores."

"Why would she tell a cop about the blackmail?" I ask, skeptical. "Let alone recruit said cop?"

The line goes quiet, because it's not just looking into an old case—she's implicating herself now. "She trusted me," Bridgers admits finally. "Same way Lem does. We'd been working together on the Parker Mountain case, on *Jessica's* case, and . . . she knew how I felt about it all, about this town and the people here. Someone was finally fighting back, and if all I had to do was hold onto an envelope and mail it to the *Star-Tribune* if anything happened to her . . ."

"Why haven't you, then?"

"Quinn, I don't think you understand the kind of information your aunt has on these people. Once this bullet's fired, there's no taking it back."

"Do you?"

"Are you asking if I've looked inside the envelope? No. Cora trusted me with it because she knew I wouldn't."

There's so much information swirling, so many different leads and roads to venture down. Did Cora blackmail the wrong person? Did she solve the Parker Mountain case? Is that what she had on the mayor, what he was willing to pay ten thousand dollars for—to cover up the fact that he killed his

own daughter and pinned it on Holly Prine? It's also possible
that the thing she was blackmailing him for eight years ago
isn't the same thing as what she's doing it for now.

"The mayor didn't kill Jessica, if that's what you're thinking, Quinn."

"How do you know that?" I ask Bridgers.

"You're just gonna have to trust me on this one."

There's that word again—and so much hinging on it.
Trust this woman I barely know, who has a million reasons to
lie to me. Trust her like I trusted Elain. Like I trusted Cora.

"Why are you helping us now?" I ask.

"My family and I don't exactly get along, if you hadn't
already picked up on that. And my divorce hasn't exactly
helped the situation. You've already figured out all the things
I wasn't willing to offer up, but the rest of it . . . seems like fair
game now."

"So why haven't you come forward with your investigation?" I continue. "Why didn't you tell everyone that the
Parker Mountain case had been mishandled?"

The line goes silent once more, but I already know the
answer. *I didn't want to ruin anyone's reputation. I didn't
want to cost a good officer their job. No good would've come from
exposing it all.* Madison Bridgers just keeps proving my point
again and again.

"Cora didn't give up on the Parker Mountain case,
though," Hunter says when Bridgers doesn't reply. "Not until
a couple months ago."

"I had no idea about that—not until you two showed up
at the station and announced it for all the world to hear."

"If she'd kept it up for all these years," I say, thinking out
loud, "hiding it even from you, then why did she stop after so
long?"

She wouldn't have stopped until she had an answer, I think.
*She could've even upped the amount she was asking for to some-
thing larger—say, ten thousand dollars if she found something*

else. Something bigger. And she had been spending all her time trying to find—

"She found Holly," Bridgers says.

* * *

The door to Cora's house is wide open when we pull up the path.

Without a word, Hunter brushes my knees to the side, pulling open the glovebox and retrieving her gun.

"Jesus—"

She slams the glovebox shut and gets out of the truck all in one motion. "Stay behind me," she orders.

The wood around the doorjamb is splintered, like someone kicked in the door. I follow Hunter into the house, moving slowly as we enter the living room. My eyes widen, and I'm barely able to stifle my gasp at the sight of it: all the furniture is flipped over, the glass coffee table shattered in the middle of the room, the rugs in crumpled piles. The kitchen isn't in much better shape. The fridge and freezer are wide open, mugs and plates broken all over the floor, the cabinet doors ajar.

Someone was looking for something—probably the very same something that's inside of Hunter's truck right now. But not just that; they wouldn't have caused all this damage if they were just looking for the ledgers or the key. No—this was on purpose. This is another warning, and it makes me pull Hunter closer to me by her belt loops.

We move methodically through the rest of the house, as one. The computer in the guest room is smashed in, like someone took a baseball bat to it. All the toiletries in Cora's bathroom are scattered on the floor, the mirror in similar shape to the computer, a giant spiderweb crack where the words *Stop looking* had once been. The drawers of her desk have been rifled through, and her bedding has been removed. When I look closer, there's a giant slash into the bed itself, and through the pillows too.

"Jesus," I breathe, picking up Cora's quilt, which is sitting near the floor of the ruined bed. *"Jesus."*

I turn toward Hunter, who clicks the safety on her gun before tucking it in her waistband. She bends down, picking up the picture of Cora and me that must've tumbled to the floor in the melee.

"Hunter—" I start, with no idea where I'm going. I could tell her that this escalation means we're out of time, that this has made it *real*, that someone is willing to get physical to make us stop. But with how hard she's gripping the photograph, I'd wager she already knows all of that.

"Get the ledgers," she says quietly, but not softly. No—there's a lethal edge to her tone that sends a chill through the air. She stares down at the ruined photo as she says, "We're finishing this now."

* * *

Hunter stands, leaning against the doorway as I retrieve this year's ledger and the key from her truck.

Taking the book, Hunter holds it in one giant hand. She opens the ledger, thumbing through it. Page by page she flips through, her eyes revealing nothing as she scans the words, the numbers, all in Cora's handwriting. The biggest clue; the last clue.

The answer to forty years' worth of questions and secrets and lies. The answer, maybe, to where Cora is now.

And all Hunter has to do is start talking.

But she shakes her head, all the anger from moments ago fading. "I don't know—"

"You've been hiding shit from me since the day I got here," I say. "There's only one reason why you'd be stopping me from finding Cora. You already told me you didn't have anything to do with her disappearance, and I believed you once. I won't make the same mistake again."

It's as if we're completely different people: the women who kissed in the truck and the women standing here, deadlocked.

"Not this," she says softly. "Not about this." She closes the ledger, then looks up at me. "Where'd you find these, again?"

"In her desk."

"And you've looked everywhere around here for answers, yeah?"

"Unless Cora's got a secret bunker—"

"She does," Hunter interrupts. I can practically see the gears turning in her head as she becomes the investigator in the room. She looks from the ledger to the desk, staring for a moment, then looks back at me and says, "The guesthouse. There's a matching desk out in the guesthouse."

*   *   *

"I don't hardly ever use the desk, which is why I didn't think about it earlier," Hunter explains as she pushes open the door to her house, leading me inside. For whatever reason, the guesthouse remains untouched, leaving me to believe either whoever was behind this knew the ledgers were in Cora's house, or they ran out of time and could only search one of the two places.

The desk is, as she said, identical to the one in Cora's room. There are a few books stacked on top of it. The rest of the space is covered in a pretty thick coating of dust, evidence of the disuse Hunter admitted to.

She pulls open the top drawers first, empty save for a couple of pens, more dust, and some sticky notes. The drawer on the bottom left holds nothing, but then she pulls open the one on the bottom right. She pauses, her body blocking me from seeing what's inside.

I hold my breath. And then, slowly, Hunter pulls out a small key.

My immediate response is "What the fuck?"

Hunter says nothing, turning the key over in her hand. It looks more normal than the one I found, like any standard-issue lock key, but it's clear this key has been used before. The brass has worn down, and if there was once any lettering on it, there's no trace of it now.

"Another key? Super helpful, Cora."

But Hunter's already shaking her head. "No, no. I know this key," she whispers, staring down at it as if trying to place it. "I've used this key . . ." A moment later she says, *"Oh,"* and looks up at me, eyes wide. "I know what this unlocks."

*   *   *

"Why is there a water slide at a high school?"

Hunter looks over at the large yellow monstrosity curling out from the walls of the high school before looping back inside the building. "It's the community pool too," she says, as if this is a completely normal sight. "Y'all don't have dual-use facilities in the city?"

"We just have enough people for two pools, actually."

She shakes her head, leading me inside. Radley High School—sits a half an hour outside Wonderland. The building is entirely unremarkable—except for the water slide, of course. It's a large, concrete rectangle with red trim, which is flaking off in some places, entirely missing in others. Functional, but certainly in need of an upgrade, which could be used to describe this entire state.

"HOME OF THE OUTLAWS!" is written in flaking red paint above the main doors.

Schools start in late August in this part of the country—we start in September up north—so at noon on a Wednesday, there are plenty of kids and parents roaming around.

"Why so many adults?" I ask.

"Orientation week," Hunter replies, opening the door to the main office.

There are so many parents crammed into the small office that there's nowhere for Hunter and me to go. They are all seemingly screaming. Some are screaming at the poor women behind the desk, who look like they're about to burst into tears at any moment. Some are screaming into their phones; some are screaming right at their kids.

Our plan was to pretend to be alumni on a little home-coming trip and sweet-talk our way into a self-guided tour of the common areas. I would do all the talking, obviously. But now . . .

Hunter must have the same idea that I do; she shuts the door, waits a moment, then starts down the hallway opposite us.

The walls are bare, small pushpin holes the only decor. Everything is tinged just a little yellow: the walls; the floors, covered in scuff marks and mud; the lighting, which is limited, as several of the bulbs have burnt out. Lockers line both sides of the hallway. They're in similar shape to everything else around here. Some are closed, some are open, and some are just slightly ajar, as if they don't close quite right, and their owners gave up on trying to secure them.

Hunter moves swiftly, knowing her destination. I trail behind, smiling politely at other adults and teens who pass by us. *Hello, we belong here! Please excuse the determined, scary-looking cowgirl in front of me!*

We hook a right, Hunter leading us down another long hallway. As we walk closer to the end of the hall, there are fewer people milling around, voices fading. There's a single door marked "Emergency Use Only," and as Hunter heads directly for it, I'm wondering if I should interject with *Are you sure this is the right way?* But at the door she stops, turning to the right, where there are three more lockers. This little alcove is completely obscured from view because of the wall. You wouldn't assume that the lockers loop around the corner either, because they haven't anywhere else in the school.

Hunter skips over the first two lockers and stops in front of the last one. They're in better shape than most of the others in the building, probably because of their obscurity and disuse. But there's still a thick enough layer of dust on the lockers and floor that it seems like no one's been here in a while.

Hunter puts her hand out, touching the metal surface. She flattens her entire palm against it. When she pulls it away, I'm sure there will be an imprint of her hand left behind from where she disturbed the dust.

"This was my locker," she says, her voice soft. "It was Cora's too. When she went here."

"All the way down here?" I ask. "Both of you were put over in this little corner?"

"They assign lockers based on where you live," she explains. "Somethin' to do with the bus schedule. Kids on the first bus have the lockers closest to the exit. Anyway, there used to only be two or three students from Wonderland, so they'd put them all together. And Cora said this corridor was popular. I was the only Wonderland kid my year, and by that time it was pretty much just me down here. The year after I graduated, they finally gave up on this section of lockers; kids kept losin' their keys, so they went to the dial combination locks."

I nod. "So the first key was for me, behind the photograph of Cora and me."

She's silent for a moment, still staring at the locker as if she's somewhere else. Some*time* else. "And the second was for me," she finally breathes, "because it was mine. Ours."

Hunter keeps her hand on the locker as we stand there, neither of us speaking or moving. She's been the one taking all the first steps here, leading us nearly to the finish line. To this place that only Hunter would know, but another key had been left in a place where I'd find it. Maybe it is all coincidence, but I have the audacity to hope it's not. That Cora left these clues for *us* to find; that she trusted *us* to save her.

There's only one way to find out.

"Let me," I say, extending my hand.

For a moment Hunter's frozen, and I think she's going to rebuff me, but then she nods, just once, and hands me the key, stepping away from the locker. The lock is as commonplace as its key, which slides right into place, releasing with a sudden click, as if no time at all had passed between now and the last time it was opened.

I didn't realize I was holding my breath until I pull the locker door open and exhale. There's as much dirt and dust inside the locker as there was outside of it. No one's been here in a long time, not even Cora.

But sitting there, all alone on the single shelf inside, is a box.

I reach for it immediately, hearing Hunter's sharp inhale. It's sturdy, one of those fireproof boxes you keep your important documents in. It's heavy too. I brush the dust off the lid, the metal cool under my fingers. It's unadorned except for a crest on the top—the same one that's engraved on all Cora's ledgers: *CC*, in brilliant gold.

Most notably, there's a place for a key.

"This whole time," Hunter says in a voice that sounds nothing like hers; it's dull and flat, detached. "This was sitting here the whole time, and I had no idea."

I shift the box in my grasp so I can grab her by the arm, turning her toward me. "It wouldn't have mattered if you knew," I tell her. "Even if you had the key, you'd only have been able to open the locker. Same for anyone who tried to cut the lock off or had an extra key. No one was getting inside this thing unless they had my key. Unless Cora *wanted* them to find it. Knowing her, she probably had the janitor or a secretary keeping an eye on it for her."

I can see it. In the hole she'd dug herself, she would've known not to store anything important at her home. The keys were only important if you knew what they opened. Only Hunter could've known about the locker key. Even if someone broke in and did find the keys, they wouldn't have known what to do with them. Bridgers got the folder of information, and her allies here kept watch over the locker connecting her to Hunter.

"Forget about the past," I tell her now, as much for her sake as mine, "and let's *bring her home.*"

I have no idea if what's inside this box will allow us to find Cora, but God does it feel good to hope so.

She nods. I close the locker, secure the box firmly between my hands, and follow Hunter as she starts back toward where we came from.

20

Kitchen Light (Then—August 1981)

IT WAS BEAUTIFUL, the spread that Jessica had prepared.

She'd driven out to Parker Mountain an hour before picking Holly up at her house. The night was warm enough for Holly to wear the one nice dress she owned, found at a thrift store in San Diego a lifetime ago. It was a deep violet sundress with spaghetti straps and a skirt that twirled when she moved.

Night was starting to fall as Jessica led Holly to the spot she'd picked out. The moon was full that night, providing plenty of light. Jessica had laid out a blanket, covering the rough ground below them. On top of the blanket was a picnic basket, and when Holly looked inside, she saw bread, cheese, dried fruit, cured meats, and apple cider.

Jessica sat down on the blanket across from Holly, tucking her legs underneath her. Dressed in a white sundress of her own, her hair falling in soft waves, Jessica looked like something out of a magazine, like a model, perfect and poised as she carefully took all the items from the basket and laid them out.

"I wasn't sure what to pack," Jessica admitted, opening the bottle of cider. Then she pulled a flute from the basket, handed it to Holly, and filled it nearly to the top, her movements fluid and graceful. "I told Mom we were having a tea party out here, and she told me what to pack."

Holly stiffened at the mention of Mrs. Coldwater, but only for a moment. All of this was so fancy. So adult, so grown-up, like they were any other people in the world, out on a date on a Friday night. They'd chosen this spot specifically—secluded, private, far away from anyone who might recognize them. At first, Holly had resented the fact that they had to hide *again*, but then she realized that privacy might not be such a bad thing. Not on this night, not with this girl.

It always sent a sharp pain through her chest, thinking about it, the uncertainty, the guessing. *Is my existence okay? Will it upset the people in my life?* If she were a boy, smiling and toasting with Jessica under the bright, shining moon, there would be no problem. It never made much sense to Holly, and it certainly never seemed fair or equal.

"It's perfect," Holly assured her.

They ate in a companionable silence, tearing pieces of bread and refilling their glasses. They listened to the breeze, blowing gently against their skin, and the animals, rustling and howling and living.

When the last piece of cheese was eaten, Holly exhaled. "So."

Jessica smiled at her. Somehow, she was even more beautiful in the moonlight. "So."

Holly leaned forward, knocking over her glass in the process. Her cheeks went hot, but Jessica just laughed softly, picking up the flute and placing it back into the basket. Then she clasped Holly's cheeks between her cool hands, skin on skin, and kissed her.

They'd kissed after school, in the gym when all the other cheerleaders had left for the day. They'd kissed at night, in the back of Jessica's car, behind Holly's house when her mother wasn't home. They'd kissed in Jessica's room, in Jessica's bed, at Flaming Gorge, on the highway—everywhere and nowhere all at once, it seemed.

But *this* kiss—this was the kiss to end all others. This was the one that made everything else, everything they'd been through and weathered and hid, finally worth it.

It was strange, like some kind of magic, Holly thought, the way that Jessica looked, naked and under her. They had the same anatomy, but staring at Jessica was like seeing it all for the first time. It was as if she was carved from some kind of precious material, so beautiful it made Holly ache just looking at her. The slope of her stomach, the cut of her collarbones, the muscles in her thighs, the flush that covered most of her body. Holly wanted to kiss and touch every inch of her—and tonight she could.

"Are you sure?" Holly whispered, resting her hand on the inside of Jessica's thigh.

"Yes," Jessica exhaled. "Yes, I'm sure."

Holly moved her hand up, bending to kiss Jessica, and the night went hazy around them.

* * *

It wasn't perfect—except in all the ways that mattered.

Holly's touch had been too firm at first, Jessica grabbing her wrist and gasping. They'd stared at each other for what felt like an eternity before Holly whispered, "Show me." There was push and pull, stop and go, but they found their way through it together.

The temperature had dropped in the time since they first sat down, and now it was too cold to laze without clothes on. Grudgingly, they both pulled their clothes back on, the process made longer by the fact that they kept stopping to kiss each other. Finally, after so much time had passed that they no longer knew which hour was closest, they gathered the basket and the blanket and headed back to Jessica's car.

There was a soreness between Holly's legs—and her right shoulder, where Jessica had bitten as she came, though she certainly wasn't complaining about that—and a fullness in her chest. Her head was racing too, thoughts of the past and the future all melding together. She almost laughed when she remembered how at one point she'd wondered if two girls could be together. Oh, *could* they.

Jessica stopped before they made it to the car. She turned to Holly, eyes bright and skin still flushed. There was a mark on her neck that resembled a bruise, and Holly realized that she'd done that.

"Can I tell you something?" Jessica asked. "Something I've never told anyone before?"

Holly's pulse kicked into high gear, in a good way or a bad way she wasn't sure. "Of course."

Jessica nodded, let out a breath. "I . . . um . . ." She swallowed, took a step closer to Holly. "I love you."

In one of her science classes in Nevada, Holly had learned about spontaneous combustion. It was when something got so hot that it exploded all by itself. In that moment, with Jessica's hand on her cheek and the way she was staring at her, her declaration hanging between them, Holly Prine swore she could've gone up in flames.

"I love you too," she told Jessica.

Nothing can touch this, Holly thought, so strongly and clearly she knew it had to be the truth. *Nothing can ever break this.*

And maybe that was the reason—maybe it was because Holly was lost in her thoughts, in her joy and satisfaction, that she didn't notice the car parked across the lot from them, the person approaching them until they were just feet apart, and then clearing their throat.

"Well, now what's all this?"

CHAPTER

21

Two Slow Dancers (Now)

THERE ARE TWO things inside the box.

The first thing: a newspaper clipping. *Coyote County Post, March 2002,* sits italicized in the top right corner. *Hospital Births* is headlined in bold, black letters. Below it, in smaller print:

> BLACKWOOD—*A baby girl was born at Blackwood Rural Hospital to Miss Lila Gregory at 6:35 p.m. last night, March 12, 2002. Miss Gregory passed away due to complications from the birth. See OBITUARIES for more.*

The second thing: a photograph. It's of a woman with short hair; it's in black and white, the photo paper worn from age, so it's hard to make out all the details. She looks thirty-five, maybe forty. Her gaze meets the camera lens, eyes wide, like she's been caught off guard, like she never wanted her photo taken in the first place. On the back of the photo, her name is written in blue ink: *Lila Gregory, Fall 1999.*

"Who is this woman?" I breathe, handing Hunter the photo, trying to keep my hand steady. We're sitting in her truck, unable to wait until we got home to open the box.

Someone likely would've stopped us on our way out if it weren't for the parents who, if possible, were shouting even louder than when we came in.

There's something eerie, something unsettling about the air around us, like opening this box has unleashed something, illuminated a path that can't be untraversed. Maybe it's the knowledge that this woman, dead for twenty-two years, is the key to finding Cora. Maybe it's the numbers, the dates, cycling through my mind.

March 12, 2002.

Hunter studies the photo. "I have no idea."

"I think . . ." I press my lips together, my mouth suddenly dry as I take the photograph back. "Where is Blackwood? In Coyote County? Do you know?"

"Colorado," she replies. "About six hours from here, southern part of the state."

"Have you ever been there?"

"Once," she says slowly, like she's reliving the events, trying to remember every old detail. "It was . . . two years ago in the summertime. I went with Cora. We had an errand to run there. I remember because it was strange—she didn't let me out of the truck, and she didn't bring back any money."

"A social visit?"

"Could've been. Only lasted about twenty minutes."

"Long way to drive for just a conversation."

I look back down at the birth/death announcement. "It couldn't have been her. Maybe her husband? The father of the baby?"

She shakes her head. "No, it was a woman. She hugged Cora when she went into the house. I saw her."

"Could it have been the baby, twenty years later?"

"No, I think she was older than Cora."

Head still spinning, I clutch at anything, something, to get that date out of my mind. "Did Cora tell you what they talked about? Or ever mention her again?"

"No," she says on an exhale, like she's been holding her breath.

I close my eyes. Here I thought this box would finally give us an arrow, a single direction to head in. Instead, all it has led to is more questions—a dead mystery woman, a place in Colorado I've never heard of, and the feeling that we've just stumbled onto something very, very bad.

"March twelfth, 2002," I say. "That's my birthday."

Hunter pauses. "That's . . . a coincidence."

My head is thumping, blood rushing in my ears, the room tilting. I take another look at the woman, trying to determine what exactly it is about this photo that has me feeling so off. Another puzzle I'm missing the last few pieces to—but at least now, I've got an idea of where to find them.

"Do you remember how to get to that house in Blackwood?"

"I should," she replies quietly.

I run my thumb over the photograph. "To Colorado we go, then."

*　　*　　*

Hunter insisted that I stay in the guesthouse with her tonight.

We agreed to head out first thing in the morning, before she said that over her dead body was I staying in the house that didn't have a working lock on the front door. Or a front door at all, really. I needed some time to think, so I told her I was going to clean up before I'd be over, and she'd relented.

My mind's running wild, full of thoughts about the box and the photo and Cora and what it all could possibly mean. A baby, a dead woman, a town in Colorado, all the clues pointing straight to one unknown woman.

I know better than to hope that maybe—*maybe*—Elain, the woman who raised and hated and abandoned me, isn't my actual mother. Still, I can't help the question that sticks in my mind: Is it better to have a dead mother or one who couldn't stand your existence?

I can't think about it anymore. Hopefully, by this time
tomorrow we'll have found Cora hiding out at this mystery
woman's house, and it'll all be over.

But there it is again. Hope.

I grab Cora's quilt from her room before slipping into my
flip-flops and shutting the door the best I can behind me.

The night sky is dark and covered in clouds, no moon or
stars peeking through. Crickets chirp, the grass rustles. It's
hard to believe that a handful of days ago I hated this view:
the sameness, the unfamiliar landmarks, the way it's so easy to
lose yourself in it all. When I look up now, all I see is the color
of Hunter's eyes, and it immediately calms me.

It's special because it isn't. The hue of the sky, unobscured
by city lights. The stillness until lightning or thunder or a
downpour shatters the illusion. The echo, paved by open
roads and miles and miles of untouched land.

I don't love it—not yet at least. But seeing it through
Hunter-colored glasses has changed my perspective, and that's
not exclusive to this state's landscape.

When I knock on Hunter's door, there's no answer. Her
response is usually automatic, ready and waiting to scold me
for something or give me one of those deep, all-knowing looks.

I wait. Wait some more, then knock again. When there's
still no answer, I briefly consider leaving and going back to the
ruined couch. But the kiss in the truck, the one that's been
playing on repeat in my mind for the past several hours, a distraction from Cora's mystery box but also so much more . . .
it makes me try the doorknob, find it unlocked, and push
inside.

The shower's running, explaining the lack of an answer at
the door. Something feels off, though—wrong. The same way
it was when we opened that goddamn box earlier.

"Lem?" I call, rapping my knuckles on the bathroom door,
letting Cora's quilt fall from my shoulders. The light is on,
seeping out from under the bottom of the door. "You okay?"

There's no response again. Every cell in my body is lighting up, warning, cautioning.

Still, I open the bathroom door, figuring better to ask for forgiveness than permission.

Steam enshrouds the entire bathroom, making it so I can't see a single thing. I prop the door open wide, allowing some of it to escape. "Jesus," I breathe into the humid air. "Lem, what is going . . ."

I trail off as I see her, completely clothed, sitting on the floor of the shower, a half-empty bottle of whiskey next to her, water cascading over her unmoving figure.

"I don't drink," she'd told me that night at Cora's table, an edge to her words I hadn't completely understood at the time. The drunk-driving father helped piece together the connection, but . . . no, this is why. She knew that *this* would be the result.

She's sitting back against the side wall, absorbing nearly all the spray. Her knees are pushed up against her chest, her hair soaked and clinging to her face. She's staring at the floor. I don't think she's even blinking.

There's a puddle of water in front of me, where it's escaped from the shower. I reach down, swearing as I take off my flip-flops and chuck them to the side. Water slips between my toes as I carefully make my way toward her.

I maneuver inside, swearing again, some of the spray hitting me as I turn it off. The water is so hot it makes my breath catch. It drip, drip, drips off, and then it's silent. Dead silent, nothing else in the tiny cabin making a sound.

I should go get help, I think immediately, but then I remember: there is no one to get. There's only me and Hunter and whatever insidious thing has overtaken her tonight.

Her monster, I realize. This is what her monster looks like when it has surfaced.

Slowly, moving like I would if I came face-to-face with one of the animals creeping outside, I sit down in front of her, completely soaking the backside of my sleep shorts.

"Lem," I whisper, trying to catch her eyes.

She doesn't respond, doesn't look up from the spot on the floor she's been staring at for God knows how long.

"Lem," I say again, inching closer. "Talk to me."

There's not so much as a blink to indicate she's heard me.

"Fine, don't talk to me," I relent. "But we need to get you out of your wet clothes."

Standing, making sure not to slip on my way out, I hurry to her dresser, grabbing a T-shirt, pants, and a pair of underwear. When I return, she's still sitting there, still staring at the same spot on the floor.

I've had my fair share of bad nights. Depression, anxiety, fear—all of it encroaching until it suddenly becomes too much. It's one of the reasons I've tried so hard to stop feeling, to put up walls so high no emotion could ever sneak through. Because in this silent, unmoving, unresponsive version of Hunter, I see so many strokes of myself. At fourteen, when Cora banished me. At sixteen, when Elain left, and I was scared and hurt out of my mind. At eleven and seventeen and five and nine—monsters under my bed and ghosts in my closet and no one to scare them off.

Putting the clothes on the sink, I throw some towels on the floor. I bend, moving the towels around, mopping up the mess—

"Don't."

My head whips up. "Lem—"

"Don't," she says again, voice breaking on the word.

"Okay," I reply, rising, wiping my damp hands on my shorts. "Do you want—"

"Leave."

"No."

She stands quicker than I would've thought possible from someone who is covered in wet clothing and most definitely drunk. She's in my face in an instant, water sloshing and pooling over our feet. *"Leave,"* she practically growls.

"There's no fucking front door at Cora's," I tell her, not backing down. All the different iterations of this woman I've seen, and none of them have scared me—I'm not about to start relenting now. "Even if there was, I still wouldn't leave you."

Her chest is heaving, as if she's just run circles around the perimeter of the ranch. Her eyes are wide, nostrils flared. In this moment, she looks every inch the feral, wild animal she's a few different choices away from permanently becoming.

"Tell me," I say, moving nothing more than my mouth. "Whatever terrible, awful thing drove you to drink and get into that shower, tell me."

My mind is racing again, but this time with its answers to that very question. *Cora's dead,* I think immediately. *My aunt is dead, and the mystery is over, and she's about to tell me it's all been for nothing, that I'm too late, that—*

Hunter blinks, sways forward the tiniest bit, and the entire length of her body softens. All the tension and fury are gone, and now all that's left is pain. She tries to take a step forward, but she stumbles. I'm there, like I promised—catching her, wrapping my arms around her drenched frame. Her hands lock at my lower back, clutching onto my shirt. She leans down, dropping her forehead onto my shoulder.

A huge, gaping sob rips through her, the entirety of her body ricocheting against mine. It happens again, then again, in quicker succession. Hunter, crying like she's being ripped apart at the seams. Through everything that I've endured and witnessed and suffered, I realize that this is it: the worst thing in the entire world. The sounds that she's making, the way this woman of stone has come crumbling down.

Cora's dead. She's dead.

It takes everything in me to keep standing, to not fall to my knees the same way Hunter has. Instead I steel myself, holding the line for the one woman I wouldn't ever let fall.

* * *

Hunter emerges from the bathroom ten minutes later, dressed in only the dry shirt I left for her, holding what's left of the bottle of whiskey in her right hand.

"Never been drunk before," she mutters, looking at the floor. Her hair is still wet, dripping down onto the floor.

"I know."

She nods. Then, before I can stop her, she lifts the whiskey to her lips, taking a long swig.

"Lem—"

"My dad died today."

The relief I feel is instant. *Cora's not dead, Cora's not dead.* But then the words sink in, the weight of what's she's telling me. "What?"

"My. Dad. Died. Today," she repeats, punctuating each of her words with a thrust of the bottle. "My drunk, son-of-a-bitch father, who killed my entire family, died today." She pauses, her brows pulling together. "I can't decide if he got to live longer than they did. Technically he did, because his heart was still working, but not his brain. So I don't know. I can't decide if I should be mad about that too. They don't really tell you how to process any of this. Especially because they called me right as I was about to jump in the shower. *'Sorry, Miss Lemming, but your father passed away this morning.'* I don't know what's worse: being told in person or over the phone. Because I've had both now. I've been told in person and over the phone that someone in my family is dead."

She moves to take another sip, but I cross the room, closing the space between us, before she can hurt herself further. When I grab the bottle out of her hand, she doesn't fight it.

"Lem—" I try, but she cuts me off, clasping my face between her hands, pressing our mouths together.

It's bruising and demanding and so different from our kiss in the truck. It aches, and not in a good way. I wrench away, but not before the taste of whiskey on her lips hits me. *Wrong, wrong, wrong.*

"Not like this," I tell her. "Never like this."

We stand there for a moment, the bottle of whiskey in my fist. Hunter's emotions and the alcohol and the news of her father's death—they've all twisted her into a completely different person, the person she would've become had she made the easier choices. If she'd given into the grief and the rage, turned into the same kind of person she's mourning tonight.

"You're the best person I know," I tell her. You have had to bear more trauma and heartbreak in your twenty-one years than most people will in their entire lives, and you've come out in better shape than any of them would be able to."

"That's not true," she gasps.

"You calling me a liar?"

"You don't know me."

"I know *exactly* who you are, Hunter," I retort. "And I don't flinch at any of it. If you need to fall apart, then do it, because I'm not going anywhere."

Hunter says nothing for a long, long moment. Then she juts her chin toward the bottle in my hand. "You stop too, then," she whispers. "'Cause you're doing it for the same reason I did tonight."

"Alright," I tell her, the easiest thing in my life I've ever given up.

She steps back as if in a daze, nodding a couple of times before moving toward the bed. She throws back the covers, stumbling beneath them.

Quickly, I dump out the rest of the whiskey in the kitchen, then get her a glass of water. I cross the room, placing the glass down on the bedside table. Hunter's eyes are already shut, her breathing calming.

I run a hand down the side of her face, smoothing down her damp hair. The gesture is as foreign to me as I'm guessing it is to the woman on the receiving end of it.

As I'm pulling away, she startles, eyes flashing open. "Stay with me," she says hoarsely.

I hesitate. "Lem—"

"Just sleep," she whispers. "So I'm not alone. Please."

"Alright," I say, relenting. I strip off my wet shorts and shirt, leaving me in just a camisole and underwear. By the time I slip into the bed next to her, she's already starting to snore.

* * *

The rain wakes me.

Pounding on the roof of the guesthouse, it rips me from the deep, dreamless sleep I'd been under. I have no idea what time it is, only that the spot in bed next to me is empty.

It's middle-of-the-night dark, but moonlight streams in through the window, helping my eyes adjust. When they do, I see the outline of Hunter's body, sitting at the foot of the bed. She sits with her back to me, staring out the window. She's thrown the curtains wide open, every inch of window exposed to her gaze.

I groan as I roll over, but the rain drowns out the sound. I stand, my feet silent on the wood floors as I settle in next to her.

I wonder how long she's been sitting here. I wonder how often she does this, staring out the window at nothing, the darkness enshrouding her.

"What's wrong?" I ask softly when the silence between us becomes too much.

She offers no reply.

"Lem, how long have you been—"

"It a crime now, to sit here and look at the rain?"

I let out a breath, heavy and slow. "Are you still drunk?"

"Ain't sure."

"Lem—"

"Not everything's got a tragic backstory."

"Tragic backstories have a habit of following both of us around."

Another pause. Then: "The rain calms me," she whispers. "The idea that everything'll eventually wash away and begin again."

I reach out, grabbing her hand and weaving our fingers together. Soft against hard, velvet sliding along steel.

"Dance with me," I say.

The words are out before the idea is even fully formed, but they get her to finally look over. Her eyes are dark and reveal nothing, such a stark contrast to the fire and flame they held hours ago.

"I don't dance," she replies.

"Dance with me."

She stares for a moment, unblinking. "There's no music," she whispers, her voice hoarse.

So many secrets and unknowns and half-truths linger between us, but the way that this woman makes me feel is the most absolute, honest thing in the world.

It's foolish to make promises, to think of the future when there are so many uncertainties, when the likelihood of pain and anguish is so high. Yet, the payoff, the endgame is having someone in my life who cares about me. Someone to come home to. Someone to build a life with, build an empire with, climb the mountain and plant the flag with.

It's so close. I can see it all so clearly, so vividly—it's brushing the tips of my fingers, breathing down the back of my neck, hot and urgent. For twenty-two years, it's what I've been searching for. It's what I've been denied, what's been given and ripped away from me, and now I have the opportunity to take it all back.

I gesture at the window without looking away. "Sounds like music to me." I stand, extending a hand out to her. "Dance with me, Hunter."

Her throat works, the expression on her face growing uncertain. She stays glued to the bed, her hands curling around the sheets.

"Why not?" I whisper.

Her gaze goes back to the window. It's raining harder now, loud enough that I'm worried she didn't hear my last question.

"We used to all dance as a family," she says. "In the kitchen, when Mom was making dinner. And now I ain't got a family, so I don't dance."

Kneeling in front of her, I place my hands on her legs. They land halfway between her knees and her thighs, and there's a bit of shock in her eyes once she finally looks at me again.

"I'll be your family now," I tell her.

She gulps in a deep breath suddenly, jerking backward, her reaction almost knocking me on my ass. "Don't say things you don't mean," she rasps. "Because you can't take something like that back."

My hands move from her legs to her face, thumbs brushing back and forth along her cheekbones. "Dance with me," I ask again.

Her entire body is shaking now, but I know it's not from the chill in the room. I know because I'm doing the same thing, my fingers unsteady along her face.

Finally, she nods, puts her hands atop mine. She takes them from her cheeks, holds them in her grip, squeezes. "Let's dance, Princess."

CHAPTER

22

Mad Woman (Then—August 1981)

"WELL, NOW WHAT's all this?"
Mrs. Coldwater stood not six feet away from
the girls, her arms tucked behind her back.

"Mom?" Jessica said, immediately dropping her hand
from Holly's face.

"No need to pretend anymore, Jess," Mrs. Coldwater said,
stepping closer. "I heard it all—started suspecting even earlier.
But Holly knew that already."

Jessica shook her head. "It's not what—"

"Not what I think?" Mrs. Coldwater continued, cutting
her daughter off. "This isn't my child being lured into a sinful,
same-sex relationship? You've insulted me enough, Jess, don't
you think?"

Holly cleared her throat. "Mrs. Coldwater, if you could—"

"What? Let you try and explain away all the ways you've
tainted my daughter?" Mrs. Coldwater sneered. "You think
I don't listen to the radio, to Pastor Dave every Sunday at
church? I know what kind of girl you are, Holly Prine. I knew
something was off about you from the first day you set foot
in my home. I should've known what you were right then.
I'm not sure I'll ever forgive myself for being so blind. But

now, *now*, I can atone. I can set this right." Her gaze turned to Jessica. "You are coming home right now. And when we get there, you're packing a bag and heading to the convent in Cheyenne first thing in the morning."

It felt like Holly's heart had stopped beating, hearing that.

"No," Jessica gasped.

"Oh, *yes*," Mrs. Coldwater returned. "I will *not* let you ruin the Coldwater name. Not after how hard your grandmother worked to deal with Kathleen. The family would never forgive me if I let them down like this."

"But school—"

"*School* has allowed this sin to fester!" Mrs. Coldwater exclaimed. "You'll finish your education somewhere more respectable. This ends right now, Jessica Anne. We're leaving."

For a moment, Holly thought that she would—that Jessica, who had just moments ago proclaimed her love, would turn her back on her. Like Lenora had, like Mrs. Coldwater was doing right now. Holly wasn't sure how she'd survive this, how she'd weather the rest of her life without the girl she was always meant to find.

But then Jessica steeled her spine. Took Holly's hand in hers. And told her mother, "No."

Mrs. Coldwater didn't even seem fazed. "I thought that might be your answer. That's what happens when the sin gets in deep." She brought her hands around to the front of her body, revealing her husband's rifle.

Jessica gasped, stepping back, pulling Holly with her. "Mom, what are you doing?"

"What I must to protect my family," Mrs. Coldwater said as coolly and calmly as if going over plans at a PTA meeting. "One day, Jessica, when you've been saved, you'll understand."

As she took aim at Holly, she said, "I warned you."

23

Not Ready to Make Nice (Now)

B LACKWOOD, COLORADO, LOOKS nearly identical to Wonderland, Wyoming.

It's a marvel that we can drive six hours southeast, look
around, and feel like we're right back where we started. The
drive from Wonderland to Denver took just under four and a
half hours, the front end of the trip nothing but highway and
rolling hills. The sameness of it all started to get to me around
hour three, the feeling that I was sitting still, even as the world
around me rushed by. It hadn't been like this on the trip up
to Boise. But then again, so much has changed since then, it's
as if someone else took that trip. It was someone else who sat
shotgun while Hunter drove seemingly endlessly, silent and
unflinching.

Things opened up a bit once we got into Colorado, actual
cities and buildings and people existing. And a three-lane
highway, my God. Hunter stopped for gas outside of Fort Col-
lins, sunglasses shielding her eyes as she gingerly got out of the
truck. Having to weather your first hangover by driving six
hours . . . not an enviable position.

I knew better than to try and ask her how she was feeling. If she wanted to say something, she would've done it

already—opened a door and let me poke my head inside. Until then, I'd decided, I'd sit in the silence and *be*. Which turned out to be all the way through the heart of the state, winding through the hills and valleys along I-25 until we exited, drove twenty minutes on a country highway, then spotted a big green sign that welcomed us to the town of Blackwood, population fourteen.

The town's even more desolate than Wonderland, a feat I didn't think could be accomplished. Hunter slows the truck to twenty-five as we pass an old abandoned gas station, a dilapidated bar, and a shack of undeterminable purpose. When I check my phone, I've got no service.

"You failed to mention this was a ghost town," I remark, the first words I've spoken in hours.

Hunter shrugs as she takes a left off the main drag, turning onto a rough road that resembles the one that leads to the ranch. "Lot of 'em in this part of the country, from when the gold mines went dry and the trains stopped running."

Wonderland could've so easily ended up like this, I think. If the Coldwaters hadn't dug their claws in so deep; if the ranches hadn't been there; if, eight years ago, they all would've gone under. People who had been there their entire lives, forced to relocate or become ghosts, the land regaining its control.

The truck rattles ferociously, as if in warning. There's nothing concrete that separates this road, this place from any of the others that Hunter and I have traversed trying to solve this mystery. Still—there's an undeniable difference. Maybe it's the unknown, the way neither of us have any idea what lies ahead. Maybe it's *Cora*, the way she could be a handful of minutes away.

Finally the road ends and a house appears. Small and quaint and in a far better state than the rest of the town. There are flowers planted in front of the narrow porch, reminding me of the ones at Irene's house.

Hunter pulls into the unpaved driveway, turns off the truck, lets out a breath. "We're sure about this," she says.

It's not a question, and we both know that. We've come this far, Cora's clues finally converging into focus, leading us to this house, hundreds of miles away from our starting point, even more in the middle of nowhere than where we started.

I reach over, take one of her hands in mine. "We're sure about this."

* * *

My heart is beating too hard, too fast.

No breath is deep enough to calm it or steady the way my hands are shaking as we walk to the door. I've never been this nervous, this unsure in my entire life. I've never felt so clearly that something bad is about to happen. Even the gun Hunter has tucked in her waistband—this all coming full circle—doesn't seem like protection enough.

We're gonna wish we kept the monsters under the bed.

Sweat runs down the back of my neck, and I tell myself it's just from the heat of the midafternoon sun hanging high above us. There isn't a cloud in the sky, no threat of rain anywhere near. A perfect, clear day in August—the month most cursed in this part of the country.

We stand on the porch. When I take Hunter's hand once more, it's trembling as much as mine is.

Hunter knocks, just once, as if she's scared to. Footsteps echo from behind the door. Hunter squeezes my hand.

"Quinn, I think—"

The door opens, cutting Hunter off. A woman appears, and for a moment I think, *Cora.*

No, not Cora.

Same hair, same nose. But different demeanors, different postures. Close, so close, but not quite right.

It's only Hunter's grip that keeps me standing, that keeps me from collapsing on the porch, and I breathe, *"Mom?"*

* * *

Elain's eyes widen at the sight of me. "Quinn?"

The world is spinning, tilting, my mind unable to process what's going on.

The woman in front of me opens the door a little wider, takes a step closer. "What are you doing here? How did you find me? Why aren't you in—"

"Is Cora here?" Hunter interrupts.

Elain turns her gaze to the woman standing next to me, taking in Hunter for the first time. "No," Elain says. "Why would she be here?"

"Because—" I start, then cut myself off. *Because we thought she was here. Because this was our last shot. Because we needed her to be here.*

Maybe this isn't the end. Maybe this is just another step in the right direction. "What do you know about Lila Gregory?" I ask.

Elain's attention is drawn back to me. "How do you know that name?"

"I know that she gave birth to a daughter and died on March twelfth, 2002," I say. "But what I don't know is how all of this connects. And I sure as hell don't know where Cora is, so you better start *talking*."

She says nothing for a long moment, staring at me with something that I can only describe as wonder in her eyes. "You followed in Cora's footsteps, didn't you?" she whispers.

"Of course I did," I bark, the time for decorum long passed.

Elain—my *mother*—closes her eyes, tilts her chin up to the sky. As if reveling in this moment, the last moment before the dam breaks, before the tide takes us all out to sea. The moment she's been preparing for for the past twenty-two years—maybe even longer.

She opens her eyes. Looks at the bright blue sky as if gazing at a friend. "Cora found Holly Prine, alright," she says, calm and even. "She found her when she found me. Because *I'm* Holly Prine. And Lila Gregory was the fake name of the woman who gave birth to you, then died in a hospital the next town over. You probably know her better by her real name: Jessica Coldwater."

CHAPTER

24

We Sink (Then—August 1981)

IT ALL UNRAVELED very quickly in the moments after Mrs.
Coldwater trained her gun on Holly.

Jessica lunged at her mother, and Holly lunged after
Jessica. A shot went off, missing Holly's ear by mere inches.

"*Stop!*" Jessica screamed. "Mom, *stop*! I'll go with you—
just don't hurt her!"

The night was suddenly very, very still. The wind ceased,
and the animals quieted to a hush. All of the attention, it
seemed, was on the scene unfolding between the Coldwater
women and Holly Prine.

The rifle was still in Mrs. Coldwater's hands, the barrel
pointed to the ground that she stared at. "Do you know the
number of people who would kill to have this information?"
she said very quietly. "Who would use it to destroy this family? To send us to ruin?" Her gaze rose back to Holly. There
was nothing there, no soul, no reason—and that was the exact
precise moment that Holly realized all three of them would
not be making an escape from Parker Mountain.

"She won't tell," Jessica exclaimed, tears clogging her
voice. Crying, she was crying. "Mom, I promise. I'll go to the

convent and Holly won't say a word, and this can all be over. Please, *please*."

It was futile, Holly knew. Mrs. Coldwater, the woman who had welcomed Holly into her home with open arms, was dead. Maybe she'd never existed at all. Maybe it had been a ruse, a persona that she'd used to lull Holly into comfort. Into trusting her. Into *believing*.

Mrs. Coldwater raised the gun once more, and Jessica screamed. Holly was still, even as her heart clattered in her chest.

She looked at Jessica. The girl she'd never thought she would be allowed to love, the girl who had changed everything. The girl who she had been searching for forever.

At least we had tonight, Holly thought, closing her eyes. *At least I know she loves me.*

Another shot sounded. Holly waited for the pain, for the bite of the bullet, for the end.

But none of it came. Instead, when she opened her eyes, she saw Mrs. Coldwater on the ground, blood pooling around her head. She saw Jessica Coldwater, the girl she loved, the girl who had saved her in so many different ways so many times over, standing above her mother, rifle pointed right at the woman who had set her own demise in motion.

Part 3

The Missing Leader

25

Killer (Now)

AFTER FORTY YEARS and three generations, the final true story of Lenora and Holly Prine, Jessica Coldwater, Cora Cole, and Elain and Quinn Cuthridge unravels at a dining room table in Blackwood, Colorado.

"It was Jess I heard," the woman I now know is Holly Prine tells us, wiping tears from her eyes. "She hit her mother in the head with the rifle and knocked her unconscious. She'd grabbed it from her in those last seconds before she could shoot me."

She'd told us the story, from the day she'd arrived in Wonderland with her mother forty years ago, to the moment that she'd almost died in the shadow of Parker Mountain.

"And then what?" Hunter continues, her voice sounding haggard.

Elain's—no *Holly's*—hands drop to the table, tracing an indentation. Holly Prine—*Holly Prine*, the missing girl, the supposed killer, the most wanted person in Wyoming, the woman who raised me, who called herself my mother for so long, says, "We drove to my house, stole Lenora's car, then left Jess's at her house and drove straight here. It was one of the places Lenora and I had stayed along the way, only for a couple of nights, and she was so drunk during that time, I knew she'd never remember staying here."

"Her mother never said anything?"

"Of course not," Holly scoffs. "Rebecca Coldwater was willing to kill me to protect her family. Telling the truth wasn't an option. With her husband as the mayor and her brother-in-law running the police department, they made up the truth."

"That her daughter was dead and you had killed her?" I manage.

Holly nods. "All she had to do was love her daughter more than her family's reputation. Yet here we are."

"You'd certainly know something about not loving your daughter enough."

Hunter's hand comes down on my thigh under the table. Not to stop, but to soothe, to reassure. I can tell the difference, even though she hasn't said a word.

Holly, to her credit, doesn't try to deny it. She looks up at me, holds my gaze for a moment, and says, "You know the love stories you grow up reading? Or see on TV? The ones that seem too good to be true? That was Jess and me. There aren't words to describe how much I loved her and what she meant to me. She was the only person I had."

"You had your mom," I counter. "You had *me*."

She shakes her head. "No, I never had Lenora. I had motel rooms and stolen library books and the same pair of sneakers for six years, but I never had a mother."

"And what about me? I didn't deserve any better than what you'd gotten?"

But she'd already answered that question. Jessica was the only person she'd had, the only person she'd loved.

And I was the one who had killed Jessica.

"When Jess died," Holly starts, "there was nothing left of me. We had survived so much. We'd managed to flee here and live for so long. We were so happy, she and I. When she decided she wanted a baby, I agreed because it was what she wanted. I never cared either way, truly. Her older sister—she was a doctor in Denver at that time—arranged everything. All I wanted in this life was her. The day she died . . . I died too."

"No, you didn't," I insist, ignoring the lovelorn sentiment. "You lived. You raised me, hating me, teaching me every day that I wasn't worthy of love or attention or *anything*. You could've given me up for adoption, you could've—"

"Adoption?" she whispers, her brows drawing low over her eyes in confusion. "No. You were Jess's. I couldn't do that."

"But you could wish I never existed," I counter. "You could wish I had died that day instead of her."

It's the truth. A terrible one, but the truth, nevertheless. It's the reason she is the way she is, the reason why *I* am the way I am. Even if I don't understand it, even if I don't forgive her for it in the slightest.

"Did Cora know?" Hunter asks when a silence falls.

"Lenora never told her because she didn't raise her," Holly replies, looking back down at the table. "Cora got her last name from her father. He was the one who owned the ranch in Wonderland, took Cora in after Lenora skipped town right after Cora was born. I thought she might stay—when she found out she was pregnant, she told me she would, if for nothing else than the money Cora's dad had. But Cora told me the money dried up because of her father's divorce, and after that Lenora had no interest in sticking around. Goes to show people never really change after all.

"When Cora's dad died and she went back to the ranch, Lenora showed up out of the blue—asking for money, of course. They got to talking, and Lenora let it slip about me: that Cora had a half sister named Holly Prine, and I was one of the most wanted fugitives in the state. Lenora said that if they found me and turned me in, there'd probably be a reward. After Lenora left again, Cora got to work trying to find me. Money was tight for the ranch even then, but she loved her daddy and wanted to keep that damn place going, even if it killed her. It took her a while, but she tracked me down through the phone calls that I had been making to Jessica's sister. That was the one thing Jessica could never let go of, her relationship with her sister. She helped us keep our secret, sent us money. It always comes back to the money, doesn't it?

"Anyway. Cora showed up in Spokane while you were at school one day," she continues. "She told me she'd met with Lenora, knew that we were sisters. I told her everything. After so long without Jess, it felt good to have someone to talk to. She told me about her plans to turn me in for the reward money, but after hearing my story, she said she had a better idea—and asked if Jess's daughter would like to spend the summer in Wonderland, Wyoming, with her. Except for Lenora, we were the only family she had left. She was so excited to get to know us, especially you.

"This woman, who barely knew me from Adam, willing to bring Jess's daughter *home*. For three months every year, at least. I agreed, of course. And during the summers, when she had you, I got to come home."

"This is where you came," I say softly, another puzzle piece clicking into place. "When I was sixteen, when you left for good. You've been living here for the past six years."

"Yes."

"You abandoned me, *at sixteen*, to play house with a ghost? Why?"

Her hands, clasped together on the table, fall to her lap. "I never . . ." She's shaking her head so hard that her shoulders sway too. "This wasn't what I wanted. None of it. I tried, but this version of my life, one without Jess . . . it wasn't how any of it was supposed to go. And when you turned sixteen, it seemed like the right time to . . . you were fine on your own. You had your license and were almost done with school, and you've always been self-sufficient. I was *waiting* for you to be fine, because I wasn't. It wasn't—"

"I was *self-sufficient* because you forced me to be!" I yell. "You didn't even tell me you were leaving or give me a reason or—"

"Quinn—"

"No," I snap. "For the past twenty-two years, you've woken up every morning with a choice. And every morning, you made the same choice that Jessica's mother did. You chose to love something else, something you could never even have, more than your own daughter."

When she flinches, I almost feel bad. But then I remember all the nights I needed her, all the times she stared through me, all the mornings she could've woken up and chosen *me*.

"Where's Cora?" I ask, suddenly so tired.

"I don't know. I haven't spoken to her in months."

Useless. Coming here, running into another dead end and all the wrong answers to questions I wish I'd never asked. "We're going now," I say, standing. Hunter rises with me, her hand gripping mine. "We won't bother you again. We'll leave you with your ghosts."

"Wait," Hunter says, freezing us in place. "You said that it was Jessica's sister who arranged everything for the pregnancy?"

Holly lifts her hands from her lap to the table once more, then spreads them flat, palms facing downward. She traces an indentation with her finger, looping up and back. I watch as she does it, studying the movement. It takes me a moment, but then I realize she's making two *C*'s: *CC.*

"Yes, the one who sent us the money," Holly answers. "She helped Jessica get pregnant, . She passed away from cancer three years ago, but she said that her daughter would keep sending the checks, every month, even though Jessica was gone. Jessica wanted me taken care of, and they agreed. This place too—Jessica's sister gave us the money for it, to make sure no one ever showed up and tried to take it from us. It was in her name before she died. Then it passed to her daughter, to keep us out of it as much as possible."

"So Jessica's niece?" Hunter asks. "She still sends you money?"

"Yes. She's the county sheriff, I think. Madison Bridgers."

I knew it. I fucking knew it.

"She's known," I breathe, turning to Hunter, who has gone pale, her grip on my hand significantly tighter than it was before Holly had spoken the words. "She's known that Jessica didn't die that night, that Holly didn't kill her. All this time, she's been playing us."

"No," Hunter whispers. "No, I grew up with Maddie. We're friends, we're—"

"We'll find out," I tell her, tugging her toward the door.

She nods, letting me pull away from Holly, from the table; from this place that has suddenly become the most nightmarish haunted house I could ever imagine.

"Quinn."

When I turn, just my head to look over my shoulder, Holly is meeting my eyes at long last. Her gaze travels up and down the length of my body, as if she's saving it to memory.

"I'm sorry," she says, the words floating across the room much like I imagine the ghosts float around this place. "I'm . . . I never wanted any of this. It was just . . . you reminded me so much of her. Between that same birthmark you all share, and your *eyes*, Quinn. You have those Coldwater eyes, and every time I looked at you . . . I couldn't do it. I couldn't look at you and see her for the rest of my life."

Jessica's eyes. Coldwater eyes. My *mother's* eyes. The same ones I've been looking into every time I have a conversation with Bridgers, the same ones that stared at me through the portrait of Jessica at her fundraiser. This whole time, I've been thinking Jessica and Bridgers resemble each other—but not that they resemble *me*. And the birthmark—that's why Mrs. Coldwater reacted so strangely at the fundraiser when she saw my wrist: she knew who I was, right then and there.

"Just family things, dear"—the fact that I was a part of hers.

The three of us. Coldwater women, separated by so much, yet irrevocably linked by something as simple as the color of our eyes and a brush of pigment on our skin. The people I've been hating and judging—I'm one of them.

"It ends here," I tell her, already turning back toward the door. "You'll be the last one in this long line of hateful, selfish women."

And then Hunter and I are gone, as if we were never there in the first place.

* * *

"Are you alright?" Hunter asks me an hour into the drive back.

The ride's been a blur so far, even more disorienting than the ride here was. Which has far less to do with the monotonous landscape than the empty, aching feeling in my chest. Finally: something I can't blame on Wyoming.

Or maybe I can. If Lenora had never brought Holly here forty years ago. If the Coldwaters hadn't made a name for themselves, been so hell-bent on protecting that name above everything—and anyone—else. If the homophobia hadn't raged, as potent and lethal as any California wildfire.

Wyoming. How it has taken, and given, so much to me. The blame, then, can't be placed on the state itself—but the people who inhabit it. The people who choose hate over love again and again; the people who flee and cheat and lie and hide.

The people who burn, then wonder why they're only left with hands full of ashes.

The vastness of this place was never my enemy. No, all this wide open space is the opposite. It's my chance to roam, to start again, to give myself the life I've always wanted. The big sky is endless, and so am I.

"No," I answer Hunter.

She nods, understanding exactly what I'm saying. "I'll wait until the morning to call Maddie," she says, readjusting her grip on the steering wheel. "Get everything straightened out. Maybe there's an explanation, or she didn't know who she was sending money to, or . . . something else."

"Pull the truck over," I say suddenly.

"What?"

"Pull the truck over, Hunter."

I don't even wait for her to come to a complete stop before I'm pushing my door open and hurling on the side of Interstate 50.

I dry heave, nothing left in my stomach, as Hunter comes around and puts her hand on my back. I stand there, hunched over in a crouch, sweat drying on the back of my neck, the sound of cars passing behind us.

How many are families? How many are happy? How many are mothers and daughters, singing along to the radio, making plans for school the next day or doctor appointments or what they want for dinner?

I lurch again. Hunter puts her other hand on my hip, attempting to steady me.

"You're alright," she says softly, rubbing small circles into my back. "It's over. It's all over."

I shake my head, spitting as I right myself. "All this time I've wanted to know," I breathe, my voice dry, my throat on fire. "I convinced myself that once I knew why she never loved me, why she left, I'd be fine. I'd be able to move on."

"Don't—"

"It was never me," I continue, my body shaking as I wrap my arms around myself. Even now, after twenty-two years of learning how to live this specific life, my first instinct is still to protect myself—because no one's ever been there to do it for me before. "There was never anything I could've done to make her love me or make her stay."

It should comfort me to know that none of it was my fault. But I'm still standing in the middle of a Colorado highway, shaking and throwing up and so close to falling apart for the last time that I can taste it, as acrid and disorienting as the nausea.

Hunter grasps my hips, turning me toward her, takes my chin between her fingers, and the panic fades—as simple as that. It's the softness of my face and the roughness of her callouses; the blue of her eyes that I haven't been able to forget since the first time I saw her; knowing that everyone else is going, going, gone, and yet here Hunter is, again pulling me back from the edge.

"Remember what you said last night about bein' my family?" she whispers, brushing my wind-jostled hair out of my face. "That runs both ways, Quinn. So forget about that woman in Blackwood, because she ain't your family. You got me, and I ain't goin' nowhere—I swear that on my family's grave."

I had not quite been able to deduce why my feelings for Hunter have been so strong, why they've come on so quickly. But as she says those words, as she vows never to leave me, I know exactly why: because the fear that I've always had with every single relationship in my life—*leaving, left, abandoned*—does not exist with Hunter. I know that even if this doesn't work out, even if she comes to hate me one day, she won't run. We are bound, wholly and unequivocally, to this place and to each other.

As it all hits me, the final piece of the puzzle sliding into place, I realize that I understand Holly Prine a bit more now. I don't forgive her or love her or want her back in my life, but the kind of love she had for Jessica, the things she felt for so long . . .

If Hunter asked me, I'm not sure there's anything I wouldn't do. We've only had a shred of the time Holly and

Jessica had together, and we can do what they never could: we can be anything, anyone, out and open and *alive*.

"I love you, Hunter Lemming," I say, fearless, flying.

"And I love you, Quinn Cuthridge," she replies, beautiful, forever.

CHAPTER

26

Wildest Dreams (Now)

"YOU KNOW THAT folds out, right?"

I look up from the couch, over at Hunter. She stands in the doorway of the ranch house, the night behind her a backdrop fit for a cowgirl queen. In under an hour she was able to fix the door, using wood, nails, and some glue—another magical skill I'd still be trying to learn on YouTube. The rest of the house is still a wreck, but I've gotten the living room back into livable condition. "Are you serious? Why didn't you tell me that the first night?"

She hangs her hat on the hook by the door, right next to mine, then makes her way over, gesturing for me to stand. I do, and she pulls out the bottom of the couch to reveal an additional section. "Hated you too much to lend any tips."

"And now?"

Hunter angles her body toward mine. "Now," she says, leaning toward me, "I'd do anything you asked me to, Princess."

"Even staying the night with me? On this incredibly uncomfortable couch?"

She presses her lips to mine, softly, just once. "Even that."

I start to pull away, but she grabs me by the elbow. There's something in her eyes, something I've only seen a handful of

other times—namely, when we made out in the truck yesterday afternoon.

"Hunter," I exhale. "It's been . . . a day."

Nodding, she steps even closer, so there isn't an inch of
space between our bodies. "I know you've . . . been with people before," she says. "And it didn't mean anything to you.
That's fine. I ain't judgin'. But this means somethin' to me.
The idea that we'll do this, and then you'll leave and—"

"Who said I was leaving?"

Her eyes crinkle a bit at the edges. "To Spokane. After we
find Cora, you're gonna go back—"

"Maybe I like Wyoming."

Hunter snorts. "Maybe pigs can fly."

"Maybe," I say slowly, tipping my head to the side, leaning
a fraction of an inch closer, enough to let her know that I'm
here, with her in this moment, ready for anything and everything, but not enough to scare her away, "I've found a reason
to stick around."

I know it's the truth because I've found what I've been
searching for all this time: someone who won't ever hurt me.

Hunter's tongue darts out, wetting her lower lip. "This
ain't proper."

"Was it proper of you to stick your tongue down my throat
in the truck yesterday?"

A low sound crawls out of Hunter's throat. "Can we . . .
can you . . ."

"Tell me."

She swallows. "Can you kiss me?"

I don't need to be asked twice. My hand curls around the
back of her neck, the other resting on her hip, as I bring our
mouths together.

The kiss is softer than the one in the truck, more explor-
atory, leisurely. As if we've got all the time in the world to be
here, doing this. I run my thumb up and down the column of
her neck, tickling the soft hair there, pulling her even closer.

I can't remember a time when I kissed a woman like this, when a woman kissed *me* like this. When it wasn't about rounding bases or getting off, but about the moment, about the kiss, about the pressure of her lips on mine, the sound of her gasp. It's somehow so much more intimate than anything I've ever done.

Hunter pulls away, her breathing ragged, cheeks a bright, blazing red. "Should I . . . do you want . . ."

Gently, I rest my hand along the side of her face. "It's me, Lem."

She lets out a long breath. "I want you to touch me, but if you don't want to—"

"I want to—trust me," I interrupt. My hand drops to the bottom of her shirt. "Can I take this off?"

"Yes," she says without hesitation.

I smile again, pulling the material up as Hunter raises her arms over her head. Once it's gone, I go still.

Hunter takes my reaction as something other than wonder. She goes rigid, reaching for her shirt. "I know I'm not—"

I stop her with a hand on her arm, pulling her back. "You're beautiful," I say simply, because that's all there is to say.

Some of the tension leaves her body, and she relaxes into my touch. She says nothing as I move my hand up her arm to her shoulder, to her bra strap. The one she wears is plain white cotton, cut high and sensible, no frills, no lace or bows.

She stiffens again. "I know they're not much—"

Whatever self-loathing thing she was going to say gets choked off as I move my fingers south, tracing along the inside of the bra cups, my knuckles brushing against the skin on the other side.

I reach the center of her chest, then meet her gaze. "If you say one more insulting thing about the woman I'm crazy about, you're going to have to leave, and I really don't think you want that."

That, finally, seems to get through to her. Hunter's breathing picks up as I trace my way back up her chest, following the line of the other cup until I've reached the strap on her left shoulder. I slip the tips of my fingers under it, pulling gently.

"Will you take this off?" I ask.

Hunter reaches behind her back and unhooks her bra, but doesn't let the material fall from her body. When I move closer, she stares at me with an intensity that I've never seen from her.

"Don't screw this up," she's saying with her gaze. *"Because this is important, and if you screw it up, I won't be the same."*

I nod, acknowledging the weight of what we're doing here, and Hunter lets another breath escape, letting the bra drop between us.

My gaze falls. For the first time I'm seeing all the dips and valleys, all the freckles and lines and scars, the muscles in her shoulders and her arms, her stomach and her chest.

Hunter covers herself, and I make a clicking sound with my tongue. "I wasn't done looking."

Slowly, with a blush spreading back over her cheeks and down her neck, she lowers her arms. I tip my head to the side, then reach out, delicately tracing a faint scar with my thumb.

It runs from the bottom of her left breast all the way around to her back.

"Razor wire got me," she explains. "When I was younger. Mistake I didn't make again."

I bend, kissing along the scar. She sucks in a breath, her back arching toward me. I steady both of us, resting my hands on her hips.

"Lie back," I murmur.

Her back hits the couch in a flash. I press my grin into her skin, kissing along her stomach and her abdomen, up and down the length of her collarbone, through the valley in the center of her chest.

I finally reach the crease between her thigh and her hip, my teeth digging into the band of her underwear—plain white cotton, but somehow still sexy—tugging it from her skin. She twitches, gasping, "Yes, okay, touch me."

I pull back, toying with the elastic of her underwear. "I am touching you, Lem."

"You know what I mean."

"I'm afraid I don't."

Hunter exhales roughly through her nose, the way she does when she's upset. Then she sits forward, bringing her chest closer—which I'm entirely too thankful for—as she grabs my hand and puts it between her legs.

"You know what I mean," she repeats, looking me right in the eyes. It may be the single hottest thing I've ever experienced in my life: her taking control like this, showing me exactly what she needs, demanding I give it to her.

I don't even try to stop the laugh that erupts from my throat. I let it ring throughout the space around us, a space that once felt so foreign and now couldn't be more familiar. A space that has been heaven and hell and home. A space where so many bad things have happened for so many years. I think back to what Bridgers said about why she helped Cora: *"Someone was finally fighting back."* Maybe it's time for me to do that too—stop hiding from the pain and the bad things and embrace them instead. Fight back. Be the thing that goes bump in the night instead of the one cowering away from it.

Time for us *to do that,* I think as we start to move, together finally.

* * *

In the middle of the night, Hunter wakes, stirring next to me. When I look over, she's staring at me, blue eyes dark and wide.

"What?" I murmur, my voice still gravelly with sleep.

"Where do you think she is?" she asks. The anguish in her voice makes my chest ache.

I want to give her an answer that will soothe her, let her sleep through the night. There's too many possibilities to even try lying about it, and Hunter would see right through it anyway.

I'm not my aunt, and I'm certainly not my mother. I wonder for a moment, with Hunter tucked up against me, what would've happened if Jessica Coldwater had lived twenty-two years ago. If she and Holly and I would've been one big, happy family or if we would've been trapped in that little Colorado ghost town, me slowly learning the horrors my moms had experienced. Would Cora have ever found out about us? Would I ever have come to Wyoming and met Hunter? Without all the pain and the anguish, would I still have let the monster inside me rage so freely? Or would it be tucked away a little deeper, a little safer for everyone else around me? It's a unique kind of hopelessness to know that I'll never get an answer to any of those questions. But it doesn't stop me from wondering who I could've been if fate had taken pity on me just once.

It did, I think, then, Hunter's hands wrapped around me. *It just took twenty-two years.*

"I don't know," I reply, pulling her closer to me.

She burrows her face into my neck, inhaling deeply. "You and me?" Hunter whispers, lips on my neck.

"You and me," I tell her, bringing her mouth to mine.

27

Getaway Car (Now)

WHEN I OPEN my eyes again, there's an empty spot next to me on the couch.

I sit up, stretching out my neck, reaching for my shirt, rested and sore in all the right places. Hunter's clothes are gone, but there's no sign of Hunter.

I lean forward, looking out the window. She's there, pacing back and forth, fresh set of clothes on and hat atop her head, phone firmly pressed to her ear. Her lips move fast, so there's no chance in hell that I'm making out what she's saying to the person on the other end, who I'd bet this whole ranch on is Sheriff Madison Bridgers.

As if on cue, my own phone rings from its spot on the coffee table. Seeing who it is, I nearly don't answer. "Carson," I say shortly.

"Nice to hear from you too."

"Calling to see if I'm on a plane back to Spokane yet?"

"And to make sure you're doing alright."

Can't answer emails and book appointments for them if I'm dead. "I solved it" is all I allow. "Well, the old murder case, that is. I still have no idea where Cora's currently at."

"And?" Carson prompts.

I shift on the couch, swinging my legs off the side and staring down at my toes. "Turns out it was Holly," I lie. "I tracked her to a tiny town in Colorado. Well, her grave. She died six years ago."

The best lies always have a shred of truth in them—made easier by the fact that Holly is dead to me.

"Well," Carson replies. "Alright, then. Sounds like you'll be back home soon."

Home. As if Spokane has ever been more than a city to me, more than a place to tread water. "I won't," I tell them.

"What do you mean *you won't*? You hate Wyoming, and you've run out of leads, and . . . oh." Their laugh is low, almost mocking. "It's the ranch hand, isn't it? You've fallen for her?"

"What do I have back in Spokane anyway?" I demand fiercely. "The apartment my mother left me in? A job that I can do anywhere in this country?"

"Me," they say lightly, almost hesitantly. "You've got me."

There's no doubt that Carson saved me when Holly left and I was a lost, lonely sixteen-year-old. I'll always be grateful to them for that. But a job and a few Thanksgivings of micro-waved turkey dinners at the office isn't a family. It isn't love.

"You're my boss, Carson," I tell them. "My mentor. I've learned so much from you, and it's been a great run. But . . . I've got a chance for something here. A fresh start. A real life. I can't apologize for wanting that."

Silence. I think for a moment that they've hung up, left me like everyone else in my life has.

Everyone but Hunter.

"You can tell yourself what you like, Quinn," they continue, "but you're not staying there for love or family or whatever you've convinced yourself of. You're staying in Wyoming for an *opportunity*. Because your aunt has this perfect little scheme going, and she's missing, and you can slide right in and take it all over. I don't quite know how that ranch hand fits into it all, but God help her. God help that whole state, going up against you—and they don't even realize it."

They hang up without another word.

*   *   *

"I just got off the phone with Mad—"

"We're calling a meeting," I say, standing, turning to Hunter. My heartbeat ricochets in my skull, but I'm steady on my feet. "Call the sheriff back. Noon, at the station."

Hunter's eyes narrow. "You alright? Who was that on the phone?"

"No one," I reply. "Not anymore."

"Alright," Hunter says. I can tell she's unconvinced, but she strolls toward me, grabbing me by the hips and pulling me into her. "Care to clue me in about this meeting?"

"Yes," I say, immediately feeling more solid, more sure, with the one person in this world who's never doubted me, never left me, never failed me, holding onto me. "And tell the sheriff to bring her grandmother to the meeting too."

"Her grandmother? That'd be—"

"The woman behind all of this," I say. "Rebecca Coldwater."

*   *   *

The secretary at the sheriff's department ushers Hunter and me into the conference room, at the very back of the station, with decidedly less enthusiasm than she received us with the last time we were here.

The sheriff is there, sitting at the head of the table, with her legs crossed and her hands folded in her lap. And to her left, a woman with the same all-seeing look in her eyes—*my eyes*—the same cool, watchful demeanor.

"Coldwaters," I say, sitting at the opposite end of the table from Bridgers. Hunter sits in the chair next to me on the right side. We're in mirrored positions, four women all holding different pieces of the puzzle.

"Quinn Cuthridge," Mrs. Coldwater replies, voice raspy. She's dressed impeccably, not a gray hair out of place, her cotton dress pressed and wrinkle-free. A set of pearls is looped around her neck, and her wedding ring stands out starkly against the pale white of her skin. "Twice that we're meeting now. A rarity, for me. If my husband hadn't been too drunk to stand, I wouldn't have even been at the fundraiser. I don't make many public appearances anymore."

So that's the real reason he wasn't there that night. "Is that since you tried to kill Holly Prine and then lied about the death of your daughter because you found out they were lesbians?" I return. "Or is it more recent?"

Mrs. Coldwater doesn't flinch. To her credit, neither does Hunter—at least she's learned a thing or two from me about a poker face. But Bridgers: her eyes flicker to her grandmother—only for a moment, but it gives away so much.

"I see," Mrs. Coldwater replies. "And who told you that fanciful tale?"

"My mother," I reply, not missing a beat. "I knew her as Elain Cuthridge, but you knew her by her given name, Holly Prine. I know that Jessica lived, because twenty-two years ago she died giving birth to me."

They were willing to give me the first secret because they'd been keeping it for so long. It might even give them some sense of relief, particularly Bridgers, to have it out in the open, in the hands of someone who will do the right thing with it.

But the second . . . you can't feel relief about unleashing a secret you never knew about in the first place.

They both knew only half of it: Bridgers that Jessica was dead, and Mrs. Coldwater that I was her kin. It's as simple as any chemical reaction: mix the reactants, sit back, and wait for it to go *boom*.

"Now wait just a minute—"

"Lem, you didn't tell me she was—"

I flip my wrist over, toward Bridgers, and she stops mid-sentence. "That night at the fundraiser," I say. "Your grand-mother saw my birthmark. She's known since then. Which makes me *your* granddaughter," I say to Mrs. Coldwater, then turn to Bridgers. "And your cousin."

"No, Holly told me . . ." Bridgers trails off, shaking her head. "Holly told me Jessie died in a car accident. She would've told me if she had a baby, if—"

"You knew Jessie was dead?" Mrs. Coldwater asks the woman next to her. "And you didn't *tell me*? You didn't tell me that my own daughter had *died*?"

I want to feel bad for this woman, but she's made it wholly impossible. "Didn't she die that night, in your eyes? You never contacted her again, never saw her. And I'm pretty sure you were never gonna tell anyone that there was another Coldwa-ter running around.

"Quite the scandal, wouldn't it be? Especially considering the long-lost Coldwater is a lesbian, like her mothers. The entire reason you almost killed a seventeen-year-old forty years ago and made your daughter flee her entire life—and it's all come back to stare at you from across a conference table."

Mrs. Coldwater's hands, folded so nicely on the table in front of her, start to shake. "You don't understand," she says, trying to keep her voice even, but I hear the waver in her tone. "It was a different time back then. I did what I had to do to protect my family. I saw what it did to our family when Kath-leen . . . when she . . ."

"So there was another gay woman in the Coldwater line?" I reply. "Sounds like it runs in the family." I resist the urge to look over at Bridgers as I say it.

"This . . ." Mrs. Coldwater is shaking her head as if she can make this all go away if she does it hard enough. "This was supposed to be over. It *was* over."

"You told me that they left together," Bridgers says. "That it was their choice to fake Jessica's death. You told Mom that. Forty years, you've been lying."

"That's how you knew that the mayor didn't kill Jessica, because *Cora* knew he didn't," I say, working it all out. "Eight years ago, when her ranch was about to go under, she decided to use her knowledge that Jessica Coldwater and Holly Prine lived, in order to blackmail him. And in the process, because of the danger, another Coldwater was made to leave the state."

"And you knew they were alive this whole time too," Hunter interjects.

Bridgers nods but doesn't take her eyes off the woman next to her. "I did, but I thought they ran away. Right before Mom passed, she told me her sister didn't die that night—that she'd escaped to live with her wife in Blackwood. She'd set money aside to be sent to them every month."

"You were sending them *money?*" the elder Coldwater hisses. "After what they did to this family?"

"Stop!" Bridgers barks. "After what *you've* done to this family, I don't know why you're still talking." Then she turns to me. "So. Cora Cole's niece, Jessica Coldwater and Holly Prine's daughter. What's your next move?"

So many secrets and lies passed down among friends and families and strangers, disfigured and barely holding on. It's a miracle this town hasn't collapsed under the weight of them all. Now here I am, the blood of both sides in my veins. The linchpin, the one with all the chips in front of her. All the power. Finally.

"Why did you become a cop in the first place?" I ask Bridgers.

"I told you, it was my only option," Bridgers says, sounding surprised by the question. "They needed someone in the office."

"You could've left," I offer. "Cut ties and started your own life somewhere where they've never even heard of Wonderland,

Wyoming. Instead, you stayed, and you've done their bidding for all these years."

"If I didn't, I wouldn't have been a part of the family anymore."

"And what a family it is."

She presses her lips together, staring at me through my own eyes. For her entire life, she's made choices that have secured her own protection and damned everyone else. She could've easily walked away, not been her family's pawn for all these years—instead, she's chosen the safety of this town and the Coldwater name. She's chosen to *stay*.

"I could go public," I say slowly, laying it all out. "Between the eyes and the birthmark, it wouldn't take too much to convince people. I could ruin the reputation your grandmother has spent so long safeguarding and finally clear Holly's name after forty fucking years."

That would be the kind thing to do, the gentle thing. "If you could do it all again," I ask, pinning my eyes on Mrs. Coldwater, "would you do anything differently?"

The room goes still as we all await the Coldwater matriarch's answer. The woman who would very much like you to believe that she was simply backed into a corner, making the best out of a bad situation. She's done a good enough job of putting up that facade for the past forty years.

But it all crumbles at my question. The weight of her lies and hate unspooling from her ugly, rotten center.

"If I hadn't done what I did . . ." She shakes her head again, toying with her wedding ring. "I wouldn't still be here. Maddie wouldn't be sheriff. Todd wouldn't be mayor. That's what Jessica was asking us to give up, was *demanding* that we give up. No one would've voted for us, tolerated us—"

"Like the way you *tolerated* Jessica and Holly?" I return. "You were afraid of the very same thing you were doing to them."

"That's not—"

"And what does all of that mean?" I continue. "Jobs? Titles? That's what you traded your daughter for?"

"It's more than that!" she exclaims. "Once I married Todd, it became my responsibility to care for the name, for this town. That was what I wanted and what I signed up for. When that was threatened, what else was I supposed to do?"

"You were supposed to love your daughter regardless of what she did or who she loved."

"You don't understand," she practically sneers. "That old, run-down house that Holly Prine and her mother moved into when they first came to Wonderland—that was my house once upon a time. I came from nothing. My family name meant nothing in this place. It was only once I became a Coldwater that I became *something*, that I had power and money and a say in things."

"And that's how you got away with it for so long."

"My brother-in-law was the sheriff. I was a grieving mother—that part wasn't a lie—and my husband was the mayor. The county medical examiner went to school with Todd and signed the death certificate without any issue. He was told one of the Jane Does at the morgue was Jessica, and he didn't even blink. The story was sad and easy to believe— no one ever liked Holly Prine to begin with. There was no one in town who was asking questions, and anyone from outside town was firmly dissuaded from following up." She shakes her head again. "Jessica wanted us all to forsake the very fabric of what it means to be a Coldwater—for what? For her *sin*? No, I gave that girl a choice. At the gala that year, I pulled her aside and told her to leave my daughter, my family, and my town *alone*. She dug her own grave—all three of them did."

Bridgers's brows furrow like she's surprised. But I'm not. No, that was precisely the answer I was looking for.

I was wrong, I realize. Wyoming is not to blame for all the anguish I have had to endure; that Holly Prine and Jessica Coldwater had to. No—it comes down to something so much smaller, so much more insidious than any midnight-dark, wide-open sky in this state could ever be.

Rebecca Coldwater, choosing hatred over her daughter; Holly Prine, choosing love over hers.

"And you," I say, looking this monster of a woman right in the eye, feeling more like myself than I ever have before, "just dug yours."

"Wait," Hunter says as I start to stand, her hand on my arm. "You said all *three* of them—Holly, Jessica, and . . .?"

"Oh," Mrs. Coldwater huffs, eyebrows raised. "You haven't figured it out yet? Maybe if *you* had taken the advice I'd given your aunt then—"

"What did you do?" Bridgers interrupts.

"Cora was blackmailing the mayor, not you," I say, looking right at the Coldwater matriarch as I fill in the blanks. "That was her mistake. She aimed for the heart, not the head."

"He'd been pulling the money from his own account until that last time," she says. I can hear the anger in her tone, the indignation. Maybe that's the reason she's telling us now. Just like that night so many years ago, her rage has reached a fever pitch, and there's nowhere for it to go but *out*. "That ten thousand dollars she asked for. She got too greedy. I probably would've never found out if she'd kept asking for smaller amounts. But this time Todd had to pull it from our joint account. He came clean as soon as I asked him about it. If he'd have let me handle it from the start, then I would've taken care of it."

"What did you *do*?" Hunter repeats.

Mrs. Coldwater doesn't even flinch as she says, "I *handled* things. The way I intended to handle things all those years ago."

CHAPTER

28

Garden Song (Now—One Week Later)

PARKER MOUNTAIN IS quieter than I'd imagined it being. The mountains stand high and majestic above us. We had to hike a bit to get out here, to what Rebecca Coldwater described as the exact location she shot and killed my aunt over a month ago. Rocks and dirt and wild grass crunched and sighed under our feet as we walked in silence. I wanted to come sooner, but it was only this morning that Bridgers called Hunter, saying that the police had officially cleared the area.

They'd found Cora's remains—and the bullet that killed her, lodged in her skull. Along with her confession, it was more than enough to put Rebecca Coldwater away for the rest of her life.

The story that Rebecca told us that day seemed too *simple* to be true. After everything that we'd done to find Cora, she was arguably in the most obvious place of all.

The ten thousand dollars. The number that was too high to be ignored. Cora drove out to Flaming Gorge that night— her and the mayor's normal meeting place—but when she got into the mayor's car for the exchange, it was Rebecca waiting. And not with a briefcase full of cash, but with the same shotgun she'd brought with her to Parker Mountain so many years before.

"*Get in the car, and talk to me about all these things you think you know,*" she'd told Cora. "*Because if you don't, I'm pulling the trigger—and I won't miss this time.*"

To Parker Mountain they drove. It was perfect, leaving Cora's truck behind—it would give the police somewhere to look when they finally found it.

At gunpoint, Rebecca forced Cora closer to the mountain, away from the lot where visitors tended to congregate. She had Cora turn toward the mountain, get on her knees, and after she shot her, Rebecca Coldwater released a breath she'd been holding for forty years, walked back to her car, and drove home to her oblivious, fast-asleep husband.

"*What about the threatening messages?*" Bridgers had asked her grandmother while Hunter and I sat on the other side of the table, too shell-shocked to do anything but listen.

That was Rebecca too. After the fundraiser, after seeing *me*, she started getting nervous. That maybe she hadn't thought of everything. That maybe, this girl from Washington with the Coldwater birthmark and the Coldwater eyes, would find something she never should've. She'd left the message on the mirror and called me, but Rebecca had instructed one of Bridgers's supposedly upstanding officers to trash the house, searching for proof of Cora's blackmail or something else she could use to get me out of town.

And that was it. Here was our answer. Here was everything we had been looking for. But it was wrong . . . Cora couldn't be *dead*. Cora was smart and precise and thought she was meeting the idiot mayor that night, not his wife. Not the woman that had been ready to commit murder for her family for forty fucking years.

Now, I squint under my sunglasses as I look up, toward the very top of Parker Mountain, thinking of all Rebecca

Coldwater's secrets it's kept over the years. *What else do you have to tell me?*

Hunter is silent as I close my eyes, tipping my head back, letting the sun hit my bare skin. It's just starting to peek through the gray clouds overhead, making a midmorning appearance.

"This feel like closure to you?" I ask.

I hear her boots against the hard ground, brushing against the grass. She takes my hand in hers. "No," she replies softly. "It don't."

It should, though. Rebecca's gone; all her work for nothing, her family in ruins. The mayor has been shut up in his house since the news broke.

And yet. It is nowhere *near* enough. The things that Cora's death has left behind are both big and small, but I see them all. Hunter still stops before coming in the main house, her jaw tightening as she rests her palm on the front door. I can't go into Cora's bedroom, can't look at the ledgers I left on her desk. The past three nights I've woken up in the middle of the night, Hunter's spot in her bed next to me empty, only for me to see her staring out the window again, like she's just waiting for Cora's truck to come rumbling down the long path.

These are the things that "justice" can't fix. The things that I can't fix, as much as I'd like to be able to. Time will do some of the work, maybe—but what about the rest of it? The grief that neither Hunter nor I have words for; the sudden, jarring ending to Cora's disappearance that's left me with an ache so deep I can feel it in my teeth.

Those nights when Hunter's pretending she's asleep next to me, sometimes all I can do is stare at the ceiling and play it over again and again in my head. Why did she ask for so much money? How could she have let her defenses down like that? Why wasn't she anticipating Rebecca Coldwater eventually finding out?

And then, of course, my thoughts turn inward. Why didn't I just pick up the phone *once* in eight years? Maybe I could've helped her. Maybe I could've saved her.

Questions I'll never be able to answer. Questions that won't bring Cora back. Questions that serve no real purpose other than to drive me even further out of my mind, but I'm helpless to stop.

Hunter—the only person I've got left—grips my hand a little tighter, and I open my eyes, looking over at her. I wait for her to say something, but she doesn't. Not for all the time we spend standing there in the mountain's shadow or on the ride home, so much looming in the rearview mirror, so much we are both unable to forget.

* * *

Bridgers is waiting for us when we get back to the ranch.

She's sitting on the steps that lead up to the main house, her head hanging low, her elbows resting on her thighs. She stands only when Hunter and I approach her.

"How y'all holding up?" she asks. Her voice sounds rough, and the bags under her eyes are heavy, like she too hasn't been sleeping much lately.

"How the fuck do you think, *cousin?*" I snarl.

Bridgers presses her lips together as Hunter gently grabs my arm. "It's been a long day, Maddie," she tells the sheriff.

"Just wanted to let y'all know that I won't be running for reelection in the fall," she tells us. "The mayor—well, former mayor, now; he resigned an hour ago—is relocating to Casper."

"Big news," I reply.

"And I'm here to apologize," she says. Her blue eyes land on mine, and I wonder how it took me so long to realize they were the same ones I saw every day in the mirror. *The same way Cora missed what was staring right at her too.* "For what my family's done. For what I've done."

"You can cut the bullshit, Bridgers," I tell her. "You're really here to see how much Hunter and I are gonna talk about your involvement in what your family's done, right?"

She doesn't have an answer to that. Instead, she reaches back toward the porch, grabbing a thick, manila envelope that she'd had resting besides her. "Don't think Cora'd want me to have this anymore."

I take the envelope from her. It's heavier than I was expecting. "The blackmail folder she gave you."

"That's right," the sheriff says. "Yours to do with what you choose. Though if it was up to me, I'd burn it first chance I got."

I run my hand over the front of it, tracing my fingers along the word *Maddie* in thick, black marker. Cora's handwriting.

"What *are* y'all planning to do?" Bridgers asks after a moment.

There are bills to be paid, a ranch to be kept up. Hunter's assured me that there's enough money to keep the ranch going for at least another year, and we agreed to reevaluate in a few months.

I'm standing in the same place that Cora was all those years ago, when she sent me away. The cost of running a ranch, the answer to all those dollar signs now clasped between my palms.

I know what this place means to Hunter. I know it's the last piece of Cora we've got left. There was still a piece of me that wondered why Cora didn't just sell the ranch and walk away when her father died. Not anymore.

I don't have an answer for Bridgers. Not tomorrow and not next week. For now, I only know that this envelope isn't going anywhere near a burn pile.

Rebecca and Todd Coldwater are gone. But the woman looking back at me and the mark on my wrist proves that the Coldwaters aren't.

"What do you think, Lem?" I ask, turning to the woman beside me, who's already got her eyebrows raised, waiting for me. "Seems to me the police haven't been doing their jobs for quite some time. I think this town might need its very own private investigator."

29

Run (Then—August 1981)

WHEN SHE OPENED her eyes, Holly Prine was sure she was dead.

But no—there was Mrs. Coldwater's lifeless figure on the ground in front of her. There was Jessica standing eerily still, clutching the front end of the rifle in her hands like you would a baseball bat, as if she was waiting for her mother to move so that she could hit her again and finish the job.

The world started spinning violently in front of Holly's eyes. She was sure she was hyperventilating, her chest beginning to heave, as she stared down at Mrs. Coldwater. Mrs. Coldwater, who had baked her cookies and told her to stay away from her daughter and *tried to murder her.*

Holly could barely get the words out as she asked, "Is she . . ."

Jessica bent down, pressing two fingers to her mother's neck. "No," she said, soft and calm. It was as if she were relaying information about the weather or the score of the football game.

When she rose, Jessica was not shaking. She was strong and still, like a statue. No—like a phoenix rising from the ashes. That's exactly what the scene around them was: ashes of a life they could never, ever return to. Things that would never be the same again.

"We have to go to the police," Holly said, willing her hands to stop shaking. "We have to tell them that she tried to kill me. That you were acting to protect me, that—"

"They won't believe you," Jessica said matter-of-factly. "My family runs the police like they run this town. No, they'll do exactly what my mother tried. They'll send me away and do God knows what to you."

Horror gripped Holly. All this over . . . over . . . *love*. Over two people who had refused to be what the world demanded of them, and had almost been punished in the most severe way because of it. All because of the times, because of the world's narrow view, because two girls loving each other was apparently enough to warrant cold-blooded murder.

She'd known the risks. Of dancing with Jessica that night at the gala. Of every kiss, every touch. Of every night spent in Jessica's bed. Of not staying away when Mrs. Coldwater had warned her off. Of coming out here tonight, of crossing that final line, of being a teenager in love.

She'd known the risks. They both had. And if this was how it ended . . . then so be it. Better to go down in a spectacular blaze than be safe and miserable.

Jessica put the gun down, then stepped toward Holly, raising her hands to cup her cheeks. "Remember that talk we had in my car before the gala?"

Holly nodded. She remembered everything when it came to this girl. "Of course."

"Run away with me, then," Jessica breathed into the cool night air. "My sister can help us once we get settled. She knows people at the college who can make sure we stay hidden. It can be you and me for the rest of our lives."

It sounded crazy suddenly—running away. It was so much easier to agree to when it was in theory, when it was talk, when it was a fantasy. But now, here Jessica was, holding onto Holly as if she would never let go, begging her to run.

"Say yes," Jessica whispered. "Say yes and run away with me and be mine, Holly."

For a split second, Lenora's face flashed across her mind. The baby, her future sister or brother. Lenora was the only other person in her life besides Jessica, and Lenora was ready to start over. To start fresh, with her new baby and her married, ranch-owning boyfriend.

Lenora wanted a clean slate, so why shouldn't Holly get one too? They could get in Jessica's car and drive, with nothing but the shirts on their backs. They could start a life together. Jessica was eighteen, and she'd be, too, in a couple of months. It was perfect. It was what she had always wanted, what she'd been searching for. A home. A family. A love so whole and devastating it overwhelmed everything else in its path.

All she had to do was run. If there was one thing that Holly Prine knew how to do, had been *raised* to do, it was run. Fast. Constantly. Without looking back and without apology.

Holly leaned forward and kissed Jessica hard. She pulled back, pressed their foreheads together and said the one word she'd never regret uttering once in her whole life: "Yes."

ACKNOWLEDGMENTS

As MANY OF you know, the lore of my fiction career started when my eighth-grade English teacher offered extra credit to anyone who wrote fifty thousand words for NaNoWriMo. Like a complete nerd, I got to work! Fourteen years and seven unpublished manuscripts later, somehow we're here. Believe me when I say that I truly thought this day would never come. I'd like to thank everyone who believed otherwise.

My family. Dad, who believed in me as much as when I was in a press box in Casper as right now. Amanda, my first bestie, who has been my first reader for as long as I've been writing. Zack, who has not read a novel since high school but hopefully is reaching this part of the book after reading it all! Mr. Jake, just for existing. No notes, king—I love you!

The wonderful team at Crooked Lane Books. My editor, Terri Bischoff, for believing lesbians should be on the shelf solving crime too. This process has been far beyond anything I could've dreamed of.

My wonderful agent, Michelle Richter, who found me in the slush pile, and even after two projects didn't sell, never wavered in her dedication to sell the third. Without her time, effort, and keen eye, none of this would've been possible.

My friends, of whom I am blessed to have so many I could not manage to name them all here. Whether you've been around long enough to remember sticky notes on the wall in 230 or are just joining the party, thank you. However, I must mention Remy and Noodles (the OG white, feral, pudgy cat) because he needs to be acknowledged in as many published works as possible.

My teachers, professors, and all the other educators I've met in my life. Now that I'm working as a substitute teacher, I can confidently say there's no way I'd be able to do what you all do day in and day out. Thank you for inspiring the writers of tomorrow.

You, fabulous reader, for picking up this book. Whether you're my best friend's mom's third cousin who was told to read this, or if you saw two lesbians in leading roles in a mystery and automatically put this on your TBR, or if you're here completely by accident and maybe a little lost: thanks for making twelve-year-old Hannah's dreams come true.

Finally, as most people who follow me on Twitter know, I've struggled with my mental health for as long as I've been writing. I've tried therapy and medication and yoga and mindfulness, and still—I never thought it was going to get better. If not for a very special group of loving, caring, patient people, this book would not be here because I would not be here. The same goes for the mental health professionals who work so hard to help all of us sad, anxious ladies, including the wonderful Dr. Amie Smith, who helped get me through the worst of it.

Maybe some of you are dealing with something similar. I hate when people say, "It gets better," because it felt so long like a lie or something that was only true for other people. But right now, I'm talking about how it did finally get so much better in my debut novel. I believe that it's going to be true for you too. I believe in you; don't give up.